Suits and Skates

Sena Voss

Want to read the **FREE** prequel to the Puck Bunny series?

Sign up for the Sena Voss newsletter and get the story delivered straight to your inbox. Scan the QR code below or go to SenaVoss.com

To the ambitious woman who was told she had to choose, and decided to take it all instead.

Contents

1.	Sloane	1
2.	Sloane	6
3.	Garrett	15
4.	Sloane	21
5.	Garrett	35
6.	Sloane	41
7.	Sloane	48
8.	Garrett	54
9.	Sloane	61
10.	Sloane	67
11.	Garrett	85
12.	Sloane	101
13.	Garrett	109
14.	Sloane	120
15.	Garrett	129

16. Sloane   138

17. Sloane   147

18. Sloane   157

19. Garrett   162

20. Sloane   169

21. Garrett   178

22. Garrett   193

23. Sloane   200

24. Sloane   211

25. Sloane   220

26. Sloane   228

27. Sloane   238

28. Garrett   243

29. Sloane   248

30. Garrett   251

31. Sloane   256

32. Sloane   261

33. Sloane   268

34. Sloane   281

35. Garrett   290

36.	Sloane	302
37.	Sloane	308
38.	Sloane	311
39.	Garrett	317
40.	Epilogue - Garrett	329
Acknowledgements		348
About the author		349

1

Sloane

The man on my screen is committing career suicide, and I can't stop watching.

Garrett "Tank" Sullivan hasn't blinked in ten seconds. I've been counting. The reporter asks about team morale—an easy question, the kind you answer with two sentences and a smile—and he responds with silence. Just silence. Long enough that I check if my stream froze.

"So, Garrett, what's the team's mood heading into this weekend's series?"

His jaw ticks once. "Fine."

The reporter's smile twitches, falters. "And the power play improvements we saw in practice?"

"Yep."

I grip my coffee mug, the one with Minnesota Mammoths wrapped around the team's emblem, and my knuckles go white. For a man paid millions to communicate on the ice, he's apparently allergic to the English language when there's a camera involved.

The reporter clears her throat, clearly hoping for more. When nothing comes, she pivots with forced brightness. "Well, I know our viewers—especially your incredible fan base—would love to hear more about what you've been working on. What would you say to the young hockey players who look up to you?"

Garrett's eyes narrow slightly, like the question personally offends him. He leans back in his chair, and when he speaks, his tone could freeze water. "They should focus on their own game instead of looking up to anybody."

The reporter blinks, clearly thrown by the dismissal. "That's... refreshing honesty. Speaking of your fans, attendance has been incredible this season. What does that kind of support mean to you?"

"Means they have tickets." He shrugs, and the gesture manages to convey both indifference and contempt. "They can do what they want with them."

My coffee goes cold in my hands. This isn't just bad. It's catastrophic. He's actively alienating the very people who buy jerseys, concessions, and premium seats. The people whose loyalty pays his salary.

But the reporter isn't done. She's got one more grenade to lob, and I watch in horror as she pulls the pin. "Before we wrap up, I'd love to talk about your partnership with Northstar Bank. They've been such incredible supporters of the team's community outreach programs. What's it been like working with them on initiatives like the youth hockey clinics?"

For maybe half a second, blink and you'd miss it, his whole posture changes. His eyes drop to his hands. He looks like someone who actually has an answer to that question.

Then it's gone.

His entire face hardens, and he does something I've never seen a professional athlete do in an interview: he rolls his eyes. Not a subtle look of annoyance, but a full, theatrical eyeroll that screams disdain for the camera to capture.

"Community outreach." He says the words like they taste rotten. "Right. Look, I play hockey. That's what I get paid to do. I'm not a guidance counselor or a role model or whatever else people want me to be." His voice goes flat and final. "And I'm definitely not a spokesperson for some bank's PR campaign."

The reporter's face cycles through shock, panic, professional desperation. "But the youth programs—"

"Are not my job." Garrett cuts her off clean. "Northstar Bank can find someone else to smile for their commercials. I'm here to win games, not hold hands with kids who probably can't even skate."

The silence that follows lasts long enough for the reporter's mouth to open and close twice. Somewhere off-camera, I can hear what sounds like muffled cursing from a producer.

When Garrett stands abruptly, his chair scrapes against the floor. Sharp, violent, final. "We done?"

The reporter stammers through her closing, but he's already walking away, pulling off his microphone and dropping it on a nearby table without bothering to hand it to anyone.

I snap the laptop shut, then open it again a beat later, masochist that I am, and rewatch the disaster. My brain logs the missteps automatically. Poor eye contact: negative five engagement points. Hostile tone: ten-point drop in trustworthiness. The full-body eyeroll at the mention of community outreach? Catastrophic. He wasn't just tanking an interview; he was torpedoing our entire Q4 brand strategy. This wasn't apathy. It was contempt, delivered like one of his trademark wrist shots, high glove side.

Six floors below my office window, the practice rink sits dark and empty, waiting for tomorrow's morning skate. I'm already dialing Vivian.

"Sloane." Her voice is velvet over a blade. "I was just about to call you. I trust you saw the... performance."

"I've got a mitigation plan," I say, already mapping it out: a three-part 'Behind the Pads' content series highlighting his charity work, leaning into the 'strong, silent' archetype. "We can pivot this to authenticity—"

"No, Sloane." The velvet vanishes. "You need to handle him. Garrett Sullivan is now your sole priority. Get him in line."

An order. Not a discussion. I open my mouth to respond, but she's not finished.

"And Sloane," she adds, her voice dropping low, "you know how Coach Kowalski is."

The line goes dead. I'm left staring at the phone, her words settling over me like a weight I can't shrug off. That wasn't advice. That was a threat in stilettos.

I swivel back to my computer and start typing. My marketing brain shifts into crisis mode, running damage scenarios while my fingers move across the keyboard.

Subject: Mandatory – Media Synergy & Brand Strategy Session Attendee: Garrett Sullivan

My cursor hovers over the send button. This meeting isn't just a PR exercise. It's a gamble. My job, my promotion, and my entire reputation are riding on whether I can fix a man who doesn't want to be fixed. The reputation I fought tooth and nail to build, to prove I was more than just Easton's little sister who got lucky. I click send.

The invite vanishes into the ether. Below me, the practice rink glows under the lights, a pristine, untouched sheet of ice. Up here, my office is a command post.

You have no idea what's coming, Sullivan.

2
Sloane

The fluorescent lights in the corporate wing buzz with their usual morning aggression, casting everything in stark angles. I pace the polished marble corridor with my second coffee of the day, reciting talking points for the Sullivan meeting like incantations.

Then I pass Vivian's office.

Something stalls my stride.

She's not typing. Not talking. Not issuing rapid-fire orders or dissecting spreadsheets. She's just sitting. Perfectly still behind her glass fortress, staring at her computer screen with an expression I've never seen on her before.

Unshielded. Hollow.

This is the woman who never shows anything but polished control. But right now, her armor has cracked wide open.

From my angle, I can make out what has her so transfixed: a photograph on her monitor. It shows a much younger Vivian, barely out of her twenties, standing beside a man in a Columbus Blue Jackets jersey. My mind flips to the right card: Jake Morrison, star defenseman, early retirement, off-ice scandal that swallowed his career whole. But it's not him I'm focused on. It's her.

Her arm is looped through his, but her body leans subtly away. No smile. Her expression is taut, brittle, eyes narrowed in a way that suggests possession rather than pride. It's not a snapshot of love; it's a study in control. Of someone holding too tightly, desperate not to lose whatever grip she has.

In the stillness of the present, Vivian's gaze on the image isn't wistful. It's bitter. She's staring at a ruin she helped build and wondering whether the fire was worth it.

I'd seen the same look on my mother's face in the months after my father left. The look of a woman who'd had her entire identity ripped away by a man and had rebuilt herself into something harder. It wasn't just ambition; it was survival. And standing there watching Vivian, I felt like a threat.

The moment holds until she senses me.

Her head snaps up. Eyes lock with mine through the glass. The photo vanishes with a single, sharp click.

Vivian rises and opens her office door, her voice cutting through the corporate quiet.

"Don't you have a multi-million-dollar asset to babysit, McKenzie? Or are you planning to stand there gawking all day?"

The venom is disproportionate. Personal. I hurry toward my office, filing away this moment as another piece of the puzzle that is Vivian. One I don't yet understand, but that feels important.

I check my laptop for the third time in five minutes. 2:27 p.m.

Garrett Sullivan is now twenty-seven minutes late to a mandatory meeting.

The sixth-floor conference room is a tomb: high-gloss mahogany table, gleaming glass walls, and one solitary chair facing mine. My first slide waits frozen on the screen: "Media Synergy & Brand Strategy." An empty seat stares back at me.

My phone is silent. No texts. No calls. No lies about practice running long or last-minute emergencies. Just nothing.

I've been spinning since the interview yesterday, fielding increasingly terse messages from Northstar's executives. The sponsorship deal that could propel my career hangs by a thread, and he can't even show me the basic courtesy of a rejection text.

Vivian's words from yesterday slither back into my mind. She didn't just want me to handle him; she was watching to see if I'd fail. Right now, sitting in this empty room, I feel like I'm walking straight into her trap.

This is Pittsburgh all over again. Different city, same playbook. When the quarterback decided he "preferred Mike for media strategy," I didn't argue. I swallowed it. Watched Mike pitch my campaign, watched him get the glory while I got shuffled into "special projects."

Six months later, I was updating my résumé and packing my life into boxes.

It wasn't just about the promotion, or the fear of another failure. It was about the work I knew I could be doing if

I just had the latitude. My gaze drifts to a locked folder on my desktop labeled "MCCP - Master." The Mammoth Community Champions Program. My real passion project. A meticulously researched plan to weave the team into the fabric of the city through youth scholarships and mentorships, the kind of legacy-building work that actually matters. I'd pitched the concept to Vivian last month, and she'd dismissed it with a wave of her hand. "Stick to the metrics that move the needle, Sloane," she'd said. "Northstar cares about ROI, not your sentimental charity projects."

I can't let that happen again. Not when I'm this close. This Northstar deal isn't just a sponsorship. It's proof I can navigate the minefield. That I belong in the room. That I can survive this league.

Thirty minutes.

I snap the laptop closed. The sound ricochets through the stillness. I stand with such purpose that my knee clips the edge of the desk, sending a jolt up my leg. Hissing, I grab my bag, shoving my laptop in with more force than necessary. My hands are steady but my blood simmers, and apparently my coordination has already clocked out for the day. If he wants to drag this down to his level, fine. I'll meet him there.

The elevator button to the rink level gets a jab that borders on assault.

The equipment room hits me all at once: sweat, leather, adrenaline. Racks of gear loom on either side. Somewhere deeper in the room, someone's practicing stick handling, the rhythmic thwack echoing off the walls.

I refuse to be intimidated. I've earned my place here just as much as any of them.

I find him exactly where I expected: standing between two equipment racks, casually peeling off his practice jersey like he doesn't have a care in the world. Like he didn't just blow off a meeting that could determine whether I keep my job.

"Garrett Sullivan."

His name leaves my mouth like a shot across the bow.

He glances up. Recognition flickers across his face, and that's what makes it worse. Not confusion, not the blank stare of a stranger trying to place me. He knows exactly who I am. I can see it in the way his jaw sets, the way his eyes do a quick sweep of my blazer and heels before dismissing the whole picture.

"Hey, Sloaner." He tosses the sweat-damp jersey onto a hook, reaching for a clean T-shirt. The old nickname lands like a pat on the head, the same one he's used at every team barbecue and Christmas party for years, designed to keep me in the box marked "Easton's kid sister, do not engage." "Look, I don't have time for corporate fluff. Whatever slideshow you brought—"

"Stop right there."

I step into the narrow aisle between the racks, blocking his exit. He's even bigger up close, six-foot-three of ice-hardened muscle that makes the aisle feel half its actual width. When he straightens to his full height, I have to tilt my chin to meet his eyes. I don't blink.

"You cost us twelve million dollars yesterday with that interview."

He laughs, but it's hollow. "Twelve million? That's some creative accounting. Nobody cares what I say to a reporter."

"Northstar Bank cares. They're our title sponsor. Their executives watch every word that comes out of your mouth. And yesterday, you told the world you 'don't really think about the fans' and that sponsorship logos are 'just noise.' It went viral, for all the wrong reasons."

His smirk fades, but I'm just getting started.

"You think media doesn't matter? Your teammates are carrying your weight every time they step in front of a camera because you've made yourself unavailable. Lucas spent twenty minutes yesterday explaining why you're not actually an arrogant asshole, which is time he should've been talking about his own achievements."

I step closer, watching his posture adjust. The lazy slouch sharpens into something engaged. His gaze narrows, and I can see the exact moment he stops seeing Easton's sister and starts seeing the person who just cornered him in his own territory.

"When free agents choose teams, they look at three things: leadership, chemistry, and public perception. You know what torpedoes all three? Players who act like they're above the business that pays their salaries. You want to focus on hockey? Great. But the business side funds everything from your equipment to the plane that takes you to games."

His stance has shifted completely now. Feet squared, shoulders set, bracing for a hit. But his eyes are sharp, calculating, fully engaged for the first time since I walked in.

"So when you torpedo a major sponsorship deal because you're too cool to engage with the media, you're not protecting the team. You're undermining it. And when Northstar pulls funding and we can't afford to keep the depth players who make your stats look good? That's on you."

Silence fills the aisle. Garrett stares at me, and I watch him recalculate. He's seen me across tables at Easton's birthday dinners. Heard me argue hockey stats with his teammates over drinks. But he's never had me square up in his face like this, and we both know it.

When he finally speaks, his voice is quieter.

"You sound more like a general manager than a marketing director."

"I understand hockey. That's my job."

He pushes off the equipment rack, standing straight now instead of leaning. His eyes narrow, and I catch something I don't expect: he's re-filing me. I can see it happen. Not Easton's sister anymore. Something he doesn't have a label for yet.

"Most suits I deal with," he says, "couldn't tell a forecheck from a face-off."

"I'm not most suits."

He closes the distance between us. At six-three he blocks out the fluorescent light entirely, and I notice a pale scar along his forearm I've never seen before. In all those years of team dinners and rink-side proximity, I've never actually been this close to him. I've watched Garrett Sullivan from a careful, self-imposed distance for as long as I can remember.

That distance just collapsed to about six inches.

"Fine," he says. "I'll do the training."

The tension in my chest loosens so fast it's disorienting. But before I can exhale, he adds, "But I'm only doing it with you. No one else."

It's not a concession. It's a provocation.

"That's not how this works. We have a whole media relations team—"

"Then I guess we don't have a deal."

He starts to brush past me, and I don't move. We're close enough now that I can count the gold flecks in his irises. This is exactly the kind of proximity Coach Kowalski warned me about. The kind that gets staff reassigned, demoted, erased.

"Why?" I manage.

A smile, barely there, ghosts across his mouth. "Because you actually get it. Most people in your position don't." He clears his throat, the sound rough in the quiet aisle. For a moment his gaze darts down the row of equipment before locking back on mine. The easy arrogance is gone, replaced by something more focused.

Then he moves past me. His shoulder brushes mine, intentional, unhurried, and I hold my breath until he's three steps gone. My hands find the edge of the nearest equipment rack and grip it, knuckles white, while my heartbeat does something I'm not going to think about right now.

"Looking forward to it," he tosses over his shoulder, leaving me standing alone in the narrow aisle.

3
Garrett

The leather of the steering wheel is warm under my hands, sun-heated from sitting in the arena garage for the past ten minutes. I haven't turned the radio on. The engine clicks softly as it cools, the only sound beneath the low hum of fluorescent lights overhead.

She had invited me to a meeting called "Media Synergy & Brand Strategy Session." Corporate for: "Fix your attitude, or we'll find someone who will." The phrase makes my jaw clench—but not because of the threat. I've faced worse pressure than a marketing exec trying to polish my public image for sponsor money.

What gnaws at me is how she handled it.

I've known Sloane McKenzie for years. She's Easton's sister, which means I've seen her at team dinners, watched her demolish his hockey takes from across the table, nodded at her in hallways. She was wallpaper. Background. Someone I filed under "teammate's family" and never thought twice about.

The woman who just cornered me in my own equipment room was not that person.

She didn't lead with buzzwords or fake charm. No tight smile, no shallow flattery. She walked straight into my territory and called me out. Told me, point-blank, what my behavior was costing the team. Told me why it mattered—to the locker room, the franchise, the bottom line.

Twelve million dollars. Northstar Bank cares. Your teammates are carrying your weight every time they step in front of a camera. The depth players who make your stats look so good.

She did her homework. Knew the figures, understood the dynamics. Most suits focus on the star players and have no clue how important the rest of the guys who fill out the roster are, but Sloane? She gets it.

She's not most suits. Apparently she never was, and I just wasn't paying attention.

I shift into drive and pull out of the garage, muscle memory guiding me through the familiar streets toward home. The city's quiet at this hour—past rush hour, before the dinner crowd. Just the way I like it.

The thing that's really grinding at me isn't that she was right about the media stuff. It's that she didn't flinch. Not when I crowded her space in that narrow equipment room aisle. Not when I used every inch of my size to intimidate. She just tilted her chin up, looked me in the eye, and dismantled my argument piece by piece.

Made me feel like a rookie again. Getting read the riot act by a coach who actually gives a damn.

My phone buzzes on the center console.

Lucas Martinez

I don't answer. By morning, half the locker room will know Tank Sullivan got verbally tackled by someone half his size wearing designer heels.

The elevator to my loft is slow, giving me too much time to think. About her voice, low and clear, saying she understands hockey. About the way she called me out not to score points, but because she actually gave a damn.

About the fact that I'm thinking about Easton's sister at all, and what that means.

My front door swings open and the silence wraps around me like armor. This space is sacred. Here, there's no crowd, no cameras. No Tank. Just Garrett.

The loft opens around me—exposed brick, iron beams, soft lighting that warms the bones of the place. Floor-to-ceiling windows overlook the Mississippi, the river dark and slow under the weight of twilight.

The west wall is lined with books—real books. Spines cracked, pages dog-eared. Hemingway leans into Dostoevsky. Atlas Shrugged still has a bookmark jammed three-quarters in because Rand's philosophy makes my teeth itch, but I'm too stubborn to let her win.

On the mantel above the concrete fireplace, my grandmother's snow globe collection gleams under the dim lights. London. Paris. A ridiculous little Zamboni in a miniature rink she picked up in Montreal. They're sentimental, absurd—and completely mine. I'd break fingers if anyone touched them.

Keys land in the ceramic bowl by the door, a small echo in the quiet. My shoulders drop an inch. The ritual begins.

Shoes by the mat. Phone facedown on the charger. Messages can wait.

In the kitchen, I check my sourdough starter—alive and bubbling in its jar, a quiet thing that needs care and patience. Not performance. Not power plays. Just time and attention.

I pour two fingers of bourbon—eighteen-year, amber and smooth—and head for the leather chair by the window. The record player calls to me from the corner, and I flip through vinyl until I land on what I need.

Bill Evans Trio. Waltz for Debby.

The needle drops. A soft pop. Then jazz pours into the room, piano drifting like memory.

This is my world. Quiet. Controlled. Mine.

The laptop opens with a familiar chime. I pull up video footage—tomorrow we've got Chicago. That means three periods of controlled brutality. I scan their recent games, looking for patterns, weaknesses, anything that might give us an edge.

The footage starts, and I watch with the detached focus that's made me one of the league's top defensemen. Chicago's power play, their breakout patterns, the way their forwards cycle in the offensive zone. It's chess at ninety miles per hour, and I'm looking for the move they don't see coming.

Then I pause the footage.

Zac Torres. Six-foot-four, and every ounce of it mean as a snake. The camera caught him mid-check, shoulder driving into some unlucky forward's ribs, the kind of hit that borders on dirty but stays just clean enough to avoid a suspension.

I know that look in his eyes. I've worn it. But his is different. Where I hit to protect, he hits to dominate. He plays with a chip on his shoulder the size of the Sears Tower, like he has to prove something on every single shift.

Last year, he blindsided our rookie with a late hit. Three weeks on injured reserve. I made sure he paid for it the next time we met.

Guys like Torres think intimidation is the only way to earn respect. They don't realize that for some of us, the only response is to hit back harder.

I sip the bourbon, eyes scanning his stance on the screen. He keeps his left shoulder tucked in, just slightly, favoring it on the follow-through. That's the tell. The shoulder's not 100%.

I rewind the clip. On the forecheck, he lunges—all power, no finesse. For a split second after he commits to the hit, his entire right side is exposed. A passing lane. An opportunity.

The jazz piano fills the quiet loft, a gentle counterpoint to the violence frozen on my laptop. The two worlds never get less strange, living together in the same room.

My phone buzzes. Probably my agent trying to catch me when he knows I'm not at the gym, or maybe Coach with some last-minute adjustment to tomorrow's lineup. I don't check it. Tonight, the outside world can wait.

I close the laptop, the city lights glittering through the glass beyond. The city moves, but in here, I'm still.

Tomorrow, I'll lace up. I'll become Tank Sullivan again. I'll absorb the hits and give the media exactly the nothing they expect from me.

But not now.

Now, I'm just Garrett.

4

Sloane

The parking lot at Mammoth Center is empty except for a handful of trucks and SUVs that cost more than my annual salary. Six forty-five in the morning, and I'm clutching a travel mug of coffee that's already gone lukewarm, my tablet loaded with a half-finished content calendar that needs actual footage to mean anything.

Vivian wants "authentic behind-the-scenes material." Fine. I've spent half my life in rinks watching Easton's practices. Time to see what I'm actually marketing.

The cold hits me the second I enter, that particular arena cold that settles in your bones regardless of the season. Ice and rubber and industrial cleaner, the smell of every rink I've ever known. I climb to my usual vantage point three rows up from the glass and settle in.

The Zamboni makes its final pass, leaving the ice pristine and gleaming. Players start filtering out in twos and threes, the hierarchy obvious: veterans taking their time, younger guys with that hungry energy. Coach Kowalski is already at center ice, whistle around his neck, clipboard in hand.

The players form up without being told. Twenty men moving into position like they've done this a thousand times before.

Because they have.

"Line rushes," Coach barks. "First unit."

The drill starts simple. Forwards working on breakout timing while defensemen practice gap control. Reid leads his line up ice, taking a pass at the red line and driving wide. The defenseman backs up, maintaining position, forcing Reid to the outside. Reid tries a toe-drag to cut inside. The defenseman's stick is already there, breaking up the play.

"Again," Coach calls. "Kowalski, you're cheating inside. Trust your edges."

Reid resets. This time he sells the outside harder before cutting back, and the defenseman bites just enough. Reid's shot goes high glove. Would've beaten most goalies.

The puck hasn't settled before the next line is already moving.

I've watched thousands of these drills with Easton. But the speed here is different. Not just faster but more compressed. Decisions made in half the time with twice the consequence.

A younger forward, can't be more than twenty-two, tries the same move Reid just executed. Gets the defenseman leaning, makes the cut, but his hands aren't quite quick enough. The puck rolls off his stick.

"Keep your hands soft!" Coach yells. "You're gripping it like a baseball bat!"

The kid nods, face red, and skates back to the line.

Three more rushes. Then Coach switches to breakout patterns.

"Defensive pairs, let's go. Work against the forecheck."

This is where it gets interesting. Two forwards pressure the defense, trying to force turnovers. The defensemen have to move the puck up ice under pressure, and if they mess up, Coach will make them run the drill until they get it right.

Garrett and his partner take their positions in the defensive zone. The forwards come at them hard, sticks active, cutting off passing lanes. Garrett takes the puck behind his own net, scans the ice for maybe half a second, then makes a tape-to-tape pass to his partner at the far boards. The partner immediately wheels and hits a forward breaking up the wing.

Clean. Efficient. Done before the forecheck could establish position.

"That's how it's supposed to look," Coach calls.

The next pair isn't as smooth. The defenseman panics under pressure and throws a blind pass up the middle. It gets picked off immediately. Coach's whistle screams.

"What the hell was that? You looked at nothing and passed to no one." Coach skates over, tapping his temple with one finger. "Your eyes are your first move. See it, then make it. Again."

They run it five more times. Each rep a little cleaner, a little faster. The fourth time, the defenseman makes the right read: chip it off the glass to relieve pressure instead of forcing something that isn't there.

"Better. That's patience."

The drill evolves. Now forwards are crashing the net on odd-man rushes while defensemen try to break up plays without taking penalties. Bodies start hitting boards. The hollow boom echoes through the empty arena, a sound I've heard my entire life but one that never gets old. Skates carve hard, throwing ice spray. Someone takes a cross-check in the corner and responds by finishing his check twice as hard on the next rep.

This is where you see who's willing to pay the price. Board battles aren't pretty. They're won by whoever wants it more, whoever's willing to take the punishment and come back for more.

A forward gets tangled up with a defenseman along the wall. Both going hard for the puck. Sticks slashing, shoulders grinding, neither giving an inch. The forward finally muscles it free and shovels it to a teammate in the slot.

"That's compete level!" Coach shouts. "That's what wins games in March!"

Reid steps in for the next rush, takes a hit along the boards that I feel in my seat, and still manages to make the pass. The forward one-times it. The goalie makes the save but gives up a rebound. Another forward crashes the net, jams it home through traffic.

"That's a goal because Reid sacrificed his body to make the play," Coach says, pointing at the sequence. "Nobody remembers pretty passes. They remember who wanted it more."

Twenty minutes in, and I can see the fatigue setting in. Breath coming in clouds. Faces flushed. But the intensity doesn't drop. If anything, it ratchets up, because everyone knows the real test is operating at this level when your legs are screaming.

Coach blows the whistle. "Power play units. First group, let's see some puck movement."

They run through set plays, practiced sequences where everyone knows where they're supposed to be. Except under pressure, those clean patterns fall apart. A pass is a second late. A guy's not quite in position. The whole thing breaks down.

"Reset. Run it again until it's automatic."

They do. Seven times. Eight. On the ninth rep, it finally clicks. The puck moves fast, the defense can't adjust, and someone finds the seam for a one-timer that beats the goalie clean.

"That's the rep that matters," Coach says. "Not the pretty ones. The one where you're exhausted and you execute anyway."

Then comes the part I knew was coming but still makes me wince.

"Conditioning. Bags on the line."

The collective groan ripples through the team. I've seen Easton skate these enough times to know they're brutal.

"Blue line and back, red line and back, far blue and back, goal line and back. Five sets. Move."

They line up across the goal line and explode forward on Coach's whistle. The first sprint looks clean. Strong strides, good form. By the second set, the technique starts to slip. By the fourth, it's pure survival. Faces red, mouths hanging open, legs heavy.

Garrett keeps pace with players ten years younger. He's not faster, but he doesn't slow down. When a rookie starts to fade, Garrett drops back beside him.

"Come on, kid. Mind over matter."

The rookie looks like he might die, but he finds another gear.

The final set is carnage. Everyone's dead on their feet, but nobody quits. They finish, then collapse at center ice, pulling water bottles from their helmets and gasping.

This is the job. Not the games. Not the highlights. This. The work nobody sees that makes everything else possible.

Coach gives them thirty seconds, then calls them to center ice for video review. They drag themselves over, still breathing hard, and cluster around his tablet while he breaks down yesterday's game film.

I catch fragments: "gap control," "weak side support," "lose the puck battle, lose the shift." But mostly I'm watching the way they absorb information while their bodies are still recovering. How they nod at corrections, ask questions, stay locked in even though every muscle probably wants to shut down.

Practice ends at eight-fifteen. Players skate off toward the tunnel in groups, some chirping each other about blown plays, others silent with exhaustion.

I'm packing up my tablet when I realize what I just witnessed.

I came here for content. For footage. For marketing angles.

What I got was a reminder that hockey isn't a product. It's work. Brutal, repetitive, unglamorous work done at six forty-five in the morning when no one's watching. And the difference between good and great is who's willing to do that work when it hurts.

My tablet is full of notes, but the real takeaway won't fit in a content calendar: these guys earn every dollar, every cheer, every moment of glory with hours of suffering in empty rinks.

I look back at the ice one more time. The Zamboni's already making its rounds again, erasing every trace of the morning's work.

Like it never happened.

But it did. And tomorrow they'll do it again.

The familiar smell of garlic and basil wraps around me as I push through the heavy wooden door of Marcello's. The restaurant hasn't changed in the year since Easton and I first started coming here: same checkered tablecloths, same Dean Martin crooning from hidden speakers, same elderly hostess who always pretends not to recognize us before breaking into a grin.

"McKenzie, party of two," I say, even though we both know she's already spotted Easton's unmistakable frame folded into our usual booth.

"Ah, Sloane! Your giant is already here, stealing the breadsticks as usual."

I laugh, weaving between tightly packed tables toward the corner where Easton is doing his best impression of a linebacker trying to fit into a dollhouse. At six-four, he makes everything in this cozy place look miniature, but it's always been our sanctuary. Neutral ground. A place where I'm just his sister, not the Mammoths' marketing exec walking a corporate tightrope in the same organization where he guards the net.

"You're late," he says without looking up, mid-demolition of what must be his second bread basket.

"You're early," I retort, sliding into the booth and snatching the basket before he can demolish the rest. "Don't you have a game tomorrow? Shouldn't you be eating quinoa and visualizing puck trajectories or whatever weird goalie zen you do?"

"My weird goalie zen includes carb-loading and stealing my sister's breadsticks." He grins, that easy smile that got him out of trouble our entire childhood. "Besides, I was hungry. You said six-thirty."

"I said seven." I check my phone. "It's six forty-five."

"Potato, po-tah-to."

The conversation is familiar, comforting. It dissolves the edge I've been carrying all day. After a week of corporate landmines and trying to crack the Garrett Sullivan code, this place, with its marinara-stained tablecloths and wax-drenched Chianti bottles, is a needed reprieve.

Our server, Maria, appears with my pinot grigio and Easton's sparkling water with lemon. She doesn't even ask anymore.

"The usual?" she says, already writing.

"Please," we echo, then laugh at ourselves. Some rituals never change.

But when she disappears toward the kitchen, Easton's expression shifts. The playful mask slips away, replaced by something more serious. I know that look. I brace for it.

"So," he says, leaning forward and lowering his voice. "How are you settling in? Really settling in, not the corporate-speak version you gave Mom last week."

I sip my wine.

"It's good," I say carefully. "Challenging, but good. The Northstar account's going to be huge if I can land the pitch."

What I don't say: that I spend half my energy threading needles in rooms where credibility is assumed for everyone except me. That "challenging" is the word you use when you can't say "exhausting" without sounding weak.

"That's not what I asked." His eyes study my face the way he tracks a puck in the slot. "You've been pulling late nights for three weeks straight. When's the last time you had a weekend without a spreadsheet?"

"Says the guy who watched game film in his underwear last Sunday."

"Different. I love my job."

It lands like a soft challenge. Do I?

"I love my job too," I say, but even to my own ears it sounds defensive. "I'm just... it's a lot of pressure. New role, new expectations. I have to prove I belong there."

Easton reaches across the table and covers my hand with his massive one. His fingers are scarred from years of deflecting pucks, warm and solid and completely familiar.

"Slo," he says gently, using the nickname only he's allowed to use. "You've been in overdrive since you were a kid. Ever since Dad left, you've been trying to build a life so perfect that nothing could ever touch it."

I pull my hand back, reaching for my wine glass instead. "That's not—I'm not—"

"You were nine years old making five-year plans," he continues, relentless but soft. "Color-coding your school supplies. Paying Mom's bills when she couldn't get out of bed. You've been the adult in every room since elementary school."

"Someone had to be." Sharper than I meant, but I don't take it back. "Mom was underwater for two years. You were barely keeping your head above it. I kept the lights on."

"You shouldn't have had to—"

"But I did." I lean forward, meeting his concerned gaze with steel in my own. "And you know what? I was good at it. I am good at it. Taking care of business, managing crises, making sure everything runs smoothly. That's what I do."

"I know that. But when do you get to just... be? When do you get to want something just because it makes you happy, not because it fits into some master plan?"

The question lodges under my ribs. Because the truth is, I don't know how to want things without calculating the cost first.

Maria arrives with our food, my chicken parm, Easton's outrageously large calzone, and I'm grateful for the interruption. I let the practiced expression slide back into place.

"Speaking of high-stakes diplomacy," I say, slicing into my chicken, "I've got a new assignment testing every skill I've got."

Easton arches a brow, picking up the cue. "Oh?"

"Garrett Sullivan. Media training for the league's least cooperative player." I keep my voice light, like this is just another box to check, not a problem that's been consuming my every thought for days. "He treats reporters like they're hostile interrogators."

"Tank?" Easton's posture changes. Alert, protective. "What's wrong with his media game?"

"Everything. One-word answers, stone face, enough hostility to tank a sponsor relationship. Vivian wants me to turn him into a human brand ambassador."

I expect him to laugh. Instead, his expression darkens.

"Be careful with that one, Slo."

I pause, fork halfway to my mouth. "Why?"

"Because I've been his teammate for six years and I still don't know what's actually going on in his head." He pushes his calzone around his plate. "He came to my birthday last year, brought this bottle of bourbon that probably cost more than my goalie pads, stayed for exactly forty-five minutes, talked to maybe three people, and left. That's Tank. Generous, loyal, shows up when it counts, but there's a wall there that nobody gets past. And if the front office wants you to get past it?" He shakes his head. "That could get ugly."

"Ugly how?"

"The kind that ends careers." He meets my eyes. "You know what this business is like. It doesn't protect the staff. It protects the assets."

My stomach drops.

"You think I can't handle one difficult player?"

"I think you can handle anything. But I also think you're ambitious, and that makes you a threat. Add in a player with a complicated reputation and a GM with a history of scapegoating, and you're playing with fire."

I want to argue. But the worst part is, I know he's right.

"Thanks for the confidence," I say, trying to keep the hurt out of my voice.

"Hey." He reaches across the table again, but this time I don't pull away. "I'm not doubting your abilities. I'm questioning their commitment to protecting you if things go sideways. There's a difference."

"Things aren't going to go sideways. It's media training."

"Just promise me you'll be smart about it," Easton says. "I love Tank, but the last person who tried to get close to him got burned pretty bad. I don't know the full story, he won't talk about it, but something happened with his ex, and ever since then he's got the shutout mentality off the ice too. Nothing gets through."

Emma. I've heard the name in passing. Caught a fragment of locker room gossip once, something about an article and a betrayal. I filed it away and never asked Easton about it because it wasn't my business.

It still isn't.

"I'm not trying to get close to him," I say. "I'm trying to get him on camera without causing a diplomatic incident."

"I know. Just..." His expression softens. "You have a good heart, Slo. And players like Tank, they're used to people wanting something from them. They don't always know how to handle someone who's just trying to help."

"Message received. Keep my distance. CYA. Don't give anyone ammunition."

"Exactly." He smiles, but it doesn't reach his eyes. "Now stop stress-eating my breadsticks."

I glance down at my plate, sheepish. Half the basket has mysteriously migrated to my side.

"Okay, maybe I'm stress-eating a little."

"Maybe?"

We drift into easier conversation: road trips, presentation timelines, Mom's latest matchmaking attempts with her book club's grandchildren. The kind of normal that smooths over raw nerves.

But just as the check arrives, Easton's phone buzzes with a team alert. His expression shifts, subtle but sharp.

"What?"

"Nothing," he says too quickly. "Just... team stuff. Sullivan had a run-in with a reporter after practice. Daniels said it got heated. Looked like he was ready to drop gloves with a mic."

The chicken parm in my stomach turns to lead. "Do we know what happened?"

"Not yet. But it's probably going to be your problem tomorrow."

I stare at the melting candle between us. A test, I think. Vivian knew this might happen.

"You sure you're ready for this?" Easton asks quietly.

No.

"I'm ready," I say, the lie tasting foreign in my mouth.

5

Garrett

The sixth-floor conference room is a vacuum. Quiet, sterile, the kind of space built to mute emotion. I push through the glass door and get hit with recycled air, dry and chilled, a poor imitation of the clean bite of rink-level ice.

Afternoon sun slices through the windows, turning the polished mahogany table into a blinding slab of reflected light.

Sloane sits behind her laptop. That auburn ponytail is pulled tight and clean, not a hair out of place. She doesn't look up. Just types, fingers moving fast and precise.

"Right on time," she says, eyes still on the screen.

I drop into the chair across from her, the leather sighing beneath me. "Let's get this over with."

Now she looks up. Cool green eyes, sharp and giving nothing away. "Good. Because we need to deal with your media presence using actual data, not guesswork."

She taps her keyboard, then swivels the laptop toward me. "In the last forty-eight hours since your interview aired, your social sentiment dropped thirty percent. Your Q-rating among the eighteen-to-thirty-four demo, Northstar's core demographic, is down fifteen points. And the comments you made last night haven't helped matters."

Then she opens another tab. "This is what their exec sent us."

I lean forward. The email is short but brutal: Concerned about brand alignment... need to see significant improvement in public perception... reviewing partnership terms.

My hand clenches into a fist under the table. "Point made."

"We're not done." She clicks again, and a familiar, bitter taste rises in my throat.

The interview.

My voice fills the quiet room, low and detached, as I offer up shrugs and one-word answers. The silences drag. The reporter's fake smile trembles. I watch myself dismiss a question about community outreach like it was beneath me.

She freezes the video. "This is what we're working with."

"So?"

"So," she says, eyebrows lifting, "this isn't about camera charm. These partnerships fund everything from the sticks in your hands to the gym you train in. When you tank an interview, you don't just hurt yourself."

I sit back, arms crossing. "Media training isn't going to change who I am."

"I'm not here to change who you are." She clicks to another tab. "I'm asking you to tell your own story before someone else does it for you."

The screen changes, and the air goes out of me.

"The Iceman: All Talent, No Heart."

The conference room falls away.

I'm twenty-two again. The locker room reeks of sweat and grief and something sharper, metallic. Miller, our captain, a guy who seems carved from granite on the ice, has his face buried in his hands. His shoulders heave in waves I can hear more than see, each one landing in my chest. Our coach stares at a spot on the concrete floor, mouth working silently, like the words died before they reached his tongue.

Someone has to hold the center.

I move. One foot, then the other. My hand lands on Miller's shoulder. The padding gives under my grip, foreign and too soft. I open my mouth. Sound comes out. I don't know what I'm saying. My jaw aches from clenching so hard my molars grind. My ribs feel wrapped in steel bands, tightening with every breath I force in and out, measured, even. If I let the rhythm slip, the pressure behind my sternum will crack me open.

A reporter materializes as I push through the exit. Microphone first, then his face. Sharp. Hungry. He already has his story.

"Not much emotion from you, Sullivan. How does a loss like that feel?"

My vision tunnels. I can feel my heartbeat in my temples, behind my eyes, matching the white-hot pressure building at the base of my skull. My hands curl into fists at my sides, nails biting half-moons into my palms. The pain centers me. Keeps everything locked down.

I give him nothing. Just a flat, dead stare. Because if I open my mouth, if I let even one word slip past the barricade, the rest will follow. The howl will come. And I will shatter in front of everyone.

So I don't.

The harsh light of the conference room snaps me back. Sloane's watching me, those green eyes seeing too much. My hand clenches under the table. Heat climbs my neck.

"What the hell is this?"

"This is what happens when you let someone else control the narrative," she says, voice even. "One bad interview. One cold expression. And suddenly, you're the villain."

"You think because you read some clickbait from a decade ago, you understand who I am?"

"I don't claim to know you." Her tone is calm, unflinching. "But I know how fast this machine chews up reputations. And right now? You're handing it the ammunition."

I slam my palm onto the table. The laptop jolts. "That article was bullshit. Written by some hack who decided I wasn't sad enough. It cost me endorsements, cost me the captaincy on my last team when they decided they needed someone with more 'leadership presence.'"

I surge to my feet, my chair rolling back against the windows. "You have no idea what you're talking about."

"Then tell me." Her voice is steady, but there's something else there now. Not pity. Closer to patience. "Because I can't fix what I don't understand."

I lean over the table, jabbing a finger at the screen. Close enough now to catch something clean and sharp cutting through the recycled air. Her, not the room. "You want to understand? That reporter had his headline written before he asked a single question. My team was a mess. Our captain was sobbing. Our coach couldn't speak. I was trying to hold the damn center. And because I kept my shit together in front of a camera, I was branded as the asshole with no heart."

Her lips part, just slightly. The steel in her expression gives way for half a beat. Not sympathy. Recognition.

"Garrett—"

"No." I shake my head, run a hand through my hair. "I'm done. We're done here."

I stalk toward the door, every muscle taut. I should leave. I want to leave.

But my hand lingers on the doorknob.

Because I gave my word. And Tank Sullivan doesn't break his word, not even when every instinct tells him to run.

Behind me, the room goes quiet.

She doesn't speak. Doesn't move. Just waits.

I turn back, jaw tight. "Not here."

She blinks. "What?"

"If we're going to keep doing this," I jerk my chin toward the screen, "I need a beer."

I don't wait for her answer. I push through the door and the hallway air hits me. Still recycled, still cold, but at least it's not that room. Not that article. Not those green eyes that looked at me like they could see every lie I've ever told a reporter.

My boots are loud on the tile. I keep walking. Past the elevator, past the vending machine, all the way to the stairwell at the end of the corridor. I push through and stand on the landing, one hand braced against the concrete wall, and just breathe.

Three breaths. Four.

Easton's sister. My teammate's sister. She works for this organization. And I just told her the worst article ever written about me still keeps me up at night. Told her in a voice that cracked on the word "heart."

What the hell is wrong with me.

The stairwell is silent. Cold concrete, dim lighting, the faint hum of ventilation. Upstairs, a woman I've spent six years nodding at across Easton's dinner table just watched me lose control, and she didn't flinch. She didn't use it. She just said "tell me," and for one second I wanted to.

That's the part that scares me.

I hear the conference room door open somewhere above me. Her heels, faint on the tile. Then nothing. She must have gone the other direction.

I push off the wall, roll my shoulders, and start down the stairs. The Penalty Box is three blocks east. It's dark enough to think, loud enough to hide, and they don't ask questions.

If she's smart, she won't follow me.

If I'm honest, I'm hoping she does.

6

Sloane

Two days after the conference room disaster, I'm back in the same chair, same table, same recycled air, with a completely different plan.

The Iceman article was a mistake. I knew it the second his face changed, and I've spent forty-eight hours figuring out how to recover the ground I lost. Vivian doesn't know about the blowup. If she did, I'd already be updating my résumé.

My laptop is open to a fresh exercise file. No clips of bad interviews. No articles. No ambushes. Today is a standard media training session: mock questions, camera work, message framing. The stuff I should have led with instead of going for the jugular.

I check the time. 3:01.

He's late. Again.

I'm rehearsing my opening line, calm, professional, pretend the last session never happened, when the door swings open.

Garrett fills the frame. Hair still damp from practice, gym bag slung over one shoulder. He scans the room like he's checking for threats. His gaze lands on my laptop, then on me.

"No ambush this time?"

"No ambush."

He drops into the chair across from me. Same spot as last time. Same leather sigh. But his posture is different. Still guarded, but he showed up.

"Okay." I turn the laptop toward him. "Here's what we're doing. I'm going to ask you questions the way a reporter would. You answer. I give you notes. We go again until you stop sounding like you'd rather be having a root canal."

"Can't promise that."

"I'll settle for mildly inconvenienced."

His mouth twitches. Not a smile. But close.

I start with softballs. Hometown. How he got into hockey. What his pregame routine looks like. He gives me answers that are technically correct and completely dead. Flat voice, flat eyes, sentences that end like they've been cut off with garden shears.

"What does this team mean to you?"

"It's a good organization."

"That's a press release, not an answer. Try again."

"It's a very good organization."

I stare at him. He stares back. His expression isn't hostile. If anything, he looks like he's enjoying this.

"You're doing this on purpose."

"Doing what?"

"Giving me nothing so I'll give up and leave you alone."

He leans back, arms crossed. "Is it working?"

"Not even a little." I close the mock-question file. The scripted approach is dead on arrival. Feeding him canned questions and expecting polished answers is like asking a shutdown defenseman to play forward. Wrong position. Wrong instincts.

"All right. New approach." I pull up the game footage I preloaded this morning, Tuesday's third period against Detroit. The Murphy hit. "Walk me through this play."

He frowns. "That's not a media question."

"Humor me."

I hit play. On screen, Detroit's Murphy builds speed behind the net, lining up the Mammoths' rookie center. The hit is coming. Anyone who knows hockey can see it.

"What are you seeing here?" I ask.

Garrett leans forward. The crossed arms drop. His eyes sharpen, tracking the play the way they must track it from the ice, reading lanes, calculating angles.

"Murphy's got thirty pounds on Daniels and a full head of steam. He's been running guys all night, and nobody's answered the bell. That's a problem, because if he puts Daniels into the boards there, it's a separated shoulder. Maybe worse."

"So what do you do?"

"I abandon my position." He says it like it's obvious. "Coach will kill me for it later, leaving the point wide open with two minutes left. But Murphy's not making a hockey play. He's hunting. And if nobody steps up, Daniels pays the price."

"And the hit itself?"

"Legal." He doesn't hesitate. "Shoulder to shoulder, feet on the ice. I just got there first and hit harder. Murphy wasn't expecting someone to come across the zone for a rookie."

He's talking with his hands now. Actual gestures, mapping the ice in the air between us. And his voice has dropped into a register I haven't heard from him before. Lower. Unhurried. Like he's forgotten I'm holding a laptop and not a hockey stick.

"Why that rookie?" I ask. "You've got twenty guys on that bench. Why risk a penalty, risk the coach's wrath, for a kid who's played twelve NHL games?"

"Because that's the job." He looks at me like I should know this. "I've been in this league fifteen years. Daniels has been in it for three months. The first time a guy like Murphy takes a run at you and nobody responds, you learn something about your team. You learn nobody's coming. And that stays with you."

He pauses. "Someone came for me when I was a rookie. I'm still here because of it."

The room is quiet. I realize I haven't typed a single note in two minutes. Excellent work, McKenzie. Very productive use of company time.

"Hold on," I say. I reach over and turn the laptop screen toward him. The camera's been recording since I hit play on the game footage. "Watch this."

He watches himself. The lean-forward posture, the hand gestures, the way his jaw unclenches and his eyes go bright when he talks about protecting his team.

"That," I say. "That's what a reporter should be getting."

He's quiet for a moment, studying the playback. "I didn't know you were recording."

"I know."

"That's sneaky."

"That's marketing." I close the laptop halfway. "You don't have a media problem, Garrett. You know how to explain what you do and why it matters. You just shut down the second someone points a camera at you and asks a scripted question."

"Because scripted questions are bullshit."

"Most of them, yeah. But you know what's not bullshit? What you just told me about Daniels. About someone coming for you when you were a rookie. A reporter asks 'what does this team mean to you' and you say 'it's a good organization,' you're giving them nothing. You tell them that story, why you did it, what it means to protect the kid who reminds you of yourself at twenty? That's a headline. And it's one you wrote."

He looks at the laptop. Then at me.

"You could've shown that recording to Vivian."

He's right. I could have.

"That's not what it's for," I say.

"No?"

"It's for you. So you can see what you look like when you're not performing for someone. That's the version of you I'm trying to get in front of a camera. Not a polished act. Just this."

He holds my gaze for a beat too long. I watch the recalculation happen, the same one I saw in the equipment room when he stopped seeing Easton's sister and started seeing someone else. Except this time, I feel it land.

I look away first. Pull up the exercise file.

"Okay. Let's try the mock questions again. But this time, when I ask something generic, don't give me the press-release answer. Tell me the real one, and we'll figure out together how to make it camera-ready."

"Together," he repeats, testing the word.

"It's a collaborative process."

"Sounds like corporate speak."

"It is. But the sentiment's real."

We run through eight more questions. He's not perfect. Still clams up on anything about his personal life, still defaults to monosyllables when a question catches him off guard. But the hockey answers are looser now. More specific. When I ask about the upcoming playoff push, he talks about the young guys finding their game, about the energy in the room shifting as the stakes get higher. It's rough. But it's real.

"That's a wrap," I say, checking the time. An hour and twelve minutes. It felt like thirty.

He stands, reaches for his bag. Pauses at the door.

"Thursday?" he asks.

"Same time."

He nods once and leaves. The door clicks shut behind him. His footsteps fade down the corridor, and then it's just me and the hum of the air system.

I sit back in the chair. Open the laptop. I should be logging session notes, building the progress report Vivian will eventually demand. Instead, I pull up the footage and hit play.

I watch his hands sketching plays in the empty air. The way he leaned forward when he talked about Daniels. How his voice dropped when he stopped performing.

I close the laptop.

I press my palms flat against the mahogany table, fingers spread. They're not shaking. But they want to.

I have a job to do. I have a career to protect. I have a brother who would lose his mind if he knew I was sitting alone in a conference room replaying footage of his teammate's hands.

Get up, McKenzie. Write the report. Go home.

I get up. I write the report.

I don't go home for another hour.

7
Sloane

The silence in my apartment is starting to get loud.

After a full day of dodging Garrett, I still haven't figured out what I'd even say if I saw him. Last night left a mark I'm not ready to look at too closely. I just need to flush the tension from my system, clear my head.

My phone buzzes on the counter.

Puck Bunny Podcast: New Episode!

Perfect.

I grab my coffee, collapse onto the couch, and hit play.

Brynn's voice fills the quiet. Bright, biting, full of satirical glee. A balm in podcast form.

"Welcome back, you beautiful degenerates, to the Puck Bunny Podcast, where we analyze the only stats that really matter: penalty box fashion and post-game interview meltdowns," Brynn chirps over the upbeat intro music.

"And where I provide the stats," Riley's voice cuts in with dry precision, *"and she provides the chaos."*

"Today, we're inducting a new member into our Worst Hair Hall of Fame," Brynn continues without missing a beat. *"We all thought Jaromir Jagr's mullet was the peak of follicular*

chaos, but folks, we have a new contender: Zac Torres and his... well, his hair looks like a sad, wet Zamboni that just gave up on life."

"Torres is also riding a twelve-game point drought," Riley adds with deadpan delivery, *"so his performance matches his grooming choices."*

I snort into my coffee.

"But speaking of players who actually know what they're doing," Brynn says, her voice shifting into formal presentation mode, *"let's talk about today's main topic: the physical protector in modern hockey. Riley, want to give us the boring, technical definition first?"*

"Gladly," Riley replies, and I can practically hear her adjusting her glasses. *"A physical protector is a high-skill defenseman who combines elite defensive play with strategic intimidation. They're shutdown players, capable of neutralizing the opponent's top lines while also protecting teammates from aggressive or illegal plays. They deter dangerous behavior through physical presence, devastating body checks, and when necessary, fighting. But unlike traditional enforcers, these players are on the ice because of their skill, not just their fists. It's strategic deterrence backed by actual hockey IQ."*

"Okay, okay," Brynn jumps in, her voice bubbling with mischief. *"Let me translate that coach-speak for everyone listening while they fold laundry or pretend to work. Picture this: you know that grumpy, overprotective best friend in every romance novel? The one who shows up when some douche is bothering the heroine at a bar? But he's not just muscle. He's also*

brilliant, capable, and devastatingly competent. He doesn't want to fight, but he will absolutely throw hands if someone threatens his person. That's your old-school shutdown D-man with a mean streak. He's the human embodiment of 'touch her and die,' except he can also solve a Rubik's cube while doing calculus."

"That's... *surprisingly accurate,"* Riley admits. *"And speaking of the perfect example of a physical protector with elite defensive instincts, we need to talk about what Tank Sullivan did in Tuesday's game against Detroit."*

"Oh my GOD, yes," Brynn practically purrs. *"Riley, tell them what happened first, then I'll explain why every woman in America needs to see that replay."*

"Third period, Detroit's Murphy lined up what looked like a dirty hit on our rookie center, Daniels," Riley recounts with clinical precision. *"Sullivan spotted the setup from across the ice, abandoned his defensive position, and intercepted Murphy with a perfectly legal but absolutely devastating check. Murphy went down hard. Sullivan skated away without even looking back."*

"WITHOUT EVEN LOOKING BACK," Brynn repeats, her voice going dreamy. *"Folks, I've watched that clip seventeen times, and every time, I need to fan myself with my stat sheets. This man saw a threat to his baby teammate from forty feet away and turned into a six-foot-three missile of righteous fury. The casual way he destroyed that guy? The complete indifference afterward? Pure alpha energy. Tank Sullivan said 'not today, Satan' and meant every word."*

"The statistical impact was significant too," Riley notes. *"Detroit attempted fourteen fewer hits on our forwards after that play."*

"Because they learned!" Brynn exclaims. *"They learned that Tank Sullivan is watching, and Tank Sullivan does not play. That's the beauty of a guy like Tank. Half his value is just existing. Just being this looming presence that says 'try me, I dare you.' Except unlike those old-school goons, Tank can also quarterback a power play and read plays three steps ahead. He's the whole package."*

This is why their podcast is a phenomenon. Riley brings the sharp, technical analysis that gives them credibility, and Brynn translates it into something everyone can understand: loyalty, protection, drama. They make the game about the stories, and they're damn good at it.

The podcast's still going when my phone lights up with a call. The contact photo is a selfie of us from college, arms draped over each other, cheeks flushed from too much cheap wine and too little sleep.

Brynn.

I pause the episode and answer, still smiling. "If you're calling to defend the Zamboni look, I'm hanging up."

"Defend it?" she scoffs. "I'm submitting it for federal disaster aid."

I laugh. "Honestly, they should just retire his helmet out of pity."

"But that's not why I'm calling. I need to vent before I go on a corporate-mandated rampage. I just got off a 'notes call' with the new network liaison."

I tuck my legs under me, fully settling in. "Oh no. Is this the guy from LA with the perfect teeth who thinks 'synergy' is a food group?"

"So much worse," she groans. "He told me the podcast needs to be more 'aspirational for the male demographic.' His big idea? A segment where I rate players' 'off-ice style,' but," she drops her voice to a pompous baritone, "'in a way that doesn't alienate the fantasy league guys.'"

I wince. "Ugh. The dreaded 'make it for the boys' note."

"He suggested I do less 'deep-dive analytics' and more 'quick-hit hot takes.' Said my last episode on defensive pairings was 'too in the weeds for the casual fan.' I think I blacked out from a rage stroke."

"Honestly, that sounds like a refreshing break from my day," I mutter, swirling the last of my coffee. "I've spent the past eight hours translating grunts and scowls from the human embodiment of a penalty box."

"Oof. The Sullivan situation," she says, instantly sympathetic. "Has he used a full sentence yet?"

"Not without looking like it caused him physical pain," I say. "Honestly, after this week, a guy whose big idea is more 'hot takes' sounds like a great conversationalist."

"And on top of it, I have to deal with that trashy copycat podcast, The Sin Bin Scoop, trying to steal my bits. They'd probably give that network suit his own segment on 'aspirational male content.'" I can hear the smile in her voice. "Want me to come over with wine and takeout? We can burn effigies of annoying men."

"Tempting, but I have to prep for another session with Captain Monosyllabic tomorrow." The thought makes my shoulders tense. "I need to be sharp."

"Ugh, fine. Be a responsible adult." There's a pause, then her voice softens. "You okay? You sound wound tight."

"It's just work," I lie, too tired to untangle the real answer. "Big project. Difficult client. The usual."

"Right." She doesn't push, which is one of the reasons I love her. "Well, if you change your mind, I'm only one spillable coffee away from 'accidentally' body checking him in the hallway."

I laugh, the knot in my shoulders easing. "You've been practicing your 'oops' face, haven't you?"

"Religiously."

"Thanks, Brynn. Really."

"Always. That's what best friends are for. Now go be brilliant and make that human cinderblock look good for the cameras."

Hanging up, I can't stop smiling. Talking to Brynn is always the perfect antidote. But her final words echo: make that human cinderblock look good. The smile fades as the reality of my task settles back in.

Tomorrow, the easy part is over. Tomorrow, I have to go to work on the cinderblock.

8
Garrett

Thursday's session runs long.

Not because she's pushing. The opposite. Sloane asks me to walk through our neutral zone breakout, and I forget to stop talking. Forty minutes on forechecking strategy. She keeps the camera rolling and doesn't interrupt once.

When we wrap, she's packing up her laptop and I should be heading to the parking lot. Instead I hear myself say, "I still owe you that beer."

She looks up. "What?"

"From the other day. The conference room." I lean against the doorframe, keeping it casual. "I said I needed a beer. Never followed through."

"That wasn't an invitation. That was you storming out."

"It was both."

She studies me for a long moment. I can see her weighing it, her eyes narrow, her jaw sets, the same look she gets before she makes a call in a meeting.

"One beer," she says. "And we're talking about Northstar."

"Sure."

We both know that's not what we'll be talking about.

The walk from the arena to The Penalty Box is three blocks. Neither of us speaks. Sloane keeps pace beside me, her heels clicking against the sidewalk.

The Penalty Box delivers what I need: low lighting, the smell of grease and stale beer, the ambient murmur of a game playing overhead. Familiar. Uncomplicated. Hockey sounds.

I claim a corner booth with a fresh pint, watching Sloane settle across from me with her untouched club soda. She's taken off her blazer. Her sweater clings to her shoulders, and when she tilts her head to glance at the game overhead, I follow the line of her throat before I catch myself.

Neither of us reaches for a menu. Neither of us mentions Northstar.

I take a long drink. The beer is cold and bitter, grounding.

"The article. It's a sore spot."

She doesn't rush in with apologies or small talk. Just watches me, hands wrapped around her glass, steady as a goalie in net.

"It's not just the nickname," I say, eyes on the foam. "It's how fast the world decides who you are in a headline, and how long you spend trying to prove them wrong."

Her expression softens. "I shouldn't have used that article. It was a shitty move."

"You were making a point."

"A bad one," she says. "And you're right. The media loves a good villain."

Her fingers trace the rim of her glass. A nervous habit she probably doesn't realize she has.

I don't know why I keep going. Maybe it's the beer. Maybe it's the fact that she had me on camera two days ago, unguarded, talking about things I don't talk about, and she showed it to me instead of marching it straight to Vivian.

That's not nothing. That's the opposite of nothing. That's the opposite of Emma.

"My ex-fiancée," I say, and the words feel like pulling a tooth. "She used stuff like that article during our breakup. Built a whole campaign on it." I can still see the headline from the gossip blog that ran with her exclusive interview. *He lets other people tell our story because he's too cold to write his own.*

"Twisted my silence into admission of guilt," I hear myself say. "Made me out to be this cold bastard who couldn't love anyone. She fed quotes to reporters, painted herself as the victim who tried so hard to reach me but couldn't break through."

Sloane's fingers still on her glass. "Jesus."

"She sold it. That whole poor-girl, heartless hockey player. They ran with her story because it was better copy." I drain half my beer. "I learned my lesson. Don't give them anything to work with."

She's quiet for a long moment. I watch her turn her glass slowly on the table, thinking.

"If I can't fix this Northstar deal, I'm probably out of a job," she says. Her voice is steady, but her thumb is pressing a dent into her club soda's napkin. "Vivian's looking for any excuse to cut me loose, and failing with their biggest sponsorship would definitely qualify. I've been fighting to be taken seriously since my first day in sports marketing, and this..." She gestures between us. "This could end everything I've worked for."

After that, it's easier.

I lean back in the booth, studying her face. "Why sports?"

"Easton was always on the ice. The rink raised me." She talks faster when she talks about hockey. Her hands move, her posture opens up, the careful corporate composure just falls away. "I know hockey from the inside out, the business, the players, the fans. But half the executives I deal with think I'm just some arena rat who got lucky."

"Are you?"

She grins, and it transforms her entire face. "Absolutely. And I'm damn good at my job."

I believe her.

I lean in, catching every word as she tells me about hiding in the bleachers to eavesdrop on coaches as a kid.

"And then my last boss," she says, puffing out her chest and dropping her voice into a deep, patronizing tone, "told me to 'circle back with a more synergistic approach.' I think my soul left my body."

A real laugh escapes me. Low, surprised, straight from my gut. She's laughing too, eyes bright in the dim bar light. She leans closer to be heard over the crowd, her knee brushing mine under the table. I don't move away.

"He was the worst," she continues, gesticulating, and the back of her hand brushes against my knuckles on the table. She stops talking. Her gaze drops to where our hands are almost touching, then comes back to my eyes.

Neither of us moves away.

By the time we leave, the air outside is a slap. Cold and raw under the orange wash of streetlights.

We stop by her car. Frost clings to the windshield, breath visible in puffs between us.

"Thank you," she says quietly. "For telling me. About the article. About everything."

"I don't hate media," I say. The words are out before I can stop them. "I just don't trust it."

She looks up, and the city noise, the cold, everything just stops. Her eyes are bright under the streetlight, her cheeks flushed from the wind. Or not from the wind.

I know better than this.

But then she just looks at me, and I don't give a damn about better.

I take a half-step closer, the crunch of frost under my boot the only sound.

"This is a terrible idea," I murmur. My hand lifts, hesitant for a fraction of a second before I commit, my fingers brushing the rough wool of her coat before finding her cheek. Her skin is warm despite the cold.

"Terrible," she agrees.

But she doesn't pull away. She leans into my touch, just slightly, and every reason I have to stop disappears.

Just as I lean in, a phone rings. Sharp and jarring in the frozen air. We spring apart. Sloane fumbles in her coat pocket, eyes wide as she glances at the screen. "It's Easton," she whispers, before swiping to answer.

I can hear his voice in the cold air, suspicious and sharp. "I thought I was giving you a ride home but then I saw your text. You're at The Penalty Box? Who are you with?"

She glances at me, panic flickering across her face. "Just... finishing up some work stuff."

"Sloane, seriously. I heard you are doing media training with Sullivan tonight." Easton's tone gets harder. "You remember what happened with Sarah."

I watch the color drain from her face, watch her whole body go rigid. She gives a jerky nod into the phone, then turns and walks away without another glance at me. Every line of her body says this conversation is over.

The name, Sarah, and the terror on Sloane's face are a combination I don't understand.

But I know a warning shot when I hear one.

I stand in the parking lot for a long time after her taillights disappear. The cold settles into my bones. My hand still feels warm where I touched her cheek.

If that phone hadn't rung, I would have kissed her. And if I'd kissed her, I would have put a target on her back in an organization that eats its own. The woman who just trusted me with her career fears, I almost made her the next Sarah, whoever that is.

That thought should kill whatever this is.

It doesn't.

9

Sloane

The team charter bus idles outside the Mammoth Center's service entrance, its diesel exhaust curling into the frozen air. I stand on the loading dock, briefcase in hand, watching the fluorescent bay lights glint off the tinted windows. My breath escapes in sharp white puffs as I mentally tick through my checklist: Northstar proposal draft. Player media stats. Travel itinerary. Everything I need to prove I deserve to be on this trip.

The engine rumbles through the soles of my boots. This isn't just transportation. It's their sanctuary in motion, and I'm an outsider being granted temporary access.

Sarah's face flashes through my mind. The look on hers that day. The way she packed up in twenty minutes flat, certifications rolled into a tube, reputation shredded by whispers and coffee proximity. Coach Kowalski's message had been crystal clear then. It should be crystal clear to me now.

I cannot afford to become collateral damage.

None of us can. This Northstar deal isn't just my career on the line. It's Miller's and Vivian's, too. Miller fumbled the last two trade deadlines. Vivian's 'New Era' campaign tanked season ticket renewals. Henderson's patience is wearing thin, and we all know Henderson has no patience for owning an unprofitable team. This deal is everyone's last lifeline.

The driver tips his cap as I board. "Morning, Miss McKenzie."

"Morning, Frank."

Inside, the air is thick and warm, saturated with old gear, fresh cleaning solution, and something distinctly territorial. Two rows of leather seats stretch before me.

I scan the layout automatically, cataloging the unspoken code. The rookies will flood the front, buzzing with first-playoff energy. The middle belongs to staff and trainers. And the back? That's veteran territory. Unwritten law. Untouchable.

I choose a seat mid-right. Safe. Strategically invisible. Close enough to observe, far enough not to intrude. Career preservation disguised as seating etiquette.

The rookies file in, voices crackling with caffeine and nerves. A few veterans offer polite nods. Easton's sister, after all. My shoulders loosen slightly.

Then Easton boards.

His goalie bag is slung over one shoulder like a second spine. Our eyes meet. His nod is a silent, complicated language I've known my whole life: pride and warning, all in one. Pure Easton. He continues toward the back, and the breath I didn't realize I was holding escapes in a slow exhale.

The bus fills steadily. I keep my eyes on my screen, tracking social media mentions, until the conversations seem to go quiet around me.

I glance up to see Garrett stepping aboard.

He's one of the last to board, veteran privilege. His hair is damp from the morning skate, clinging to his temples. He moves the way he moves on the ice: unhurried, sure of exactly where he's going.

He stops at the front. Surveys the cabin.

Plenty of open seats near the back with the other vets. A few with the equipment staff. Safe, expected options that follow the protocol carved by three decades of team culture.

His eyes find mine.

Don't. Don't even think about it. Follow the rules. Pick a seat. Keep your distance.

Garrett starts walking. Down the aisle. Toward me.

I spot Turner, one of the alternate captains, nudge his seatmate and nod toward us. A rookie cranes his neck to get a better view, mouth slightly open. Even Frank adjusts his rearview mirror.

He stops at my row.

"Thought the arena rat might need backup in enemy territory."

He slides in beside me. The leather sighs under his weight.

Arena rat. He remembered.

I stare straight ahead, body rigid. "What are you doing?" I whisper through gritted teeth. "Everyone is looking."

"Relax. I'm checking on my media coach." He says it at normal volume, easy, natural, the kind of thing anyone on the bus could hear and file away as unremarkable. Then he drops his voice. "You look like you're about to crawl out of your skin."

I hate that he can read me so easily.

He pulls out his phone and a pair of earbuds. Holds one up, the white cord dangling between us. "Music helps."

I should refuse. Taking it turns us into something on a bus full of people who will remember every detail.

But my hands are shaking and the engine noise is grinding against my teeth and he's just sitting there, patient and un-bothered, like this is nothing.

I take it. Our fingers brush. I fumble the bud before secur-ing it in my ear.

The music begins. Not the aggressive rock I expected, but something indie and thoughtful. A bass line that builds a wall between us and the rest of the bus.

"Better?" His voice is lower now, meant only for me.

Despite myself, I nod.

He catches me glancing at my laptop, the Northstar deck, still open, color-coded within an inch of its life.

"You color-code everything?"

"It's called organization."

"It's called terrifying." But the corner of his mouth twitch-es. And something about that twitch, the fact that he's teasing me, here, now, with twenty guys pretending not to watch, makes me forget, for exactly one second, that I'm supposed to be afraid of this.

I almost smile. I don't. But my shoulders drop half an inch, and he notices. Of course he notices.

We settle into the music. Not talking. His arm rests on the armrest between us, sleeve pushed up to the elbow, and I can see the pale scar along his forearm, the one I first noticed in the equipment room. I want to ask about it. I don't.

The bus hits a seam in the highway and my knee bumps his.

Neither of us moves.

I should move. This is the kind of thing that becomes a story, *did you see them on the bus?*, and I know exactly how fast stories travel through a locker room. One game of telephone and "their knees touched" becomes "they were all over each other."

But his leg is warm and solid against mine, and the music is still playing, and for ten seconds I just let it be what it is.

Garrett is the one who moves. He shifts his knee away, casual, unhurried, like he's just adjusting his position, and pulls the earbud from his ear. Stands.

"Good talk, McKenzie." He rolls his neck like he's loosening up for a shift. "Oh, for Des Moines, their regional VP was at the alumni game last month. Numbers guy. Hates fluff."

He pats the headrest of my seat once, the way you'd acknowledge a trainer in passing, and walks toward the back. Easy stride. Unhurried. He drops into the seat next to Lucas, who immediately starts talking about something on his phone. Garrett leans back, stretches his legs into the aisle, laughs at whatever Lucas is showing him.

Doesn't look at me again.

In the window's reflection, I catch Easton's face. His jaw is tight, but he's not grinding it to dust the way he was two minutes ago. Whatever he just witnessed, it was short enough to explain away.

Two minutes. That's all it was.

I pull up my Northstar spreadsheet and stare at the columns without seeing a single number. The earbud is still warm in my palm. I should put it on the seat beside me. Return it to him later through some normal, professional channel. Hand it to a trainer, leave it on the conference room table.

Instead, I close my fingers around it and slip it into my coat pocket.

The bus pulls onto the highway, and the fields open up outside my window. Flat, frozen, endless. I press my forehead against the cold glass and let the vibration rattle through me.

Two minutes. His knee barely touched mine.

So why can I still feel exactly where it did?

10

Sloane

"If a reporter asks about your leadership style, what do you say?"

Garrett tilts his chair back on two legs. "Depends. Is the reporter an idiot?"

"Assume they're all idiots. What do you say?"

"I lead by example on the ice. Next question."

"That's seven words. You can give them ten."

"I lead by example on the ice and I don't like talking about it. That's fourteen. You're welcome."

I bite the inside of my cheek to keep from smiling. We've been doing this for forty minutes, our third session since Iowa, and he's getting better at this. Not good. Better. He still makes me work for every sentence, but at least the sentences are coming.

"Okay. Last one." I check my notes. "You're at a charity event. A donor asks what motivates you to give back to the community. Go."

He's quiet for a beat. Then: "Hockey gave me everything. Makes sense to return the favor."

I look up from my laptop. That was actually good. Clean, honest, no hedging.

"What?" he says.

"Nothing. That was solid."

"You don't have to sound so shocked every time I string a sentence together."

"I'm not shocked. I'm pleasantly surprised. There's a difference."

"There really isn't."

These sessions have become the best part of my week, which is a problem I'm not going to think about right now.

"All right, one more. For real this time."

"You said 'last one' two questions ago."

"I lied. This is a media training session, not a democracy." I scroll to the question I've been saving. "A reporter asks: 'What motivates you to keep playing at this level after fifteen years?'"

He doesn't answer right away. The chair comes down from two legs to four. He looks at the window, then at the table, then at me.

"The game changes every year," he says slowly. "New guys come in with new speed, new systems. And every year I have to prove I still belong. That I can still read a play three moves ahead, still protect the guys behind me." He pauses. "I keep playing because the day I can't do that anymore, I won't know who I am."

The conference room is very quiet.

That wasn't for a reporter. That was too unguarded, his voice slower and quieter than he'd ever use on camera. And he's looking at me when he says it. Not at the laptop, not at the window. At me. Like the answer only half belongs to my question.

I reach over and stop the recording.

"That was..." I close my eyes for a second. "We should clean that up for on-camera. Tighten the middle, cut the last line. Too personal."

"Too honest?"

"For a reporter, yes."

I close my laptop. "Good session. We're done."

He doesn't stand up. "You always do that."

"Do what?"

"Cut things off right when they get interesting."

My hands are very still on the laptop. "That's because 'interesting' isn't in my job description. 'Professional' is."

He holds my gaze for one more second. Then he stands, grabs his bag, and pauses at the door the way he always does now.

"Same time next week, McKenzie?"

"Same time."

The door closes. I sit in the empty conference room and stare at the blinking cursor on my session notes for a long time. I type: *Session productive. Client showing marked improvement in message delivery and on-camera comfort.*

I don't type: He looked at me when he said he won't know who he is. I don't type: I stopped the recording because I didn't want Vivian to hear whatever came next. I don't type: This is becoming a problem.

I close the laptop and head to Vivian's office.

The lemon scent of her office hits me as I stand in front of her pristine glass desk, waiting. She doesn't look up from her monitor for what feels like an eternity but is probably ten seconds. Classic power move. Classic Vivian.

"Sloane. Glad you could make it." Vivian's voice is crisp, her posture regal against the city skyline framed by the floor-to-ceiling glass.

I clutch my portfolio tighter. "You said it was urgent."

"The Northstar Bank dinner." She finally looks up. "Tonight. Summit Club. You'll be our marketing point."

My mind clicks into motion. Q3 analytics, fan engagement metrics, renewal timeline. This isn't just dinner. It's negotiation.

"Who's the player rep?"

"Garrett Sullivan. They requested him specifically."

"Tank?"

Vivian's smile is thin. "You'll be his handler. Keep him on message. Northstar's team is data-obsessed."

Handler. Like he's a prizefighter about to punch the wrong executive.

"I can have demographic breakdowns ready in an hour. Cross-market analysis by—"

"Perfect." She turns back to her screen. "That's exactly the kind of initiative that gets noticed around here."

I'm halfway to the door when the knife lands.

"Oh, and Sloane?" Her voice softens, honey poured over glass shards. "David Kellerman from the executive board requested a comprehensive proposal deck. They'll want insights you don't have yet. Data that wasn't in the brief."

She leans back, her expression shifting into something appraising. "Senior executives anticipate the board's needs and deliver solutions before they're asked. Coordinators deliver what's in the brief. This is your moment to decide which one you are."

I nod, my mind already racing, calculating timelines and data points as I turn to leave.

"Oh, and one last thing," Vivian calls out just as I reach the door, her tone breezy, almost an afterthought. "I just got the finalized Q3 numbers from analytics. They're slightly different than the preliminary data I sent last week. Nothing major, but you know Kellerman. I'll shoot them over in an email shortly."

Slightly different. I force my expression to stay neutral. "Thank you, Vivian. I'll look for it."

The walk back to my office is the longest of my life. Every step is a countdown to the moment that email lands, the moment I find out exactly how deep the water is that she just threw me into. Back at my desk, the email arrives with an almost cheerful chime. The subject line: "Updated Numbers!" The exclamation point feels like a taunt.

I open the attachment, and my stomach drops as I scan the spreadsheet. Slightly different? The demographic breakdowns are off by fifteen percent. The engagement metrics I'd built my entire value proposition around have shifted enough to invalidate two of my key slides. I have exactly four hours before dinner to verify these numbers, rebuild my projections, and rehearse new talking points.

Deep breath. I've got this.

The Summit Club smells like expensive champagne and quiet power. Fifty floors up, the city sprawls below us in a glittering grid, and I'm nursing a club soda while reviewing talking points on my phone. Around me, conversations happen in hushed, confident tones, deals being made over thirty-year Macallan and handshake agreements worth millions.

Demographics. Engagement metrics. The Northstar renewal projections I've memorized down to the decimal point. Anything to keep my brain focused on work instead of—

"Ready to knock 'em dead, McKenzie?"

I don't need to turn around. The voice is unmistakable.

I glance up. Garrett's in a charcoal suit tailored within an inch of sin. He doesn't look like a hockey player. He looks like the man who owns the team.

"You clean up nice, Sullivan," I say, tucking my phone into my clutch.

He grins. "Don't sound so surprised."

That's when I notice the tie. Silk. Navy with thin silver stripes, corporate trust colors. Probably Hermès, if my marketing-trained eye is right. And crooked enough to make my perfectionist brain twitch.

"Hold still," I say before I can stop myself.

I step into his space.

The tie is warm under my fingers. He smells like sandalwood and something sharper underneath. My fingers aren't entirely steady as I slide the silk through the knot.

Don't let them shake. His shirt is ridiculously expensive, custom tailored, Egyptian cotton. This is one inch away from being an HR violation. Step back. Now.

But I don't step back. I smooth the tie down his chest. His gaze drops to my hands. Then lifts.

"Thanks, Sloane." His voice is rough, low enough that it lands somewhere it shouldn't. "You always notice the details others miss."

I finally look up and find his eyes dark, focused entirely on my face. Not on the room full of powerful people, not scanning for networking opportunities. Just me.

A laugh from the main dining room breaks the moment. "We should probably..."

"Yeah." He doesn't move, and for a heartbeat, neither do I. "Probably."

I flee to the bathroom.

The marble countertop is ice under my palms. I stare at my reflection. Eyes too wide. Lipstick flawless. Control, not so much.

This is how it starts.

A tie. A glance. A man in a suit who looks at you like you're not invisible.

Sarah flashes in my memory. Brilliant, confident Sarah. Right up until the day security escorted her out of the building, career destroyed, all because she let a beautiful man distract her for a split second.

You are not her. You will not lose everything for a man in a great suit.

I reapply lipstick with steady hands and go back to work.

Dinner is a masterclass in professional chemistry.

The Northstar execs are exactly what I expected: sharp suits, sharper questions, the kind of people who see dollar signs instead of game scores. Robert Blackwood, the senior VP, has the smile of someone who's made his fortune turning sentiment into spreadsheets. Jennifer Walsh, their marketing director, dissects every proposal down to the decimal.

But Garrett and I are something else entirely tonight.

"The team chemistry this season has been exceptional," Blackwood says, cutting into his dry-aged ribeye. "What's your take on the leadership dynamic, Sullivan?"

Garrett sets down his fork. Gives Blackwood his full attention.

"Leadership's about trust," he says, voice calm, measured. "About building systems where everyone knows their role. But real strategy comes from people like Sloane."

The pivot is so smooth I almost miss it.

He nods toward me. "She identified a twelve percent crossover between our season ticket holders and Northstar's premium credit card users."

He turns, that same focus now on me. "Sloane, walk them through the conversion model?"

The handoff is perfect. I launch into the numbers, riding the high of being in my element.

"The demographic overlap targets high-income professionals, ages twenty-eight to forty-five. We're projecting a fifteen percent increase in premium card applications during game weeks, direct revenue correlation tied to emotional investment in the team."

I swipe to the interactive model on my tablet. "If we time campaigns around playoff runs, we can spike conversion even higher. Sports loyalty becomes brand loyalty when the messaging aligns with emotional peaks."

Jennifer leans forward. Skepticism giving way to something closer to respect. "You're talking about leveraging parasocial relationships for financial products."

"Exactly," I say. "The trust fans place in their team becomes trust in Northstar's brand. We're not just sponsoring hockey. We're sponsoring belonging."

Blackwood smiles for the first time all night. "You two make an interesting point. I think this is the start of something bigger, if you keep bringing this level of insight."

Under the table, Garrett's foot brushes mine. Brief, deliberate. I glance over and find his gaze already on me.

There's pride in his eyes. But there's also something else I'm not going to name at a business dinner.

"But enough business," Jennifer says, signaling the server. "Robert, didn't you want another bottle of wine to have with dessert?"

"Absolutely. Garrett, why don't you two pick something special? I heard you have an eye for wine. The private collection's in the wine room."

Of course it is.

The wine room door shuts behind us with a soft click, muffling the restaurant's hum to nothing. Rows of bottles stretch from floor to ceiling in temperature-controlled glass cases. The air smells like oak and earth and aging paper.

Garrett leans against a rack of champagne. The tight discipline he wore during dinner loosens now, corporate polish falling away. What's left behind is the version of him I only see when the cameras are off.

"You were incredible out there."

The words hit lower than they should. I turn toward the wine display, trailing my fingertips along a bottle I can't afford to pronounce. "We were incredible. Not bad for a Friday night."

"Sloane."

My name in his voice makes me freeze. When I turn, he's already crossed the narrow space between us. Close enough that I have to tilt my chin to meet his gaze.

"This isn't about the job anymore," he says softly. "And I don't think it has been for a while."

My heart is hammering. "Garrett, no." The words come out breathless. "We work together. The Kowalski rule—"

"Screw Kowalski." He steps closer, blocking out the wine racks, the room, everything that isn't him.

"It's not that easy." My back hits the wine case, cool glass pressing through the silk of my dress. "For you, breaking the rule is a fine. A slap on the wrist. For me, it's a career death sentence."

I turn away, but there's nowhere to go. My fingers find the label of a Dom Pérignon, tracing its edges.

"I knew someone," I whisper, barely audible above the soft hum of the temperature controls. "Sarah Carlson. She was my mentor when I interned at the Titans."

The air behind me goes still. He doesn't speak. Just waits with the patience of someone who understands that some stories can't be rushed.

"She was brilliant. Best marketing mind I've ever seen. Could take a last-place team and make them profitable within a season." My voice catches, and I have to swallow past the tightness in my throat. "She had this corner office with windows overlooking the practice facility. Used to keep it stocked with the good coffee because she said great ideas deserved great caffeine."

I can still see her. Sharp blazers, designer heels, commanding every room she entered. Sarah who taught me that data was just storytelling with numbers. Sarah who showed me how to turn passion into profit margins.

"She fell in love with a player. Jason Pruitt. They kept it quiet, but someone got photos. Posted them on social media with captions about conflicts of interest and professional ethics."

My hands are shaking now. I press them flat against the cool glass, watching my reflection fracture in the curved surface of the bottles.

"The team fired her within a week. Said it was about 'maintaining professional standards' and 'avoiding appearance of impropriety.'" I can't look at him.

"What happened to her?" His voice is rough, carefully controlled.

"She moved to Portland. Works for a minor league baseball team now, making a quarter of what she used to earn. Jason got traded to Chicago the next season. Never missed a paycheck." The words feel thick and wrong in my mouth. "She lost everything. He lost nothing. That's the rule here. For women, ambition and love are mutually exclusive."

I hear him step closer. When I finally risk a glance in the reflection, he's right behind me, close enough that his breath stirs the hair at my nape.

"Sloane." His voice is barely above a whisper. "I'm not him."

Slowly, I turn to face him. He's right there. Inches.

He reaches up, fingertips barely grazing my jaw. The touch is careful, asking permission with every movement. But there's fire behind it.

"And you," he says, voice rough, "are not her."

"How can you be so sure?" The question comes out as barely more than breath.

His thumb traces along my cheekbone. "Because everything you said about Sarah was about what she lost. But everything I see in you is what you build."

My mind flashes to the dinner. The slides, the strategy, the confidence I wore into that room. The way I turned skeptics into believers with nothing but data and conviction.

"What you did out there tonight?" His voice drops lower. "That's yours. You didn't inherit it or sleep your way into it. You earned every ounce of respect in that room. And no one can take that from you."

His other hand comes up to frame my face, and I'm caught between his body and the wine case.

Something inside me cracks open. My hand moves without permission, settling on his chest where I can feel his heartbeat under expensive cotton.

"Garrett..." I start, but I don't know how to finish. Don't know if I'm warning him away or pulling him closer.

He leans down, and I tip my face up, and for one perfect, terrifying moment we're suspended between wanting and having. His lips are a breath away from mine, his hands warm on my skin, and every rational thought in my head is dissolving.

Then footsteps echo in the hallway outside.

We spring apart. My back hits the wine case hard enough to rattle bottles, and Garrett stumbles backward, running a hand through his hair. The spell breaks so suddenly it leaves me dizzy.

The footsteps pass without stopping, but the damage is done. Reality crashes back. We stare at each other across the narrow space, both breathing hard, both perfectly aware of how close we just came to crossing a line we can't uncross.

"We should..." I start, then trail off.

"Yeah." His voice hasn't recovered. "We should."

But neither of us moves toward the door.

I watch him straighten his tie with unsteady fingers, watch him rebuild the mask that slipped. When his eyes meet mine again, they're steady. Decided.

"This isn't over, Sloane." Quiet. Certain.

I reach for the Château Margaux with hands that barely shake. "A classic," I manage, my voice steadier than I feel.

He moves to hold the door, and as I pass through the narrow space, his hand settles on the small of my back. The touch looks professional, courteous. It isn't.

Back in the restaurant, Robert Blackwood is laughing at something his colleague said. The wine arrives with perfect timing, served in elegant crystal goblets that reflect the candlelight. We slide back into our seats, back into our roles.

Blackwood raises his glass. "To new partnerships."

The glasses clink. The wine is rich, complex, impossibly smooth.

Across the table, Garrett lifts his glass, and his eyes find mine over the rim.

When the check arrives and we stand to leave, his hand finds my elbow to guide me toward the exit.

He walks me to the taxi stand, our footsteps echoing in the quiet lobby.

"See you tomorrow, Sloane," he says.

He waits until I'm safely in the car before turning away, but as my driver pulls into traffic, I catch him in the side mirror. Standing on the sidewalk, hands in his pockets, watching my taillights disappear into the Minneapolis night.

My phone buzzes against my purse. A text from an unknown number. Three words glow on the screen:

That was real.

It's past midnight when I finally get back to my apartment. The Northstar dinner was a success. I navigated Vivian's data sabotage, and Blackwood seemed impressed.

But I'm not celebrating. I'm terrified.

I stand in my kitchen, the navy silk of my dress feeling slick and cold against my skin. All I can see is the look on Garrett's face in the wine room. All I can hear is my own voice, telling him the story I never tell anyone.

She lost everything. He lost nothing. That's the rule here.

I've spent my entire career proving I'm the exception to that rule. But tonight, surviving Vivian's sabotage and then nearly kissing Garrett at a client dinner, it all feels like I'm walking straight into a trap.

Vivian didn't just try to make me look bad tonight. She tried to make me fail. This isn't professional rivalry. This is targeted sabotage. And now Garrett is a factor.

I've moved past reactive. I'm done being a target. If I'm going to protect my career, I need to know why she's so threatened by me.

I toss my heels onto the rug and head to my office. Sleep is impossible.

I'm not just curious about Vivian's past. I'm a strategist gathering intelligence. And the only clue I have is that single photograph on her monitor, her standing next to Jake Morrison, wearing an expression that had nothing to do with love. I remember that Morrison used to play for the Columbus Blue Jackets, so that must have been where she worked before. She never talks about it.

I type a search into Google: *Vivian Lamore Columbus Blue Jackets*

The first three pages give me nothing but generic press releases and archived game recaps. I refine the search, add quotation marks, try different combinations.

On page six, buried beneath layers of irrelevant results, I find it.

A staff photo from the Columbus Blue Jackets' 2019 holiday party. The image quality is poor, clearly taken from an old website slideshow, but I zoom in anyway. There's Vivian, younger but wearing that same controlled expression. I scan the other faces, looking for anything that might—

Three people down from Vivian stands Anna Reyes. One of the junior coordinators from marketing operations, the one who never speaks in meetings and always looks terrified of her own shadow.

Not might-be Anna. Not someone who looks like Anna. It's unmistakably her. Same delicate features, same dark hair. But the woman in this photo is different. Confident. Open. Her smile reaches her eyes in a way I've never seen at the Mammoth Center.

I screenshot the image. Anna worked in Columbus. With Vivian.

Too late to approach her now. But tomorrow.

I catch Anna at the coffee machine the next afternoon, timing it for that liminal window between meetings when the office empties out for lunch. She's pouring cream with careful precision, her movements contained.

"Anna?" I keep my voice light, curious. "Quick question. I was digging into some of Vivian's old press, and I saw this."

I pull up the screenshot on my phone, angling it so she can see.

The cream keeps pouring. Over the rim. Across the counter. She doesn't move to stop it, doesn't seem to notice. Her eyes, locked on my screen, go glassy with something beyond fear.

"You worked with her in Columbus, right?" I press gently.

When she finally looks at me, the color has drained from her face so completely I can see the fine tracery of veins at her temples.

"I..." The word dies in her throat.

She catches herself, forcing her shaking hand to set the coffee pot down with deliberate care. When she speaks again, her voice is flat. Dead.

"Yes. I worked there."

"Anna, did anything happen? I've been trying to understand Vivian better..."

"I don't know what you mean, nothing comes to mind." She says it to the counter, not to me. Each word lands like a door slamming shut.

"Anna, I just need to know if—"

"I have a two o'clock meeting I need to prepare for."

She turns, dumps her ruined coffee in the sink, and walks back to her desk. Not fleeing. Not running. Just gone.

I stare at her rigid back as she disappears around the corner.

11

Garrett

The booth in the back corner of Murphy's Tap House has been ours for three seasons. Same cracked leather, same initials carved into the table edge by some drunk college kid in 2019, same waitress who knows our orders before we sit down.

Tonight, all five of us made it. Phil Santos is holding court about his daughter's hockey practice. Marcus Webb's laughing so hard beer nearly comes out his nose. Taylor's already two deep and getting louder. And Easton McKenzie—my best friend, my goalie, the brick wall who's kept us in games we had no business winning—is shaking his head at all of them.

"Tell me the tutu story isn't true," Easton says as I slide into the booth.

"Pink tulle over full gear." Phil grins. "Coach didn't know what to do with her. I told him if she can skate in a tutu, she can skate in anything."

"That's because you're soft," Taylor cuts in. "You're raising a mini tyrant."

"I'm raising a girl who knows her own mind." Phil's voice carries that easy confidence of a man who's figured out what matters. "When she's sixteen and some junior hockey asshole tries to tell her what to do, she's gonna tell him exactly where to shove it."

"Spoken like a terrified father," Webb says.

Easton raises his glass. "To terrified fathers. May our future daughters never date hockey players."

"Amen," Phil and Webb say in unison, clinking glasses.

"Tank." Easton leans back, beer in hand. "That hit you threw on Torres in the second period—beauty. Daniels owes you."

"Kid needs to keep his head up."

"Kid needs a veteran defenseman watching his back," Easton corrects. "Which he's got. You're good with the young guys. They trust you."

Something warm settles in my chest. Easton doesn't throw compliments around carelessly. When he says something, he means it.

"Speaking of young guys," Taylor jumps in, "Mitchell tried to fight that Chicago enforcer. Dumb kid's lucky he didn't get murdered."

"Mitchell's twenty-one and thinks he's invincible," Webb says. "We were all that stupid once."

"Some of us still are." Phil looks pointedly at Taylor

The conversation flows—game breakdown, playoff positioning, the usual chirping about Taylor's dating disasters and Webb's expanding family. Easton leans back, beer in hand, looking relaxed in a way he never does on game days.

"You know what the worst part about being a goalie is?" Easton says.

"The crippling anxiety?" Phil offers.

"The fact that you're all clinically insane?" Webb adds.

"No." Easton grins. "It's that I have to watch you idiots throw yourselves in front of hundred-mile-an-hour shots and pretend it's normal."

"That's called playing defense," I say.

"That's called a death wish," Easton shoots back. "I get paid to be crazy. What's your excuse?"

"We're protecting you," Taylor says. "You're welcome."

"You're giving me premature gray hair is what you're doing." Easton runs a hand through his hair. "Tank, that hit you threw in the second? My heart rate monitor thought I was having a cardiac event."

"You wear a heart rate monitor during games?" Phil asks.

"My therapist suggested it. Said it might help with the anxiety."

"And does it?"

"No. Just gives me data on exactly how stressed I am. Turns out it's very."

This is what I came for—not the beer or the wings, but this. The rhythm of men who've bled together enough times that the distinctions between friendship and family stopped mattering.

Easton's phone rings. He glances at it, silences it, then drains the rest of his beer. "Early practice tomorrow. I'm out."

"Disciplined," Phil says with mock reverence.

"Someone has to be." Easton stands, throws cash on the table. "See you guys at practice."

He claps my shoulder as he passes, solid and sure.

The door closes behind him. For a moment, there's just the comfortable noise of the bar—someone's terrible karaoke attempt at *Don't Stop Believin'*, the crack of pool balls, the low murmur of a dozen other conversations happening around us.

Taylor signals for another round of wings. "So Phil, when's your kid's next game? I want to see this tutu situation in person."

"Saturday morning. Eight a.m."

"That's barbaric. Who schedules children's hockey for eight a.m.?"

"People who hate parents," Phil says. "But you're welcome to come suffer with me. Rachel would love the company."

"I'll be there," Webb says. "My wife's been on me about getting out of the house more anyway. Says I'm hovering."

"You are hovering," Phil confirms. "You texted me yesterday asking if it was normal for pregnant women to cry at insurance commercials."

"It was a very moving commercial about life insurance."

Taylor's already crying laughing. "What was she insuring? Her feelings?"

"Tank, you coming Saturday?" Phil asks. "Fair warning, the coffee is terrible and the rink smells like a locker room had a baby with a wet dog."

"Wouldn't miss it."

Phil pauses mid-drink. "Really?"

"Yeah. Why?"

"Because last time we invited you somewhere, you showed up for thirty-seven minutes and then claimed you had 'a thing.'"

"I did have a thing."

"You had 'being around humans makes me uncomfortable' thing," Taylor cuts in. "But sure, 'a thing.'"

Webb nods. "My kid's birthday. You arrived, ate exactly one slice of pizza, and then vanished like a vampire at sunrise."

"I stayed appropriate amount of time."

"You missed the cake," Phil says. "Who leaves before cake?"

"Someone who hates fun," Taylor adds helpfully.

I take a long drink instead of responding.

Phil's still watching me though. "So what's changed?"

"Nothing's changed."

"Something's changed." Taylor leans forward. "You smiled at practice yesterday. Unsettling."

"I smile."

All three of them look at me.

"You really don't," Webb says.

"You do this thing—" Taylor makes a face like a constipated robot "—that's technically a smile but mostly terrifying."

"Anyway," Phil cuts back in, "whatever's going on with you, keep it up. Less corpse energy is good for team morale."

The wings arrive. Taylor immediately burns his mouth, swears, drinks beer too fast, swears again. Webb shakes his head. Phil's already telling a story about some guy from his Boston days.

"Hendricks started hooking up with someone in PR. Went bad, messy breakup, she still had to coordinate all his media stuff. Kid requested a trade within a month."

"Miller in Tampa married the GM's daughter," Webb adds. "Divorced a year later, couldn't get ice time. Coincidence, sure."

"Front office stuff gets messy," Taylor says through a mouthful of wings. "That's why I keep it simple. Tinder, bad decisions, no workplace entanglements."

"That's not a strategy, that's chaos," Phil says.

"It's *sustainable* chaos."

I'm only half-listening. Across the bar, Mitchell's waving down the waitress for another round, already slurring. I catch Daniels' eye, give him a look. The kid immediately intervenes, smooth enough that Mitchell doesn't notice his beer getting swapped for water.

"You just did it again," Phil says.

"Did what?"

"That thing. Taking care of people when they don't even know they need it."

"Kid's twenty-one and hammered. Someone needs to."

"Most people would let him make his own mistakes."

"Yeah, well." I shrug. "He's got practice tomorrow."

The check comes. We split it without discussion—same as always.

Phil catches my arm on the way out. "Saturday. Eight a.m."

"I'll be there."

"Good." He squeezes once, lets go. "Rachel's making her breakfast burritos after. You're staying for those."

"That a request or an order?"

"That's me telling you that if you pull your disappearing act, my wife will hunt you down. And she's scarier than I am."

Taylor and Webb are already arguing about the Uber route. Phil herds them toward the car.

I watch them go—Taylor still talking, Webb tolerating it, Phil making sure everyone gets home.

The scrape of my blades carving into fresh ice is a sound I've known my whole life, but this morning, it's background noise. I glide backward, pivot loose, and then it hits me—sandalwood and wine.

The cellar. Her eyes. The dim gold light on her cheekbone.

I miss the edge on my turn. My skates stutter against the ice before I recover.

A slow smile starts to form—and then my phone buzzes on the bench. Once. Again. A third time. Urgent.

I coast over, the vibration rattling against the boards. A mass text alert.

Coach Kowalski

MANDATORY all-hands meeting: team and staff.

Conference Room C.

10 minutes.

The smile is gone. Ten-minute notice means someone's in the crosshairs.

The walk from the rink to the conference hall is a pressure drop. The usual chirps from the equipment guys are replaced by tight jaws and low murmurs. In the hall, the air is stale, recycled. I find a seat with the other vets. My eyes scan the room automatically. I find her—three rows up.

Sloane.

She glances back, just once. Her posture is military-rigid, eyes unreadable. But I feel it—the same tightness cinching my chest is written all over her.

Then Kowalski steps to the podium.

The hum in the room cuts to silence.

He grips the mic with white knuckles. "There are rumblings," he says, voice gravel over steel. "Distractions."

I go still.

"My philosophy has always been to protect this team. From now on, it's not a philosophy."

I brace myself, expecting a hit from the blind side.

"It's a zero-tolerance mandate."

Behind me, whispers start up. Low, sharp. Taylor's voice.

"Heard it's Miller and one of the interns."

"Rookies," Parks mutters. "Don't know what they're risking."

"What do you mean?"

"Careers, man," Taylor answers. "Seen it happen. Player gets involved with someone on staff, chemistry goes to shit, everything falls apart."

Kowalski's voice drones on—chemistry, distractions, accountability—but all I hear is the conversation behind me.

"It burns everything down," Taylor mutters.

And that phrase—it slices clean.

You let it burn everything down, Sullivan. The GM's voice from ten years ago. The cold office. The C stripped from my jersey.

"Burns everything around it," Taylor adds.

I look back up. Look at *her*. Sloane. Her story about Sarah. She lost everything. He lost nothing.

This isn't about me anymore. It's about her.

Kowalski's voice sharpens. "I won't let personal drama poison this locker room. You risk your job, you risk the team's future. Make your choices."

The meeting ends. The chairs scrape. Players rise. Tension stretches over everything like a pulled muscle.

I catch a glimpse of Vivian up front—stone-faced, arms folded, not even pretending to hide her disdain. She's not looking at Kowalski, she's staring at a fixed point on the far wall, her expression a mask of cold, familiar fury. When her eyes briefly meet Sloane's across the room, there's no professional solidarity, only a look that says, *See? This is what they do. This is how they burn it all down.*

My first instinct, sharp and absolute, is to find Sloane.

I navigate the tense crowd, shouldering past a couple of rookies who are whispering nervously. I see her up ahead, talking with a colleague from her department, her expression carefully neutral, but the stiffness in her shoulders gives her away.

"Sloane," I say, my voice lower than I intended.

She turns, her eyes meeting mine. And I know before she speaks—she's already armoring up.

Her colleague ducks away. We're left standing in the chaotic hallway, a bubble of intense silence around us.

"Well," she says, her voice crisp and cool, a stark contrast to the warmth from last night. "That was... unambiguous."

"Are you okay?" The question feels stupid and inadequate.

"I'm fine, *Sullivan*." She uses my last name like a shield, her gaze flicking over my shoulder as if to remind me we're being watched. "I have a proposal to finish for Northstar. That's my focus."

Then she turns—cool, professional, closed.

I watch her go, pulse surging with something that isn't quite panic but damn close.

Then I see it.

A reporter, cutting her off by the media tunnel. Not one of the good ones. He's all angles and elbows, recorder in her face, his questions slick with implication about team chemistry.

The possessive heat surges through me—move. Intervene. End it.

But I freeze. Because I want to see what she does.

And she doesn't even flinch. She just offers a cool, professional smile that doesn't reach her eyes.

"Mark," she says, her voice calm and even. "I've already provided the team's official statement on our playoff readiness. Is there a specific part of 'we are confident in our roster' that you're struggling to understand?"

The reporter's smug expression falters. He starts to stammer, but she gives him a single, dismissive nod and turns away, leaving him fumbling with his recorder.

A memory flashes—Emma, crying and screaming at a blogger in a hotel lobby, making it all about her. The contrast is a physical jolt.

Sloane runs her own plays.

She disappears down the hall, and the low-grade panic simmering in my gut solidifies into something else. Something hard and clear. Kowalski's mandate. The whispers. The wall she just put up. They aren't just obstacles.

They're threats.

And I'm done playing defense.

The locker room feels different tonight because I'm different. The familiar rhythm of preparation—shoulder pads, shin guards, the methodical choreography of getting ready for war—but there's a new edge to it. A purpose that wasn't there before.

"Tank." Easton's voice cuts through my focus. He's lacing his skates two stalls down. "You good?"

"Better than good." The response surprises us both. He raises an eyebrow but doesn't push.

I tape my stick with deliberate precision, each wrap of black tape a promise. Kowalski's voice echoes in my head—*Make your choices*—and I have. The mandate was meant to scare me into submission, to make me back down and play it safe.

Instead, it's gasoline on a fire I didn't even know I was carrying.

The tunnel stretches ahead, and I'm aware of every detail with hyper-focused clarity. The ring of skates against concrete. The low murmur of preparation. The weight of the moment pressing down like atmospheric pressure before a storm.

I catch a glimpse of the press box as we emerge—auburn hair catching arena lights—and instead of pushing it away, I let it sharpen me. She's up there. Watching. And I'm about to show her exactly what happens when someone threatens what's mine.

The anthem plays. Twenty thousand people on their feet. The energy builds, and I channel it into something cold and controlled and absolutely lethal.

The puck drops.

And I go hunting.

Seventeen minutes in, Chicago's Torres builds speed on the forecheck, lining up our rookie Daniels behind the net. I see it developing—predatory veteran looking to make a statement on fresh meat.

Not today.

Every cell in my body recognizes this moment. This is exactly what I told myself in that hallway: *I'm done playing defense.* Torres represents everything—every threat, every ultimatum, every spineless bureaucrat who thinks they can dictate the terms of my life.

I angle my approach with fifteen years of controlled violence. Torres commits to his hit—too high, too late—and I arrive at the perfect moment with all the fury I've been storing since Kowalski opened his mouth.

The collision is devastating. Legal, but barely. Torres hits the ice hard, sliding into the boards with a look of genuine shock. The crowd explodes, but I'm not done. I stand over him for a beat—just long enough to make sure he understands the message—before skating away.

Touch my guys, and I'll end you.

"Beautiful hit, Tank!" someone yells from the bench.

Damn right it was. And it felt better than any hit I've thrown all season.

I'm locked in now, but not the way I usually am. This isn't the zen-like calm of pure hockey instinct. This is sharper. Meaner. Every play is personal because I've made it personal. Kowalski wanted to back me into a corner? Fine. But cornered animals are the most dangerous.

Second period, Chicago power play. They're moving the puck with crisp precision, looking for the seam that will crack our defense. I'm seeing everything three moves ahead—not because I'm calm, but because the anger has burned away everything except clarity of purpose.

You want to threaten my career? My choices? Try it.

I anticipate their cycle before they execute it. Position myself not where the puck is, but where it's going to be. When their point man thinks he's found the perfect passing lane, I'm already there, stick blade angled to deflect the puck into neutral territory.

The interception springs our counter-attack. Clean breakout, odd-man rush, goal.

This is what playing offense looks like. Not waiting for the hit to come. Taking control. Dictating terms.

"That's why you're the alternate, Tank!" Coach yells as I skate past the bench.

He has no idea. I wear the 'A' because when it matters—when someone I care about is threatened—I don't back down. I don't play safe. I go through whatever's in my way.

Third period. Game tied 2-2. Four minutes left.

Chicago pulls their goalie, flooding our zone with six attackers. The pace ratchets up to playoff intensity, and I feel it in my bones—this is my moment. This is where I prove that Kowalski's mandate means nothing. That I'm not backing down. That I'll take every hit they throw and still be standing.

Their point man winds up for a slap shot through traffic. I read the trajectory instantly, and there's no hesitation. No calculation of risk versus reward. There's only the pure, distilled truth that's been burning in my chest since that meeting:

I protect what's mine.

I drop into the shooting lane as the puck rockets off his stick. Ninety-five miles per hour of vulcanized rubber catches me square in the ribs, finding the gap between shoulder pad and elbow guard. The pain is white-hot, explosive, driving the air from my lungs.

And it feels like victory.

This is what it means to play offense. To step into the fire instead of avoiding it. To choose the pain because the alternative—backing down, playing it safe, letting fear dictate my choices—is worse than any physical punishment.

I hit the ice hard, gasping, seeing stars. My ribs scream in protest, but I'm already pushing myself back up because that's what you do when you've decided to stop being afraid.

"You okay, Tank?" Easton calls from the crease.

I give him a thumbs up, though my ribs might be cracked. It doesn't matter. This is the price of refusing to back down. And I'll pay it every single time.

Two minutes later, riding the adrenaline of earned pain and absolute clarity, I thread a perfect pass through three defenders to spring Cassidy on a breakaway. He buries it top shelf, and the arena explodes.

Game over. 3-2 Mammoths.

The horn blares, and the arena erupts in a deafening roar. The team swarms at center ice, a chaotic symphony of triumph, but I'm barely aware of it.

My eyes are already searching the edge of the ice, the mouth of the tunnel.

And then I find her.

She's standing just inside the corridor, tablet forgotten at her side. Her professional mask is gone, replaced by a smile so bright and full of undisguised pride that it hits me harder than the blocked shot. Our eyes lock across the chaos.

In that single, silent moment, everything crystallizes.

She sees what I just did. She understands what it means.

I didn't just win a hockey game. I proved that I'm done playing by their rules. That I'll take the hit, make the play, and damn the consequences.

The scoreboard says the Mammoths won.

But that look on her face—fierce and proud and completely unguarded—that's the only victory that matters. That's what I went to war for.

And I'd do it again. Every single time.

12

Sloane

Garrett's grin is the only thing I can see. The world dissolves into a blur of blue and gold confetti and the deafening roar of the victory song, but my entire universe narrows to the pure, unfiltered joy on his face. His teammates swarm him, slapping his helmet, but he just throws his head back and laughs, a triumphant, magnetic figure in the center of the storm.

A surge of pride swells through me. The campaign metrics had projected a twenty percent fan engagement lift from this milestone; a quick glance at the roaring crowd tells me we shattered that number. Every screen in this arena played the countdown videos I designed. Every fan knew exactly what they were witnessing tonight because of my work.

Our work, I correct myself, the thought a professional reflex. This is data-driven satisfaction. A successful execution of a multi-platform strategy. But the warmth spreading through me has nothing to do with analytics, and the triumphant pounding in my chest isn't about brand synergy. It's about him. And that is far more dangerous than any metric I've ever miscalculated.

Across the chaos of the arena, Garrett's eyes find mine. The easy, public grin slips, replaced by a slow smile that's just for me.

Kowalski's voice echoes in my head. Zero tolerance.

My hands shake as I grip my tablet tighter. The noise is too loud, the celebration too bright, the weight of eighteen thousand people pressing down until I can barely breathe. I need air. I need space to think without Garrett's eyes on me, without the memory of his voice in that wine room.

I slip away from the tunnel, pushing through the heavy door into the equipment corridor. The sound cuts instantly, from deafening roar to muffled thrum, like diving underwater. The contrast makes my ears ring. My shoulders drop as I lean against the cool cinderblock wall, finally able to breathe.

Harsh fluorescent lights buzz overhead, making everything look stark and exposed. A world away from the carefully orchestrated spectacle beyond that door. It's not pretty, but it's quiet. And right now, quiet feels like salvation.

Here, I can think. Here, I can remember why my promotion depends on staying invisible until the season ends.

The door opens behind me.

Every muscle in my body seizes. I know it's him before I turn. The soft squeak of his skates on concrete, each step measured and sure.

Garrett steps into the corridor, still in full gear except for his helmet. Sweat dampens his dark hair, clinging to his forehead. His face is flushed with exertion and victory, hazel eyes bright with something that makes my mouth go dry. He looks massive in the narrow hallway, broad shoulders nearly spanning the space.

He doesn't speak. Just looks at me, steady and unguarded.

The door clicks shut behind him. Suddenly the oxygen feels thin.

"Congratulations," I say, because I need to fill the space with something normal. Something safe. My voice comes out breathier than I mean it to. "Two hundred assists is—"

"Sloane."

His voice is low, rough. He steps closer. Then again. That same focused stride he uses on the ice. No hesitation. No doubt.

My brain screams: DANGER. ZERO TOLERANCE. But my feet won't move. I'm frozen, trapped between the wall and six-foot-three of determined hockey player who hasn't taken his eyes off me since he walked through that door.

He stops in front of me. So close I have to tilt my head to meet his gaze. His jaw flexes.

"I heard him," he says.

His hand lifts. Calloused fingers graze my jaw with surprising gentleness. His thumb brushes my cheek, angling my face up.

"He's asking me to choose," Garrett murmurs. "And for the first time in my life, hockey might not be the answer."

For one terrifying moment, my mask cracks wide open. Pride, want, fear, all of it right there on my face for him to see. A low groan rumbles in his chest. "Sloane."

My name on his lips is a match to a fuse. I look up at him, and my body acts before my brain can stop it, leaning in.

That's all the permission he needs.

The playful victor is gone. What replaces it is raw and unguarded and it steals the breath out of me. His gaze drops to my mouth, and then he closes the distance.

He leans down and his mouth covers mine. It's not soft. It's hungry and claiming, tasting of victory and salt and weeks of tension finally snapping free. His mouth moves against mine with the same intensity he brings to everything, focused and purposeful. The hard plates of his gear press into my chest.

His tongue sweeps against my lips, a demanding question I answer without hesitation. The kiss deepens, and he presses me back against the cold concrete, his body a hard, undeniable presence against mine. A low sound rips from his chest. "Mine," he growls against my lips, the single word vibrating through me and silencing every rational thought.

The rough scratch of his stubble is addictive against my skin. My hands, which had fisted in his jersey, uncurl. One tangles in the thick hair at the nape of his neck, pulling him closer. The other slides down his chest, feeling the solid muscle beneath the damp fabric.

My brain screams. This is insane. This is career suicide. This is—

More. I need more of this. More of him.

His hand leaves my jaw and slides to my hip. His fingers dig in, claiming the curve through the fabric of my dress. The pressure is possessive and protective all at once. I arch into it, a soft gasp escaping my lips. He swallows the sound, his own breath gone ragged against my cheek.

When he finally pulls back, we're both panting, foreheads pressed together, the world a blur of adrenaline and after-shock. The distant echoes of celebration feel galaxies away. Reality crashes down.

My gaze darts down the corridor. "Are you insane? Any-one could've seen. A camera, a trainer, Vivian—" He's still too close. His proximity fogs my thoughts.

His lips curve into a slow, reckless smile. "Worth it."

The words hit like a slap.

"Worth it?" I whisper, furious. "Worth me getting fired? Worth being blacklisted across the league? Is that what this is to you, some risk that you can afford but I can't?"

The smile dies.

"No." He steps back in. Serious now. "That kiss wasn't the risk. Walking away from it is."

"There is no 'it,'" I say, but my voice cracks.

"Isn't there?" His hand rises again, and for a second I flinch, but he just brushes his thumb along my cheek. "Don't lie. Not about this."

I can't reply. The truth burns at the back of my throat.

He seems to read it anyway.

"So we keep it a secret," he says, voice lower now, like he's already planning the play. "Until the season's over."

A brittle laugh escapes. "A secret? Garrett, we travel together. Your media training is my top priority. My brother is your teammate. You think we can just... hide?"

"I'm not naive. But I'm careful. And you're smart." His eyes lock onto mine. "This becomes a different kind of game. One with higher stakes. The goal? We both win. You get your promotion... and I get to keep kissing you."

His words hang between us, bold and impossible and thrilling.

I don't answer. Not right away. My mind spins with timelines, risks, optics.

Two months. Maybe three.

"You're talking about a total blackout," I say. "No public dates. No photos. Not my friends, not your teammates. We'd have to be ghosts."

He nods. "Ghosts."

He steps back just enough to let me breathe, but his eyes stay locked on me.

"I can handle that," he says. "Question is, can you?"

Can I?

Can I spend months pretending nothing's there, sneaking glances and stolen moments, knowing how high the cost would be if anyone finds out?

The smart answer is no. The safe answer is no. But neither of those is the truth.

"What exactly are you proposing?" My voice comes out steadier than my heartbeat. Business mode. Negotiations.

This I can handle. "Because if we do this, I need rules. Boundaries. A clear understanding of what happens if—"

"We do this," he says, cutting through my spiral with quiet certainty. "Until the season ends. Until your promotion is decided."

"I mean it, Garrett. One hint of unprofessionalism, one slip-up that puts my career at risk, one moment where someone sees you looking at me the wrong way in a team meeting, and we're done. No discussion, no second chances."

"Understood." But he's still smiling, and the confidence in his gaze makes my stomach flip. Like he's already planning exactly how we're going to navigate this. "What happens at work stays professional. What happens outside this buildi ng..." He lets the sentence hang.

"Completely separate," I agree, trying to ignore the way my pulse jumps at the implications. "This doesn't exist during business hours. We're colleagues. Nothing more."

"Deal."

He steps close again, and for a second I think he's going to kiss me. But he only reaches up and smooths a strand of hair behind my ear. The touch is maddeningly gentle.

"See you tomorrow," he says.

Then he's gone.

I stay against the wall, lips tingling, my body humming with a current I can't shut off.

In less than eighteen hours, we'll be trapped on the team jet together. Six hours. Same hotel. Same schedule.

Pretending we're nothing, while this secret burns between us.

I touch my fingers to my lips. I can still taste victory and trouble and the promise of whatever comes next.

The celebration roars on beyond the door, but the noise is a distant hum. All I can hear is the echo of his voice.

Worth it.

13

Garrett

Two weeks.

It's been two weeks since the kiss that changed the rules. Two weeks since Sloane and I made a pact to be ghosts.

Our lives have become a high-stakes game of inches and stolen glances, of living with a constant, humming wire of tension under the surface of every single day. We're both so busy it feels like we live at the rink.

Most of our connection lives on our phones—a private, ongoing conversation that never sleeps. A GIF of a cartoon spy when she sees Kowalski coming down the hall. Me sending a picture of my morning coffee and her replying with a single eyeball emoji. *Watching.*

The real torture—the *good* kind—happens in person.

It's passing her in a crowded arena hallway, the sleeve of her coat brushing my arm for a fraction of a second, sending a jolt through my entire body. It's standing on opposite sides of a packed elevator, our eyes meeting only in the polished reflection of the doors.

And then there's today.

I see her rounding the corner by the training rooms, tablet clutched to her chest, her expression carefully neutral, giving nothing away. She's heading for the media scrum, and every rational part of my brain tells me to keep walking. Give her a nod. Play by the rules we established.

But I'm not feeling rational. I'm feeling the ache of two weeks of near-misses and stolen glances.

I don't even think. I just act.

As she passes the equipment closet, I reach out, my hand closing around her arm. Her head whips around, eyes wide with shock, but I don't give her time to protest. I pull her into the darkness with me, the heavy door clicking shut behind us with soft finality.

The darkness is immediate, broken only by a thin sliver of light under the door. It smells like industrial cleaner, worn leather, and equipment tape, but all I can smell is *her*—that clean, sharp scent of citrus that's been haunting my dreams.

Her surprised gasp turns into a soft laugh against my mouth. "Are you insane?" she whispers, but her arms are already winding around my neck.

"Completely," I murmur, backing her against a rack of spare helmets that rattle softly with the movement.

This isn't the questioning, hesitant kiss from the arena corridor. This is frantic. Desperate. A thirty-second pressure release valve for weeks of pent-up need. My mouth is hungry on hers, and she meets me with equal force, her fingers tangling in the hair at the nape of my neck.

My hands slide under her blazer, gripping her waist, pulling her flush against me. The wall of her professionalism is gone, replaced by the woman who looks at me like I'm the only thing in her universe. I slide one hand up her back, feeling the delicate shape of her spine through the thin silk of her blouse. She arches into me with a soft sound, and I swallow it, deepening the kiss.

For thirty perfect, uninterrupted seconds, there are no rules, no risks—just the feel of her lips and her hands tangled in my shirt, and the sound of my own blood roaring in my ears.

Then, the sound of voices in the hallway—sharp and close. We freeze. Her eyes go wide in the dim light, the reality of what we're risking crashing back in. The footsteps pass, but the spell is broken. She pulls back, breathless and flushed, her lipstick delightfully smeared.

"We have to stop doing this," she whispers, but she's smiling.

"No, we don't," I say, stealing one last, quick kiss before I open the door just a crack. "Coast is clear. Go."

She slips out, smoothing her blazer, and is gone. I wait a full minute, leaning against the door, my pulse finally starting to slow. This is torture. The best damn torture of my life.

The memory of her lipstick, delightfully smeared, is still burned into my mind as the engines of the team jet whine to life outside the window. It's a familiar feeling, but the energy buzzing under my skin is all new. It's all about the pact. All about the fact that Sloane McKenzie sits four rows behind me, looking like the picture of professional focus with her tablet balanced on her knees, when less than an hour ago she was pressed against a wall with my hands tangled in her hair.

I do the usual scan of the cabin—habit from years of reading the ice. Vets and coaching staff in the plush seats up front. Rookies scattered throughout the main cabin. Everything in its place.

My eyes land on Sloane. Window seat. Mid-cabin, a safe, professional distance.

The urge to walk back there is physical. But I force myself to stay put, in my assigned seat up front next to Easton.

Playing by the rules. For now.

I pull out my phone and hover my thumb over her name.

> Worth it.

Four rows back, her screen lights up. I see it happen. See her shoulders tense slightly. She doesn't move right away. Then her head tilts down. From here, I can't see her face. Just the quiet precision of her posture

My phone buzzes.

Sloane

> God, yes.

> Okay done, back to work.

> For now.

The corner of my mouth twitches.

A flight attendant passes down the aisle, and for a brief moment, the path between us is clear. She glances up, and our gazes meet directly over the top of the seats. A spark of live-wire connection across the distance. Then she's looking back at her tablet.

Game on.

The ninety-minute flight becomes a silent, charged game. Her phone buzzes with work calls, and I listen to the clipped, professional cadence of her voice as she handles sponsors, metrics, logistics. There's a sharpness in her tone that cuts through the dull rhythm of travel.

She's all steel and polish.

It makes something in my chest tighten.

My phone buzzes again.

Sloane

MINNESOTA MAMMOTHS CODE OF CONDUCT. Required reading. Section 4, subsection B is particularly relevant to your interests.

Already read it. Pretty sure I'm violating at least three of those just by looking at you from four rows away.

You're a walking HR violation, Sullivan.

Just wait until we land.

By the time the jet touches down and we shuttle to the hotel, I've memorized her little tells. The way she tucks her hair behind her ear when she's focused. The tilt of her head when she's listening.

At check-in, we keep perfect distance. But when we're both waiting for key cards, I let myself drift just close enough for our shoulders to nearly touch.

We both reach for the counter at the same time. Almost.

The jolt from that *almost* shoots straight through me.

"Ice machine's at the end of the hall," I say, voice normal volume, like I'm making casual conversation. "Left of the elevator."

She nods once, studying her key card like it holds state secrets.

Room 412. I'm in 408.

Four doors. Might as well be four hundred miles.

We navigate the lobby separately, but I'm hyper-aware of her every movement—the click of her heels on marble, the way she adjusts her laptop bag, how she holds herself with that perfect professional posture even when she thinks no one's watching. In the elevator, I catch a hint of her perfume, something warm and subtle that makes me want to lean closer.

Night passes with the knowledge that she's just down the hall. I lie in the too-soft hotel bed, staring at the wall that separates us, calculating the exact number of steps it would take to reach her door. Twenty-three. I counted twice.

The morning skate is where I test our new normal. I glide through warm-ups, but my focus keeps drifting to the stands. She's already there when we hit the ice, tablet in hand, perfectly positioned to observe team dynamics.

Halfway through drills, she moves—three seats to the left. Now she's directly in my line.

Smart woman.

I skate past her section. No wave. No smile. Just three full seconds of eye contact as I coast by.

I see you.

She barely nods. Looks down at her tablet like she's studying zone entries. But I catch the slight curve of her lips.

It's enough.

During a water break, I spot her watching me with the same intensity I've been watching her, the composure she wears like armor faltering just enough to reveal the heat underneath. When she realizes I've caught her staring, she doesn't look away immediately like she should. Instead, she holds my gaze for a beat too long, her chin lifting slightly in challenge.

The arena suddenly feels ten *degrees warmer.*

"Sullivan!" Coach's voice snaps me out of it. "You here to put on a show or play hockey?"

"Hockey, Coach." But my pulse is still hammering from that look.

The afternoon game goes well—we take St. Louis 4-2—but I'm distracted. Every time I spot Sloane during media timeouts, I want to skate over and... what? Kiss her in front of fifteen thousand people? Real smart, Sullivan.

Get it together.

The mandatory team dinner at some upscale steakhouse downtown should be routine. Good food, team bonding, everyone on their best behavior. It should be easy enough to keep my distance.

I'm at a table with a few of the other veterans—safe zone. But not far enough. Sloane is at the next table over, seated with Vivian.

The restaurant lighting makes her hair glow. I'm trying not to stare when the voice hits me sideways.

"Well, well. *Tank* Sullivan."

I look up. Danny O'Malley. Blues forward. Smug. Uninvited.

He slides into the open seat beside Sloane. My jaw locks.

"O'Malley."

"Great game tonight," he says—but his eyes are already on her. One arm draped over the back of her chair. Smiling like he's doing her a favor by showing up.

"You must be the one making these guys look good on Instagram."

The casual condescension punches me in the gut.

You're just there to look pretty, Tank. Don't take it so seriously.

Derek's voice from three years ago. Right before I found him in my apartment. With Emma.

I grip my steak knife until my knuckles go white.

The urge to stand up, to put myself between them, claws at my chest. My jaw clenches so hard it aches, and I force myself to stay seated, to appear normal while my pulse pounds in my ears.

But something makes me wait. Watch. Trust.

Sloane angles her body slightly away from O'Malley, and suddenly I can see the difference between her and Emma so clearly it takes my breath away. Where Emma would have giggled and played up the attention, Sloane's spine straightens with quiet steel.

"We handle multi-platform brand strategy and partner activations," she says. "Instagram content is a small fraction of our data-driven fan engagement funnel. But I'm sure you have more important things to focus on—like tomorrow's game."

It's a masterclass in polite demolition. O'Malley flushes, mumbles something, and slinks away.

I exhale a breath I hadn't even realized I was holding, my death grip on the knife finally loosening.

She didn't need me to ride to her rescue. Didn't want it, either. She handled herself like the competent professional she is, shutting down a threat with nothing but words and absolute confidence in her own worth.

The realization hits me with startling clarity: I'm not just attracted to Sloane McKenzie. I'm not just breaking rules for the thrill of it. That spike of jealousy, that terror at the thought of losing her—not to O'Malley, not to anyone—it's real. Terrifyingly real.

The jet cruises through the dark at thirty thousand feet, the win behind us, the world a quiet blanket of clouds below.

Four rows behind me, I see her silhouette against the small porthole window.

My phone buzzes.

Sloane

> I saw you about to jump in with O'Malley.

You didn't need my help.

> Never do. That's the point.

I read it twice. Then lean back, eyes closed. *That's the point.*

But something shifts in me. It's not enough anymore. The glances. The hidden threads. I need *her.*

I open the keyboard. Type. Delete. Type again.

I need to see you. Away from the rink. Just us.

My finger hovers over the send button. This is the move that breaks the game we made. This is the one that asks for everything. I hit send.

The little "Delivered" lights up. I watch. Nothing. Five seconds. Ten. Then—the dots. Typing. Gone. *Shit.* Back again. One minute passes. Then two.

My phone buzzes.

Sloane

Yes.

14

Sloane

The Mammoth Center after hours feels like a different building entirely. I push through the glass doors of the executive wing, my heels clicking against polished floors that reflect the emergency lighting strips running along the baseboards. Most of the offices are dark, ghosts of ambition left behind by people with dinner plans and families and lives that don't revolve around proving they belong.

But not me. Never me.

I settle back into my desk chair, the leather still warm from my earlier twelve-hour marathon. The Northstar presentation spreads across my monitors like a digital war room: demographic breakdowns, engagement metrics, competitive analysis reports painting a picture I'm still not satisfied with.

Close. But not transcendent.

Not the kind of pitch that makes executives forget they're looking at numbers and start seeing possibility.

My marketing brain churns. Traditional sponsorship integrations, predictable ROI. Digital campaigns, solid engagement. CSR initiatives, on brand. But nothing that captures the visceral excitement of eighteen thousand people on their feet, screaming for their team. The raw emotion that makes fans drive six hours to away games, that makes grown men cry when their team hoists a championship cup.

I lean back in my chair, rubbing my eyes. Through my office windows, downtown Minneapolis twinkles against the dark, the city going about its evening routine while I chase perfection in spreadsheets and slide decks.

What I need is the intangible factor. The human element that separates data from storytelling, metrics from magic. And suddenly, I know exactly where to find it.

Game footage. Raw, unedited moments. The kind of split-second decisions that reveal everything stats can't. The chemistry. The grit. The belief.

The team film room is three floors down. By now, it should be empty. Coaching staff gone, players home or in bed.

Perfect.

I grab my laptop and head for the elevator, mentally reviewing which games might deliver: The November 15 comeback against Detroit. The OT win over Nashville where the team looked genuinely surprised by their own resilience. Moments where you could see something clicking, chemistry developing, the intangible team culture that makes fans invest emotionally in outcomes they can't control.

The service elevator descends with mechanical precision. The corridors down here smell different. Less like corporate cleaner and more like honest work. Ice and rubber and the lingering ghost of equipment tape. The film room sits at the end of a hallway lined with storage closets, its door marked with a simple placard that probably intimidates visiting teams more than it should.

I push the door open, expecting darkness and the antiseptic glow of dormant monitors.

Instead, I find light.

A single workstation glows in the corner. One screen plays slow-motion footage. A figure hunched in focus.

Garrett.

He's traded his jersey for jeans and a Mammoths pullover, hair tousled like he's been running his hands through it for hours. Just a man lost in the game he loves.

My chest tightens.

"Working late?" I ask.

He glances up. His concentration fades into something warmer. "Could ask you the same. Though I guess rising stars don't get to clock out with everyone else."

"Neither do alternate captains, apparently." I step inside, letting the door click shut behind me.

"What's the occasion?"

He gestures at the monitor, where Chicago's power play flickers. "They've been shutting us down all season. I figured if I'm gonna complain about our PP coordinator's system, I should at least understand theirs."

I move closer, curiosity overriding caution.

"What am I looking at?"

"See their D-man? He's cheating center, reading our guy's eyes. It's not textbook. It's instinct. He's baiting the pass, sliding over just enough to kill the lane."

The way he sees the game makes something inside me stir. Not attraction, though it's there too. Admiration.

"How did you catch that?"

"Years of pattern recognition. Same way you see trends in numbers that would give most people a migraine." He pauses the footage and looks at me. "What brings you down to the dungeon? Don't tell me you're suddenly interested in penalty kill systems."

"Game footage for the Northstar presentation," I say. "Vivian wants a standard pitch, all metrics and market share. But I'm trying to build a case for something bigger." I hesitate. The quiet of the room makes me feel bold. "I have this whole framework I've developed, the Mammoth Community Champions Program. It's about using our platform for scholarships, youth mentorships... creating real, generational loyalty. But Vivian keeps shooting it down. She says Northstar won't care and that I need to focus on what's 'commercially viable.' So I'm trying to find game footage that proves my point, that these human moments are what create the emotional investment that drives real, long-term value."

His eyebrows rise with genuine interest. "You want to show them what we are. Not just what we generate."

"Exactly." I sit beside him. Aware of the space between us. Aware of everything we're not supposed to feel right now. "Any company can slap a logo on a jersey. But if I can get them to believe they're investing in belonging... that's how I win the room."

He studies my screen. "That's the stuff that actually matters in the locker room. The part no one ever sees."

His comment shouldn't matter. But it does. Coming from him, it lands differently. Maybe because he understands both sides, the business and the passion that drives it.

"The challenge is finding the right moments," I continue, pulling up my presentation files on the adjacent monitor. "I need plays that showcase individual excellence within team success. Moments where viewers can see both skill and heart."

He's quiet for a moment, studying my rough outline. When he speaks, his voice carries the authority of someone who's lived these moments instead of just analyzed them.

"March eighteenth," he says finally. "Away game in Vancouver. Third period, we're down by two with eight minutes left. Phil takes a brutal hit, separated shoulder, everyone can see he's hurt. But instead of coming off the ice, he sets up our next goal with a pass he had no business making."

I'm already pulling up the game footage. "What makes it special?"

"Watch his face when he makes the pass. You can see the exact moment he decides the team matters more than his own pain. That's not skill. That's character. That's what turns fans into believers."

The footage loads, and he guides me to the specific sequence. As the play unfolds, I see exactly what he means. The hit is brutal enough to make me wince. But Phil's expression afterward, the grim determination, the way he positions himself despite obvious agony, it's the kind of authentic human moment that turns data into storytelling.

"Perfect," I breathe, already imagining how this fits into my narrative framework. "This is exactly what I needed."

"There's more." His usual media wariness has been replaced by genuine excitement about showcasing his teammates. "November twenty-third, when Daniels scored his first career goal. Not just the goal itself, but the celebration. Watch how the veteran guys react. Pure joy for a kid they've been mentoring all season."

He's leaning closer now, pointing out details on the screen.

"Show me the Daniels goal," I say.

He navigates to the footage with practiced efficiency. The goal itself is nothing spectacular, a deflection from the slot that trickles past the goalie. But the aftermath is pure magic. Daniels drops his stick and gloves, disbelief and joy on his young face, while veteran players converge on him like proud family members.

"See Walker there?" Garrett points to a player I barely recognize. "Guy's been in the league fifteen years, seen everything. But watch his face. He's as excited as if he scored it himself. That's what team chemistry actually looks like."

I'm taking notes, but I'm also fighting the growing awareness of his presence in this small room. The way he explains each play with genuine pride in his teammates. The thoughtful way he considers which moments will translate to my civilian audience.

"This is invaluable," I say, and I mean it.

"Because you're asking the right questions." He turns to me fully now. "Most people want highlight reels, the prettiest goals, the biggest hits. You want the human moments."

"The human moments are what create lasting relationships. Between fans and teams, between brands and consumers." I'm speaking to fill the quiet that's growing too comfortable. "Anyone can sell a product. But if you can make people feel understood, valued, part of something m eaningful..."

"You create loyalty that transcends results." His voice is quiet, thoughtful. "Even when we're losing, even when the season goes sideways, they still show up because they believe in what we represent."

"Garrett..." I start, not sure what I'm planning to say.

He stands, ostensibly to adjust something on the monitor, but the movement brings him directly behind my chair. I can feel exactly where he is without turning around.

"There's one more sequence you need to see," he says, his voice lower now. "January ninth. The game-winner against Pittsburgh."

He leans down. Points something out. His breath stirs my hair.

I stop breathing.

"Sloane."

My name. A whisper.

I turn. We're inches apart. His hand comes up, fingertips grazing my cheek.

"We shouldn't—"

"I know."

But I don't pull away.

And that's all he needs.

He leans in—

The sound of a door closing echoes through the hallway.

We freeze. Heavy footsteps approach, accompanied by the distinctive jingle of security keys. My blood turns to ice as recognition hits. Those are Easton's footsteps. I'd know my brother's stride anywhere.

I jerk away from Garrett so violently that my chair spins. If Easton walks in here and finds us like this...

"The penalty kill rotation," I say loudly, my voice artificially bright as I spin back to face the monitor. "That's fascinating how they disguise their intentions."

Garrett recovers instantly, stepping back to a professionally appropriate distance. "Right. Chicago's been running this system all season. Very effective against traditional entries."

The footsteps pause outside the door.

My pulse is deafening.

Then... they pass.

Just a guard on his phone.

Relief crashes through me, but I'm shaking.

"I should go." I'm already saving files. "Early meeting."

"Sloane—"

"Thank you for the footage recommendations," I interrupt, gathering my laptop with practiced efficiency. "This will really strengthen the presentation."

The formality is a shield. But as I head for the door, I catch his reflection in one of the dark monitors. He's watching me go, and what's on his face isn't frustration. It's patience. The look of a man who knows what he wants and is willing to wait for it.

15
Garrett

The walk from the arena to my truck is a slow grind, each step heavier than the last.

I grip my keys so tight the metal bites into my palm—anything to distract from the image of Sloane's face when she heard someone walking outside that door. The way she went rigid. The way her walls slammed back up so fast it left me dizzy.

I sit in the driver's seat for five full minutes, engine off, just staring at the dash. The silence in here is a solid thing, thick with everything we didn't say. Everything.

This is insane.

We're adults. Not teenagers sneaking around, always checking for a teacher or a parent. But that's what this is. Stealing moments in closets, texting in code, always looking over our shoulders.

The secrecy is a physical weight, pressing down until it's hard to breathe.

I think about how she leaned into my touch—just for a second—before reality tore it away. How her breath changed when I said her name. The heat between us, so charged, so close, before the sound of footsteps crashed it all down.

If I want to know the real Sloane—not the marketing director with the firewall gaze, not the woman managing perception like oxygen—I need to get her out. Away from the arena. Away from the surveillance. Away from the pressure to perform.

My phone feels heavy in my hand. My thumb hovers over our message thread. I type, the words coming out raw and unfiltered.

> This hiding is killing me. We need to go out. For real.

I stare at the message. Too much. Too fast. It's a demand, not an invitation, and it ignores every risk she's taking. I delete it, the frustration still simmering. I need a better play. Something that gives her an out.

Finally, I settle on something cryptic enough to maintain plausible deniability.

> Know any good places to find stories that don't involve hockey? Could use a tour guide.

I hit send before I can second-guess myself, then immediately want to throw my phone out the window. What if she doesn't get it? What if she does get it and thinks it's stupid? What if—

My phone buzzes.

A bookstore, maybe? Unless a poetry section is too much excitement for you.

Relief floods through me so fast I actually laugh out loud in the empty truck. She gets it. And she's teasing me. I grin as I type back.

Never. I know a place. Wild Rumpus Books on Grand Ave. It's... different. Sunday 2pm?

Intriguing. See you in the stacks.

Come in disguise.

Wild Rumpus Books feels like someone's incredibly well-read grandmother's house. All mismatched furniture, floor-to-ceiling shelves, and the kind of comfortable chaos that comes from prioritizing books over aesthetics. Afternoon light filters through dusty windows, casting everything in gold.

I'm early. Fifteen minutes early, because sitting in my apartment pretending to focus on anything else wasn't an option. I've been wandering the aisles, picking up books without reading them, my attention fixed on the door.

The bell chimes.

She's here.

Sloane stands just inside the entrance, scanning the store with that focused intensity she brings to boardrooms and press conferences. But something's different. Dark jeans instead of tailored slacks. A loose cream sweater that makes her look both powerful and approachable. Her auburn hair falls in loose waves past her shoulders. No severe ponytail. No corporate armor.

She looks like herself. Just Sloane.

Our eyes meet across the store, and I watch her face soften. A slight uncertainty that makes my chest tight with the urge to close the distance.

"Hey," she says, weaving past a display of local authors and a tabby cat sleeping on a stack of mysteries.

"Hey yourself." I close the book I haven't been reading, something about urban planning that might as well be written in Sanskrit for all the attention I've paid it. "Find it okay?"

"GPS and divine intervention." She glances around, taking in the towering shelves and cozy reading nooks. "This place is incredible. Very niche. Very you."

"Very me?"

"Thoughtful. Layers you don't show everyone." Her cheeks flush slightly, like she's revealed more than intended. "How did you find it?"

"Used to come here as a rookie. Needed somewhere quiet to think that wasn't my empty apartment." I gesture toward the back corner. "Come on. There's something I want to show you."

I lead her past fiction and self-help, past dusty cookbooks that probably haven't been touched in years. The history section sits tucked away, quieter and more private.

"This," I say, pulling a worn paperback from the shelf, "changed how I think about leadership."

She takes it from my hands, our fingers brushing. *Undaunted Courage* by Stephen Ambrose. She turns it over, studying the back cover with the same careful attention she gives everything else.

"Lewis and Clark," she says. "Not what I expected from a hockey player."

"What did you expect? *The Art of War*?"

Her laugh is soft, genuine. "Maybe something with more hitting."

"There's plenty of conflict. It's just different." I lean against the shelf, watching her flip through pages marked with years of reading. "Lewis is leading men into completely unmapped territory. Making life-or-death decisions with incomplete information. Keeping everyone alive and moving forward when he's probably terrified."

Her fingers still on the pages. "Sounds familiar."

"That's what wearing the 'A' feels like most days. You're making calls that affect people you care about, and you won't know if you were right until it's too late to change course." The honesty slips out easier than expected. Something about this corner, her attention, makes it feel safe.

She looks up, and I catch something shift in her expression. Recognition, maybe. Or understanding.

"The responsibility must be crushing sometimes."

"Sometimes." I study her face, noting the way she holds herself even here, even now. "What about you? What shaped how you think about leadership?"

"That's assuming I read about leadership instead of just marketing metrics."

"Sloane. I've seen your office. You have more leadership books than Harvard Business School."

Her smile turns wry. "Guilty. I think... *Hidden Figures*. Katherine Johnson, Dorothy Vaughan, Mary Jackson." She slides the book back onto the shelf with deliberate care. "They didn't just break barriers. They made themselves indispensable first. Proved their worth so completely that discrimination became an obvious inefficiency."

"Strategic brilliance."

"Survival," she corrects, and there's steel beneath the soft words. "They couldn't just be good. They had to be perfect. Every day. One mistake would become evidence that women didn't belong in mathematics."

The weight of it hits me. Of course. The pressure she lives under, the perfection she maintains. It's not paranoia. It's pattern recognition, learned from generations of women who paid the price for being human in spaces that demanded they be flawless.

"That's exhausting," I say quietly.

"That's reality." She touches the spine of another book, not meeting my eyes. "Sorry. You probably didn't bring me here for a lecture on workplace dynamics."

"I brought you here to get to know you," I say, stepping closer. "The real you. Not the version who has to be perfect all the time. Not Easton's sister. Just Sloane."

The words hang between us.

She looks up, and I see her weighing the invitation, calculating the risk of letting me see her without her armor.

"That's a dangerous proposition," she says softly.

"The best ones usually are."

For the next hour, the conversation flows easy and unguarded. I learn about the summer she spent trying to build a treehouse and the terrible poetry she wrote in high school. I watch the brilliant, guarded woman I know recede, replaced by someone with a quick laugh, and we forget we're supposed to be hiding. We get lost in the simple act of finally, truly seeing each other.

Her phone buzzes, sharp and insistent in the quiet.

She glances at the screen and sighs. "Sorry. Brynn. She's persistent when she needs advice."

"Take it."

She offers an apologetic smile and answers. "Brynn, please tell me you're not calling to complain about your assignment again."

I can't hear the other end, but I watch Sloane's expression cycle through fondness, exasperation, and concern.

"I know you think he's an arrogant Neanderthal, but he's still your subject. Professional objectivity, remember?" A pause, then an eye-roll that makes me smile. "Fine. But if this interview goes sideways, don't blame me."

She hangs up and looks at me, contrite. "Sorry. Best friend. Journalist. Currently convinced her latest assignment is going to be a disaster."

"Anyone I know?"

"Probably. Hockey player. Apparently has a reputation for being difficult with female reporters."

Something protective flares in me. "She meeting him somewhere public?"

"Already handled." Her smile is softer now. "Thank you. For caring about someone you don't even know."

"I care about you," I say, the words coming out more intense than intended. "Which means I care about the people who matter to you."

The honesty lands heavier than expected. But instead of deflecting or stepping back, she moves closer.

"Garrett..."

We're standing in a narrow aisle between towering shelves, surrounded by stories and afternoon light. The bookstore fades until there's nothing but her. The way the sun catches the copper in her hair. The soft curve of her mouth. The way she's looking at me like I'm the only thing in her universe.

"I'm not playing games anymore," I say.

"Neither am I," she whispers.

When I lean down to kiss her, it's nothing like the corridor. This is deliberate. Tender. A promise instead of a secret. Her lips are soft and sure beneath mine, and when she sighs into my mouth, I taste something that makes me not want to stop.

Her hands fist in my jacket, pulling me closer, and I'm drowning in the rightness of this. Holding her in the golden light of a place that feels like sanctuary, hidden in winding bookshelves, finally free to show her what she means to me.

We break apart slowly, foreheads resting together, sharing breath in the quiet.

"We should go," she whispers, but she doesn't pull away.

"Separately," I agree, though every instinct is telling me to keep her close.

"You first." She's smiling now, soft and slightly breathless. "I need a minute to remember how to function around other people."

I press a kiss to her forehead and force myself to step back.

"See you tomorrow."

"Tomorrow."

I walk away before I can change my mind, past new releases and sleeping cats. At the register, I buy the first book I can grab without really seeing it.

Through the window, I watch her emerge from the history section five minutes later, browsing the poetry shelf like nothing world-changing just happened. But I catch the way she touches her lips when she thinks no one is looking.

16

Sloane

An empty conference room on a Tuesday night. Not exactly romantic.

But with Garrett's apartment a revolving door for teammates, including my brother, and my place off-limits for the exact same reason, our options are nonexistent. A bar or restaurant? Too public. Too risky. The bookstore had been perfect, stolen and brief, a glimpse at something real before reality crashed back in.

So here we are. Conference Room C. Where I can pretend to work late on the Northstar account if anyone asks. Plausible. Professional. A perfect lie.

I close my laptop. The snap echoes in the sterile quiet, louder than it should be. The proposal I'd pulled up as cover stares back at me, untouched. My shoulders ache from the tension I've been holding for the last hour, waiting.

My phone buzzes against the table. Another alert from the PR team. Subject: URGENT - Caleb Jones Livestream Gaffe. I silence it without reading past the preview. Another fire to put out. It can wait until tomorrow.

Tonight, I'm choosing something else.

The door opens, and Garrett fills the frame. He's holding something small, and when he crosses to the table, he places it in front of me with careful deliberation.

A napkin. With a flower drawn on it in blue ink.

I stare at it for a beat, then look up at him, raising an eyebrow to hide the nervous flutter in my chest.

"Oh, this is a date, is it?"

"Absolutely is." A slow, genuine smile spreads across his face. He pushes a stack of printouts aside, then moves his chair from the far end of the table to sit directly beside me.

"Alright, tell me one story from when you were a child that explains everything I need to know about you," Garrett says.

The question is so unexpected, a real laugh escapes me.

"Okay, fine. When my brother Easton was seven, he refused to do his chores. So, I made a binder."

Garrett leans forward, chin resting on his hand like this is the most important story he'll ever hear.

"It had a color-coded chart. A demerit system for non-compliance. I scheduled weekly performance reviews with him in the living room. Tried to convince my parents to tie his allowance to his Key Performance Indicators."

He throws his head back and laughs, a full-bodied, joyful sound that echoes in the quiet room and settles deep in my chest.

"You put your seven-year-old brother on a corporate improvement plan?"

"He started taking out the trash," I say, mock-defensive. But I'm laughing too. "Okay. Your turn. Same question."

He turns to the window, watching the lights of the city flicker below. A smile lingers on his face.

"We had this goat on my family's farm in Saskatchewan. Chester. He had this thing for eating my hockey jerseys. Loved them. So I spent an entire weekend building this elaborate fortress around the clothesline. Scrap wood, chicken wire, pulleys, three-latch gate. I thought I was a genius."

"And was it?"

"Chester ate a hole through the gate in five minutes. Then fell asleep on my best jersey. I gave up and started hanging them in the barn."

I grin. "So we both have a history of trying to manage stubborn, uncontrollable forces."

"Seems so," he says, his voice softer now.

His eyes meet mine. And in them, I see not the star athlete, not the man with the media-wary stare, but the kid who got outsmarted by a goat.

The conversation flows easily from there. We move from childhood mishaps to family dynamics, trading stories about the people who shaped us.

"You know what's funny?" he says, leaning back in his chair. "Growing up as the only boy with three sisters, you learn things they don't teach you in hockey."

"Like what?" I ask, genuinely curious.

A small smile tugs at his mouth. "Like how to French braid hair at six in the morning before school because Emma had a presentation and Mom was already at work. Or that when your little sister comes home crying because some kid called her stupid, you don't teach her to fight back. You teach her she's brilliant and then you spend the whole weekend helping her build the best science fair project the fourth grade has ever seen."

"That's really sweet."

"Sweet nothing. They were ruthless." His laugh is genuine, affectionate. "Made me sit through hours of princess movies, used me as a practice dummy for makeup, forced me to be the groom in about a thousand pretend weddings. But they also had my back in ways that mattered. When I got cut from my first junior team, they made this elaborate 'Garrett is the best' banner and hung it in my room. Didn't ask if I wanted to talk about it. Just made sure I knew they believed in me."

He pauses, something vulnerable crossing his face.

"Hockey taught me strategy, but my sisters taught me loyalty. The real kind. Not just when someone's winning, but when they're falling apart and need you to hold them together."

I think about Easton, about the way we've protected each other, but how different our dynamic was.

"I can't imagine having sisters," I say. "Growing up with Easton was like having a bodyguard who doubled as a worried parent. He used to walk me to the bus stop every morning until I was in eighth grade. Not because I needed protection, but because he needed to make sure I got there safely.

Even now, he still texts me after every away game to make sure I made it home."

"Must've been nice, though. Having someone look out for you."

"It was. But it was also suffocating sometimes." I tuck a strand of hair behind my ear. "Your sisters sound like they saw you as a person, not a problem to solve. Easton loves me fiercely, but he's always trying to fix things for me instead of just being there while I fix them myself."

Garrett nods slowly. "That's the difference, isn't it? My sisters trusted me to handle things. They just made sure I knew I didn't have to handle them alone."

He reaches for something on the table, a forgotten bag of vending machine pretzels I didn't even notice him bring in, and offers it to me.

"Is that what you want?" he asks quietly. "Someone who trusts you to handle things?"

The question goes far beyond family dynamics. I look up at him, really look, and see something in his eyes that makes my breath catch. Patience. Waiting.

"Yeah," I whisper. "I think it is."

The conversation softens after that, meandering through smaller topics. Favorite books from the shelves of his loft, terrible movies we both secretly love, the first concerts we ever went to. The easy back-and-forth stretches, punctuated by comfortable silences, until the room feels less like a corporate meeting space and more like a private sanctuary.

Then something catches my eye through the window behind him.

"Is that... snow?" I ask, squinting at the white specks dancing under the haloed streetlights.

"Huh. Guess it is." He checks his phone. His eyes go wide. "Whoa. It's late. Past eight."

The laughter dies in my throat. Eight? We've been in this room for hours. It felt like twenty minutes.

"I should... I need to get home. I live a good twenty minutes from here—"

Before I can finish, my phone buzzes violently. An alert. EXTREME WEATHER WARNING: BLIZZARD CONDITIONS. TRAVEL NOT ADVISED.

"It's not safe to drive. I'm not letting you drive in this," Garrett says, already standing.

"There has to be another option—"

"There is." He steps closer. "My place is five blocks from here. The roads are shot, but we can walk it."

"Garrett, I can't. If anyone saw us—"

"No one's seeing anything in a blizzard, Sloane." His voice lowers. "It's this, or you sleep on the couch in the marketing office. Your call. With that big scarf of yours, no one'll recognize you anyway."

My throat tightens. "This is a bad idea."

"It's the only idea left." His gaze holds mine. "Let me get you home safe."

I give a short, sharp nod before I can change my mind.

He holds the heavy exit door, and we step into a wall of white.

The wind hits like a fist. Snow slashes across my face. Within seconds, visibility drops to near-zero.

My dress pants are soaked by the first block.

"Stay close!" Garrett shouts, grabbing my elbow. His grip is steady.

I slip once, ice hidden under fresh snow, and he catches me before I fall, his arm solid around my waist. The cold cuts through my blazer like tissue paper. My fingers are already numb despite my gloves.

By the third block, I'm breathing hard, each step a fight against wind that wants to knock me sideways. Without Garrett beside me, I'd be completely lost.

"Almost there," he says, barely audible above the storm.

When his apartment door finally swings open, warmth hits me like salvation.

I step inside and stop short, dripping snow onto hard-wood.

This is not what I expected.

Exposed brick. Industrial beams. But softness woven through. Worn rugs, warm lighting. A cast-iron radiator hums in the corner. Floor-to-ceiling windows overlook the Mississippi, now lost in the swirling white.

The air smells like old paper, cedar, and something faintly sweet. Vanilla and... bread?

"You bake?" I ask, incredulous.

He laughs, hanging our coats by the door. "You sound shocked."

I am shocked.

One wall is covered in books. Paperbacks with cracked spines, hardcovers dog-eared and leaning. Hemingway next to Dostoevsky. *Atlas Shrugged* bookmarked three-quarters through.

But what stops me is the mantel.

Snow globes.

A dozen of them. London. Paris. A tiny Zamboni in a miniature rink.

"You collect snow globes?"

"My grandmother started it. Left them to me." He touches one, gently. "Seemed wrong to pack them away."

Something in my chest pulls soft and tight.

"Hungry?" he asks, already heading to the kitchen. "I was gonna stress-bake sourdough tomorrow, but I've got stuff."

"You stress-bake?"

"Don't sound so shocked." He opens the fridge. "Pasta okay?"

I nod, still stunned.

We fall into rhythm. I chop. He simmers. We move around each other like it's instinctual.

At one point he reaches for the same cabinet I do and boxes me in. He pauses.

Our eyes lock.

His gaze drops to my lips.

For a second, no one moves.

Then he steps away slowly, leaving me breathless and wanting.

Jazz drifts from hidden speakers. Something soft and complex that I never would have imagined Tank Sullivan listening to.

This isn't Tank Sullivan's space. It's the space of a man with a quiet, hidden world, and I want to map every corner of it.

17

Sloane

"It feels like the rest of the world has disappeared," I say, curled on his couch with an empty plate balanced on my knees.

Outside, snow falls in thick, muffling sheets. We're cocooned. Safe in our own private snow globe.

"Let it," he murmurs, close to my ear.

I turn, and the look on his face unravels the last of my restraint.

He reaches out and brushes a stray strand of hair from my cheek.

It's a simple gesture. Tender. And it completely undoes me.

I lean into his touch, my eyes fluttering shut. When I open them, his gaze has gone dark.

He cups my face in both hands, his thumbs stroking my cheekbones. "Sloane."

The way he says my name shatters something in me.

Flashes of our past moments: the arena wall. The closet. Frantic, hidden, adrenaline-fueled.

But this is different. This is soft lamplight spilling into a hallway. The quiet of his hands. The deliberate, unhurried way he's looking at me, with no fear of a door swinging open or a voice shouting his name.

This isn't a secret being stolen. It's a choice being made.

I meet his gaze and nod.

This kiss is nothing like the others. It's slow. Certain. The kind of kiss that says *finally*. His lips are warm and sure, and when I part mine, he's right there, claiming, exploring, deepening with a thoroughness that makes my toes curl. I thread my fingers through his hair, tugging him closer. He groans against my mouth, a low, broken sound that vibrates through my whole body.

He kisses my jaw, then trails down the column of my throat. I tilt my head back, gasping when he finds the spot below my ear that makes my vision swim. His hands begin to move. One slides down my back, pressing me tight against him. The other drifts lower, resting on my thigh, his thumb drawing slow, deliberate circles.

Need cuts through me. Every rational thought I've ever had about professional boundaries and career risks dissolves under his touch.

My hands find the buttons of his shirt, fingers fumbling. The first button gives way, then another. He helps me, shrugging out of it and letting it fall. My palms press flat against his chest, and I can feel his heartbeat racing.

His fingers trace the hem of my blouse, a question in his eyes. When I nod, he lifts it over my head with careful reverence, as though I might disappear if he moves too quickly.

The cool air hits my skin, but his gaze makes me feel anything but exposed.

"You're beautiful," he whispers, and the words aren't just about how I look. They're about this moment. About us, finally here, finally honest.

He pulls back just enough to meet my eyes, his breath ragged. "Sloane. I want..." He stops, searching my face. "Are you sure?"

The question holds everything. Not just tonight, but what this means. What we're risking. Whether I'm ready to stop running from this.

"Yes," I whisper. "I'm sure."

He stands, lifting me with him, and I wrap my legs around his waist as he carries me toward his bedroom. My back hits his bedroom door as he fumbles for the handle, and we're kissing again, desperate now, all pretense of patience abandoned.

The door swings shut behind us.

His bedroom is clean lines and muted colors, but I barely register any of it. There's only him. Only us. Only the way he sets me down and frames my face in his hands like I'm something precious.

"Last chance," he says softly. "We can stop. We can go back to the couch and finish that movie and pretend—"

I silence him with a kiss that answers every question he could ask. There's no going back. Not from this.

When we break apart, we're both breathing hard. His hands shake slightly as he traces the line of my shoulder, and

I realize he's nervous too. This careful, controlled man who never lets his guard down is trembling because of me.

"I've wanted this," I admit, barely above a whisper. "I've wanted you. Even when I was telling myself all the reasons it was impossible."

Something in his expression cracks open. Relief and desire and something deeper. "Good," he says simply. "Because I don't think I could have let you walk away again."

What follows is a slow unraveling of everything we've held back. His hands learn the curve of my waist, the spot at the base of my throat that makes me gasp his name. I discover the scar on his shoulder from last season's injury, my tongue tracing the raised skin, and I feel his breath hitch.

We take our time. But the weeks of tension finally snap. The gentle touches become urgent. His mouth leaves my throat, trailing down my collarbone, dipping lower. When his lips close over the peak of my breast through the lace, a sharp, pulling sensation makes me arch off the bed, my fingers tightening in his hair.

"Garrett," I gasp, the word a plea.

He moves to my other breast, giving it the same attention before his hands slide from my waist to my hips. My own hands are shaking as I find the button of his pants. He helps me, kicking them away.

His fingers hook the lace edge of my underwear. He pauses, his eyes finding mine in the dim light. I answer by lifting my hips, letting him slide the last barrier away.

He moves between my legs, and my body opens for him. But he pauses again. "I've wanted to taste you since that first meeting," he rasps.

Before I can answer, his mouth is on me.

It's not hurried. He's slow. Deliberate. His tongue is clever, insistent, learning every part of me, and my world dissolves into a single, blinding point of sensation. I cry out his name, my body still pulsing as he moves back up, his skin hot against mine.

He pulls back just for a second, his breathing ragged as he reaches for the nightstand. I hear the rip of a foil packet, and then he's back, settling between my legs.

"Sloane," he groans. He positions himself at my entrance, and for a beat, we're just still. His hazel eyes locked on mine, our bodies flush, the world outside gone.

And when he finally presses inside me, it's not a fall. It's a click. A lock sliding into place.

It's home.

A completeness so total it steals the air from my lungs. I meet his first slow, deep thrust, my legs wrapping around his waist to pull him closer. He moves with a steady, powerful rhythm that's all Garrett. Controlled, strong, deliberate. This isn't a frantic, stolen moment. It's a claiming.

"You feel perfect," he breathes, his forehead resting against mine.

I whisper back, meeting every push, every slide. The tension coils again, lower and deeper, a burning, building need. He feels it, his rhythm breaking, his thrusts becoming harder, faster. He calls out my name, raw and broken, and I'm clinging to his shoulders, my own body rising to meet his. The pressure builds, unbearable and perfect, until it shatters. I feel his own release, a deep, shuddering groan that moves through my entire body.

Afterwards, I lie curled against his chest, boneless and complete, listening to his heartbeat slow. His fingers trace lazy patterns on my back, and for the first time in longer than I can remember, my mind is perfectly quiet.

"The snow's still falling," he murmurs, pressing a kiss to the top of my head.

I lift myself up to look out the window. The world is still buried in white. "We're snowed in."

"Tragic," he says, but he's smiling.

I rest my chin on his chest, studying his face in the dim light. "What happens when it stops?"

The question carries all the weight of reality. Our jobs. The team. The careful distance we've maintained for months.

He's quiet for a long moment, his hand moving through my hair. "I don't know," he admits. "But I know I don't want to go back to pretending there's nothing between us."

"Good. Because I don't think I could."

He pulls me up for another kiss, soft and sweet and full of promises we're both afraid to voice yet. Outside, the storm continues, holding the world at bay a little longer.

I wake to soft, grey light filtering through his curtains. For a long, precious moment, I don't remember where I am.

There's no dread. No alarm. No to-do list playing on repeat in my head. Just the solid weight of Garrett's arm around my waist and snow falling gently outside the windows.

My blouse is draped over his dresser. My phone waits in silence on the nightstand, full of emails and expectations I'm not ready to face. The world is still there, waiting. But for now, it hasn't found me yet.

I study Garrett's sleeping face, the way his dark hair falls across his forehead.

The snow is still falling. Our snow globe. We're still inside it.

My greatest fear used to be getting fired. Now, it's leaving this bed.

I drift back to sleep, and when I wake again, the light has shifted warmer. The storm still rages outside, but it feels distant, a white curtain drawn around our private world.

The bed beside me is empty, but I can hear quiet sounds from the kitchen. The soft clink of ceramic. The whisper of something being stirred. I stretch beneath the sheets, every muscle loose and languid in a way I can't remember feeling in years.

I slip from bed and find one of his dress shirts hanging over a chair. Soft cotton that carries traces of him. It falls to mid-thigh, and I roll the sleeves to my elbows before padding barefoot toward the kitchen.

Garrett stands at the stove, wearing nothing but pajama pants that hang low on his hips. His dark hair is mussed from sleep, and there's something fundamentally different about him. The careful control he wears in public has been set aside. He's humming, actually humming, as he works.

"Good morning," I say quietly.

He turns, and his face lights up. Not the practiced smile of his public persona, but something open and unguarded that makes me want to pull him back to bed.

"Good morning, beautiful." His voice is rough with sleep. "Coffee's almost ready."

He reaches for a mug from the cabinet. "I'm making pancakes. Sourdough ones. Figured I should put that starter to good use."

I lean against the counter, watching him work. There's something hypnotic about his competence here, the way he moves through his kitchen with quiet confidence. This is Garrett, not the carefully controlled captain the media sees. The man who reads and nurtures living things and makes pancakes from scratch on snowy mornings.

"You don't have to—"

"I want to." He hands me the coffee. "Besides, I've been wanting to cook for you."

The pancake batter is pale gold and full of bubbles. He ladles it onto the griddle with practiced ease, and the kitchen fills with the smell of something wholesome and homemade.

"This is nice," I murmur, settling onto one of the barstools at his counter. "Domestic."

"Dangerous word," he says, but he's smiling. "Might give a guy ideas."

"What kind of ideas?"

He flips a pancake with a quick flick of his wrist. "The kind where I imagine doing this every morning. Where I picture you in my kitchen, wearing my shirt, looking exactly like you do right now."

The casual intimacy of his words, the easy way he talks about a future that includes both of us, makes something flutter in my chest that has nothing to do with attraction and everything to do with hope.

"Your pancakes smell incredible," I say. "How long have you had the starter?"

"Years now." He flips another pancake. "My grandmother gave me hers when I got drafted. Said it would keep me grounded, having something that needed daily attention." He pauses, spatula poised above the griddle. "Probably sounds ridiculous."

"Not at all. It's like continuity. Something constant when everything else changes."

He glances at me, something soft crossing his face. "Yeah. Exactly like that."

The quiet settles between us, filled only with the soft bubble of batter on the griddle and the storm outside. I find myself studying his profile as he works, the strong line of his jaw, the way his shoulders move beneath bare skin. Last night feels both distant and immediate.

"I should probably check my phone," I murmur, though I make no move to do so.

"Probably." He plates the pancakes, perfect golden circles. "But the world can wait a few more minutes."

He sets the plate in front of me, along with real maple syrup warmed in a small pitcher. The first bite is extraordinary, tangy and complex, with a texture that speaks of patience and care.

"These are incredible," I say.

"Yeah?" He watches me over his coffee.

"The kind that make me want to stay in this kitchen forever."

The words slip out before I can stop them, more honest than I intended. His hand stills on his mug.

I know what he's thinking because I'm thinking it too. Last night changed everything. We can't go back to careful distance, to stolen moments and hidden glances. But moving forward means risking everything we've both worked to build.

"One step at a time," I say softly, reaching across the counter to cover his hand with mine. "We don't have to figure it all out this morning."

He turns his palm up, interlacing our fingers. "One step at a time," he agrees.

Outside, the snow continues to fall. And for now, that's enough.

18

Sloane

The familiar warmth of Marcello's should feel like coming home, but tonight, the checkered tablecloths and Dean Martin crooning from hidden speakers feel like stage dressing for a performance I'm not sure I can pull off.

I slide into our usual corner booth, my phone already buzzing in my hand.

Garrett

Miss you already. How's dinner going?

The smile hits before I can stop it. Soft, involuntary, the kind that reshapes your whole face. I catch myself and flip the phone face down on the table. But the warmth lingers in my chest like a secret I'm carrying under my ribs.

Three days.

Three days since the blizzard. Since his apartment. Since everything changed.

Three days of stolen glances across the arena, of professional conversations laced with something else entirely, of text messages that make me feel like I'm seventeen again and reckless.

Three days of walking around with this new, buzzing energy under my skin.

"You're glowing."

I look up. Easton's watching me with those sharp green eyes that miss nothing. He's already claimed the breadstick basket, some things never change, but his usual grin is gone. Replaced by something quieter. Sharper.

"What?" I laugh, but it comes out too bright. Too quick. "I'm not glowing. It's the lighting."

"Uh-huh." He tears into a breadstick with exaggerated slowness, eyes never leaving mine. "You look different."

My phone buzzes again. Another flutter. Another glance I catch before I can stop myself.

Easton catches it anyway.

"Popular tonight," he says. Mild.

"Just work stuff." The lie tastes sharp. Unfamiliar. Wrong.

I've never lied to Easton about anything important. Not when Dad left. Not when I got my first job. Not when I moved to Minneapolis. We've always been each other's safe harbor.

Until now.

Maria appears with my usual pinot and Easton's sparkling water, her smile as warm and familiar as the soup specials. "The usual?" she asks, even as her pen is already moving.

"Please," we say in unison.

But the ritual feels hollow tonight. Forced.

When Maria disappears toward the kitchen, Easton leans back against the booth, his posture deceptively casual. But

I know that look. It's the same focus he brings to reading shooters in the slot, analyzing every micro-expression, every tell that might give away the play.

"So," he says, voice carefully neutral. "How's the Sullivan project going?"

My wine glass freezes halfway to my lips. The question lands clean. Calm on the surface. Lethal underneath.

"Fine." It comes out clipped. "He's been more cooperative lately. The media training's working."

"Cooperative." He says the word like it's unfamiliar. "That's an interesting way to describe Tank Sullivan."

My phone buzzes a third time. I don't look, but the pull is there.

"People can change," I say. "Sometimes they just need the right approach."

"Mmm." He drums his fingers against the table, a rhythm that matches his pre-game warm-up routine. Controlled. Calculating. "And what approach would that be?"

Every word feels like a trap. Every pause an opportunity for him to read between the lines I'm desperately trying to blur.

"Professional. Consistent. Building trust."

Corporate jargon. Reliable as Kevlar.

But Easton's too smart for that.

"Sloane." His voice drops to that serious tone he uses when he's about to ask something that matters. "What's really going on?"

My escape routes are closing. My mind races, searching for a piece of the truth big enough to hide the rest. I find one.

I let out a long, weary sigh and drag a hand through my hair. "It's not what you think. It's work. God, is it ever work."

Easton leans forward, eyebrows drawing together. "What work? The Northstar thing?"

"I wish." I lower my voice. "It's Caleb Jones."

His expression shifts immediately. "Cal? What'd the kid do now? Post another gym thirst trap with a typo in the caption?"

"Worse. Way worse."

My phone buzzes again. This time, I glare at it with real, unscripted frustration.

"He was on a livestream last night with some influencer. Thought it ended. It hadn't. He spent two minutes mocking the away-team jerseys. Called them 'pajamas for sad clown s.'"

Easton groans, tipping his head back. "Jesus. These kids..."

"Yeah. I've been on the phone with legal and our GM all day. The league called. The other team's PR is salivating. This is what's been blowing up my phone. This is why I look like I have a fever."

He shakes his head. "They grow up with phones in their hands but don't understand how to use them without setting their lives on fire."

"And I'm the one holding the extinguisher," I mutter into my wine glass.

"What are you going to do?" he asks, all brotherly concern now. "Take away his phone until the playoffs?"

"It's in my latest roadmap. A whole digital footprint and brand management onboarding program for rookies. Caleb just became my Exhibit A."

Easton nods, approving. "Good. Someone needs to teach these guys to be careful. Unfortunately, it matters almost as much as the game now."

He pauses. Then:

"No wonder you're so stressed. Just don't let it burn you out, Sloane. Guys like Cal are a dime a dozen. You're special."

The words, meant for comfort, land like shrapnel.

I offer him a small, grateful smile. I feel like a traitor.

"I won't," I say. And I mean it in the way lies are sometimes meant.

Maria returns with our pasta, and the conversation shifts. Next road trip, his new trainer, why Mom still can't Face-Time without tilting the phone at her ceiling fan.

The danger passes.

But as I push pasta around my plate, the buzz of my phone feels different now.

It's no longer just a sweet, secret thrill.

It's a risk.

It's Exhibit A.

19

Garrett

The supply closet smells like industrial cleaner and forgotten equipment, but all I can focus on is the taste of Sloane's lip gloss and the way her fingers are twisted in my shirt.

She's pressed against the metal shelving, her green eyes dark in the dim light filtering under the door, and for thirty perfect seconds, nothing else exists.

"We have to stop meeting like this," she whispers against my mouth, but she's smiling when she says it, her thumb tracing the line of my jaw.

"Probably," I murmur back, but I don't move away. Can't. I want to memorize everything. The way she catches her breath when I kiss just beneath her ear. The soft sound she makes when my hand finds the curve of her waist.

"Garrett." My name is half-warning, half-surrender. "Someone could—"

The sharp sound of voices in the hallway slices through our bubble. Sloane freezes. Her eyes go wide with a panic that twists something ugly in my chest.

This is what we've been reduced to. Supply closets, thirty-second kisses, constant fear.

Like we're doing something wrong, instead of something right.

I step back immediately, giving her space. She smooths her blazer, checks her reflection in the dark screen of her phone. Her expression goes neutral, that same look she wears in meetings, but I catch the tremble in her hands as she fixes her hair.

"Coast is clear," she whispers after cracking the door.

We slip out separately. Her first. Me, thirty seconds later. I watch her walk away, heels clicking, posture straight. To anyone else, she's the marketing director en route to her next meeting.

They don't see the slight flush in her cheeks. Or the way her lips are still swollen from my kisses.

The pride that surges curdles almost instantly into something cold. This isn't protection. This is erasure.

&&&&&&&&&&&&&&&&&&&&&&&&&&&&&&&&&&&&&

The team meeting drags. Coach is breaking down power play adjustments, diagramming formations on the whiteboard with the kind of detail that usually holds my focus.

But I'm not locked on Xs and Os. I'm three rows ahead and two seats to the right, where Sloane sits with her tablet, taking notes.

She's in that navy blazer that makes her look like she could run a Fortune 500 company. Her auburn hair is pulled back in a sleek ponytail, baring the line of her neck.

Twenty minutes ago, I was kissing that neck in a supply closet.

Now, I'm pretending she's just another staff member.

"Sullivan." Coach's voice snaps across the room.

Heat climbs my neck. "Yes, sir."

"Need you to coordinate with Sloane on playoff coverage. Player interviews, behind-the-scenes stuff. Make sure we're projecting the right image."

Sloane glances back. Her expression is perfectly professional. But her lips curve just slightly.

"No problem," I say, holding her gaze for three seconds. Then I look away.

Any longer, and someone might notice.

The meeting ends twenty minutes later, players filing out in small groups, complaining about ice time and discussing weekend plans. I linger, organizing my notes with deliberate slowness, waiting for the room to clear.

"Garrett." Her voice is neutral. Controlled. "Coach wants us to align on the playoff media strategy."

"Right." I stand. "Your office?"

"Conference room down the hall," she says, already moving. "More professional."

Professional. The word tastes like dust.

We walk the hallway with practiced distance. Not quite together. Not obviously apart.

A choreography we've perfected. But tonight, it feels like a lie.

In the conference room, she immediately crosses to the windows, putting the length of the table between us.

The message is clear.

"Coach wants regular player availability," she says, pulling up her calendar. "Short interviews, practice footage, community documentation. Enough content to shape a strong playoff narrative."

I watch her speak. Watch the way she avoids looking at me for more than a second at a time. Even here, alone, she won't let her guard down.

"Sounds reasonable," I say. "What do you need from me?"

"Your cooperation." She finally meets my eyes. And I see the exhaustion. The strain. "I know media isn't your thing. But if we control the narrative—"

"Sloane." Her name comes out rougher than I intend. "We don't have to do this."

She stiffens. "Do what?"

"Pretend. In here, with just us, we don't have to pretend we're nothing to each other."

Her expression falters. I catch it. The flicker of something real.

Then it's gone, and her face smooths over.

"We have to pretend everywhere," she says quietly. "That's what we agreed."

"And what if I don't want to pretend anymore?"

She looks at me. Really looks. And I can see the war happening behind her eyes.

"Garrett..." Her voice is barely above a whisper. "You know why we can't."

I do. Vivian. Easton. The team's rules. Her whole career.

I know. I understand.

But understanding doesn't make it hurt less.

"Right," I say. "Professional."

She nods, but her fingers shake as she reaches for her tablet. "I'll send the content calendar. We should schedule weekly check-ins."

"Sure."

The meeting ends ten minutes later with bullet points and deadlines.

She gathers her things. I want to say something, anything, that breaks the pattern. But I can't.

She pauses at the door.

"Garrett?"

"Yeah?"

"This is worth it." Her voice is soft. Certain. "What we have. It's worth protecting."

Then she's gone.

And I'm left alone in a room full of silence and the crushing realization that protecting something shouldn't feel this much like losing it.

&&&&&&&&&&&&&&&&&&&&&&&&&&&&&&

That night, I lie in bed staring at the ceiling.

My phone buzzes now and then. Team updates, social pings. None of them are the one I want.

The loft feels too big. Too quiet. The absence of her is everywhere.

Three floors below, traffic moves through downtown Minneapolis. Headlights sketch brief patterns across my walls before disappearing again. People out there are living normal lives. Laughing in restaurants. Holding hands without consequence.

My mind drifts to Emma. And I taste the bitterness rising in my throat.

It's not a fair comparison. What I have with Sloane is real. But the shadows are familiar.

"You never talk about us," Emma had said during one of our final arguments. "It's like you're ashamed of me. Of this."

She wasn't wrong. I was ashamed. Not of her. But of what we'd become. The public show. The scrutiny. The performative affection. She fed off the spotlight. I withered.

When the rumors started, her and Derek, I said nothing. I thought silence was dignity. Turned out, silence was complicity.

"He never fought for me," she told the reporter who broke the story. "When things got difficult, he just shut down. Made me feel like I was bothering him by existing."

The words had gutted me because underneath the manipulation and the lies, there was a grain of truth. I hadn't fought for her. Not publicly. Not when it mattered.

And now here I am, making the same mistake with a woman who actually deserves fighting for.

I open our thread.

Sloane

> **Good meeting today. Sleep well.**

Clean. Safe. Sanitized.

I type:

I miss you.

Delete. *This is killing me.* Delete.

Finally, I settle on:

You too.

The dots appear. Vanish. Appear again.

She's typing. Deleting. Typing again.

Sloane

Sweet dreams, Tank.

The nickname cuts through me. Private. Tender. But distant.

It feels like a breadcrumb. Just enough to keep me going.

I set the phone aside and stare at the ceiling.

The memory of her face in that conference room returns—when I asked what if I didn't want to pretend anymore. That flicker of hope. That moment where *maybe...*

Then reality returned.

She's protecting her career. I respect it.

But every day we spend hiding feels like a slow erasure. Like I'm asking her to be ashamed of the best thing we've built.

Emma's words echo in the dark.

He never fought for me.

I push them away.

But I don't sleep.

20

Sloane

The fluorescent lights above my desk buzz with their usual aggressive hum, casting everything in harsh, unforgiving angles. I've been staring at the same spreadsheet for twenty minutes, but the numbers blur together like watercolors in rain. My coffee has gone cold, and the quarterly projections that were due an hour ago sit untouched in my inbox.

I can't concentrate. Haven't been able to since Tuesday's "meeting", where Garrett and I spent forty-five minutes pretending to discuss player interview schedules while I fought the urge to reach across the table and touch his hand.

My phone buzzes against the desk. The sound makes me jump like I've been caught stealing.

Garrett

> Need to review the playoff media rollout plan. My place? 7 p.m.?

His name on my screen is a spark hitting dry tinder. I stare at the message, reading it three times before the words register. The "playoff media rollout plan" is our code now—plausible professional cover for meetings that have nothing to do with work and everything to do with the fact that I haven't been able to think about anything but him for days.

This is dangerous. Reckless. His apartment means privacy, yes, but it also contains risk. We could be seen.

But God, I want to see him. Really see him. Not the careful, professional version he wears like armor at work, but the man who reads Dostoevsky and listens to jazz when he thinks no one is watching.

My fingers hover over the keyboard for thirty seconds before I type back.

See you at 7.

The elevator in Garrett's building climbs with mechanical precision. Each soft ding of a passing floor is a countdown. The last time I was here, I was running from a blizzard, the danger physical. Wind and ice and biting cold. Tonight, the danger is all internal.

The hallway outside his door smells like cedar. I smooth my sweater, cashmere, navy blue, chosen with more care than I want to admit, and knock softly.

The door opens, and Garrett stands there in jeans and a gray Henley that clings to his shoulders. His hair is slightly damp, like he just showered. But it's his expression that stops me. Soft, unguarded, genuinely happy to see me.

"Hi," he says.

"Hi yourself."

He steps aside to let me in, and I cross the threshold into his world.

The loft feels different without a blizzard to distract me. Warmer. More intimate. The exposed brick glows amber in the soft lighting, and the Mississippi stretches beyond his windows like a dark ribbon threaded with city lights. Jazz drifts from hidden speakers, something complex and melancholy that I don't recognize but somehow fits.

This is him. Not Tank Sullivan, the stone-faced defenseman who treats reporters like hostile interrogators. This is Garrett.

And the terrifying, wonderful truth is: I'm not just attracted to him. I'm falling for him. All of him.

"So," Garrett says, opening the refrigerator with a grin, "for our very important 'playoff media rollout' meeting... did you bring the spreadsheets?"

I lean against the counter, watching him move through his kitchen. "They're in the car. I figured we could get to them right after you tell me about the emotional state of your sourdough starter."

He laughs, that low, genuine sound that never fails to undo me. "She's thriving, thanks for asking. Bubbling with personality."

"Good to hear. I was worried our last meeting might have stressed her out."

"Nah, she's tougher than she looks." He pulls out a bottle of wine, and I catch the label. That Malbec I mentioned liking weeks ago. Of course he remembered. Of course he went out and bought it.

"You didn't have to—"

"I wanted to." He sets the bottle between us. "Besides, I'm pretty sure our fake meeting requires proper refreshments."

I trace the wine label with my fingertip. "Very thorough planning, Sullivan."

"I'm a thorough guy."

The words carry weight that has nothing to do with wine. I glance up to find his gaze on me. Not scanning the room, not distracted. Just me.

My eyes drift to the bookshelf behind him, landing on a familiar spine. "I see you're still battling Ayn Rand," I say, nodding toward the bookmark jutting from *Atlas Shrugged*.

"She's winning," he admits, following my gaze. "But I refuse to let her have the last word."

We eat at his dining table, simple pasta with fresh herbs from the garden box on his balcony. The food is perfect, but it's the conversation that feeds something deeper. We don't talk about hockey or marketing or the impossible tightrope we're walking at work. Instead, he asks about my childhood, about what I wanted to be before I discovered I had a gift for turning passion into profit margins.

"A teacher," I admit, twirling pasta around my fork. "Elementary school. I wanted to be the adult who made kids feel safe and seen."

"What changed?"

I think about it, really think, instead of giving him the polished answer I've perfected for networking events.

"My dad left when I was nine. Mom fell apart for two years. Someone had to keep the lights on, make sure Easton ate breakfast, forge Mom's signature on permission slips." I shrug, but it doesn't feel casual. "I got good at managing crises. Turned out there was a career in it."

Garrett's hand finds mine across the table, his thumb tracing slow circles on my knuckles.

"I'm sorry," he says, and I can tell he means it. "That's too much responsibility for a kid."

"Maybe. But it taught me that I could survive anything. That I was strong enough to rebuild when everything fell apart." I meet his eyes. "What about you? What did you want to be before hockey chose you?"

He laughs, and the sound fills the loft. "A chef. Seriously. I was obsessed with cooking shows, used to drive my mom crazy experimenting in the kitchen. Hockey was just something I was good at, but cooking... that felt like magic."

"You still cook."

"Still love it. There's something about creating something nourishing from nothing. About the precision and patience it requires." He pauses, considering. "Maybe it's not so different from hockey. Both require timing, practice, understanding how all the pieces work together."

We talk about his grandmother, fierce, tiny woman who taught him to read and bake bread and never let him get away with anything. About the farm where he grew up, the weight of being the oldest son, the pressure of carrying a family's hopes from the time he was sixteen.

I tell him about Easton, about watching my brother grow into this massive, protective force who still worries about me like I'm made of glass. About the loneliness of being the smartest person in most rooms, the exhaustion of always having to prove I belong.

The wine disappears. The candles burn lower. The jazz shifts from melancholy to sultry, and somewhere between his story about accidentally dyeing the team's laundry pink and my confession about organizing a protest for better vegetarian options in my college cafeteria, we migrate to the couch.

It happens naturally. One moment we're sitting on opposite ends, talking and laughing, and the next I'm curled against his side, his arm around my shoulders, feeling safer than I have in months.

"This is nice," I murmur against his chest.

"Yeah." His voice is rough with something deeper than contentment. "It is."

He tips my chin up with gentle fingers, and I see the exact moment the evening shifts. His eyes are dark, focused entirely on my face.

When he leans down to kiss me, it's unhurried. Deliberate. His lips are soft and sure, and when I part mine, he deepens the kiss with a patience that undoes me.

This isn't stolen. This isn't desperate. This is chosen.

His hand slides into my hair, angling my head as he explores my mouth. I can taste the wine on his tongue, feel the steady rhythm of his heartbeat against my palm where it rests on his chest.

For the first time since this started, there's no clock ticking in my head. No fear of footsteps in the hallway or doors swinging open. Just this. His hands in my hair, his mouth on mine, the weight of him surrounding me.

Then his phone buzzes loudly on the coffee table.

We break apart instantly. The spell shatters, reality crashing back.

The screen lights up, and I see the name before Garrett can grab it.

Easton

> Just finished film review. You still at the rink?

A wave of dizziness washes over me. The professional panic floods back—ice-cold and immediate. Easton at the rink, looking for his teammate. His teammate who's supposed to be laying low and focusing on the game, not entertaining his sister in his apartment like some kind of romantic retreat.

"Sorry," Garrett breathes, reading the message.

I'm already pulling away, smoothing my hair, my sweater, anything to erase the evidence of what we were just doing. "What are you going to tell him?"

Garrett's thumb moves across his phone screen with practiced ease.

> Nah, headed home early. Long day.

The lie comes so naturally, so effortlessly, that it sends a chill down my spine. He hits send and sets the phone aside like it's nothing, but the moment is ruined. The warm, safe intimacy we'd built lies in pieces around us.

"This is..." I start, then stop.

"Harder than we thought it would be," he says quietly.

"The lying. The constant fear. The way we have to pretend we're nothing to each other." I lean back against the couch cushions, suddenly exhausted. "I knew it would be difficult, but I didn't realize how much energy it would take. How much of ourselves we'd have to hide."

Garrett shifts to face me. "Are you having second thoughts?"

The question hangs between us. Am I? Part of me is terrified by how deep this is getting, how much it's starting to matter. But when I look at him, really look at him, sitting in his grandmother's light surrounded by books and jazz and the faint smell of rising bread, I know the answer.

"No," I say, and I mean it. "But I need you to understand what we're risking. Not just my job. My entire career. The reputation I've spent years building. If this gets out..."

"It won't." His voice is fierce. "I won't let that happen."

"You can't promise that. Neither of us can." I reach for his hands, lacing our fingers together. "All we can promise is that we'll be careful. That we'll protect each other as much as we can."

"I can promise something else." He pulls me closer, until I'm back in his arms. "I can promise it's worth it. You're worth it."

The words settle into my chest. Worth the risk. Worth the fear. Worth the exhaustion of living two lives.

When he kisses my forehead, I let myself believe him.

Outside, Minneapolis glitters in the darkness. Inside this loft of brick and books and quiet jazz, we hold each other against the cold reality of what we're attempting.

It's not enough to keep the world out forever.

But for tonight, it's enough.

21
Garrett

The tape comes off my stick in long strips, adhesive clinging to my fingers. I'm taking too long with this. Everyone else cleared out ten minutes ago, but I keep finding reasons to stay—retaping the blade, adjusting the curve, checking for splinters that aren't there.

Anything to avoid walking out into the hallway where someone might want to talk.

"You got a minute?"

Phil's voice cuts through the humid quiet of the equipment room. He's leaning in the doorway, arms crossed, still in his practice gear minus the shoulder pads.

I don't look up. "Kind of busy."

"Yeah. I can see that." He moves into the room, settling against the equipment rack like he's got all day. "You've been off lately."

Not a question. A statement.

My hands still on the tape. "I'm fine."

"You blew two coverages last game." Phil's tone stays even, matter-of-fact. "Showed up late to three practices this week. And you're checking your phone between drills, which you never do."

The observation lands heavy in my chest. I force myself to keep working the tape, unwinding it from the blade. "Just tired."

"Bullshit." He shifts his weight. "I've seen you play tired. This is different."

I look up, meeting his eyes. Phil's face shows concern, not accusation. Teammate checking on teammate. Friend checking on friend.

"Whatever's in your head," he continues, "it's showing up on the ice."

Heat crawls up my neck. I try for humor, deflection. "Didn't know you were tracking my stats."

"Your stats are fine." Phil doesn't smile. "You aren't."

The words hit harder than they should. I set down my stick, lean back against the wall. The concrete's cold through my compression shirt.

"It's nothing. Personal stuff." My voice comes out rougher than I intend. "I'll handle it."

Phil nods slowly. Doesn't push for details, doesn't demand explanations. Just accepts the boundary I'm setting. "Okay. You don't gotta tell me what it is."

Relief floods through me. He's going to let it go.

Then he moves closer, sits on the equipment trunk across from me. His knees almost touch mine in the narrow space.

"But I need you to hear something."

I wait.

"Whatever you're dealing with?" Phil's voice drops lower, more serious. "You don't have to do it alone."

"Phil—"

"I'm not asking for details." He cuts me off, not unkind. "I'm telling you how this works. We notice when one of us is struggling. Could be hockey shit, could be life shit—doesn't matter. You carried us through that Calgary series, remember? Four games, you were playing injured and never said a word."

I remember. Separated shoulder, couldn't lift my arm above my head for two weeks after.

"Now it's our turn." Phil's eyes hold mine. "We got your back. When you're ready to talk, we're ready to listen. Until then, we're here."

Something cracks in my chest. The weight I've been carrying alone—the secrecy, the constant vigilance, the fear of what happens if anyone finds out about Sloane—it all presses down harder knowing I can't tell him. Can't tell any of them.

But knowing they'd be there if I could? That matters.

"Thanks, man." The words come out rough.

Phil stands, claps my shoulder once. The contact is brief, solid. "Mean it. Whatever it is, whenever you need it."

I nod. Can't speak past the tightness in my throat.

He reads it, doesn't make me. Heads toward the door, then turns back.

"And Tank? Take care of yourself." His expression softens slightly. "We need you right."

Not just for hockey. He means *me*.

Then he's gone, footsteps echoing down the hallway.

The ice pack on my knee has gone warm, but I can't stop replaying yesterday's conversation with Sloane.

Her shoulders were too rigid, even when she laughed. Her smile too bright when she said she was "fine, just busy."

She's not fine.

She's carrying too much, and it shows—in the dark circles under her eyes, in the way she checks her phone every thirty seconds like she's bracing for impact.

I close my laptop, stats forgotten. Hockey problems I can fix with better positioning and smarter plays. *This*? This needs a different kind of strategy.

The thing about pressure is, it builds until something cracks. And Sloane's under more pressure than most people could survive.

Vivian breathing down her neck. The Northstar account riding on her shoulders. An entire corporate ecosystem judging her for doing her job too well.

And all the while, we're pretending like we don't matter to each other. Like she's not the first thing I think about every morning.

Last week, when Davies made a crack about me being "too focused on the marketing department," I wanted to shove him into the glass and explain exactly *why* Sloane McKenzie matters.

Instead, I laughed it off.

The secrecy is supposed to protect us. But watching her shrink herself to protect me? That's killing me.

I grab my phone and open Google Maps.

"Arcades near Minneapolis." Too close. Too risky.

I expand the radius.

The Pixel Palace. Forty minutes out. Family-owned. Looks like it hasn't been updated since 1985.

Perfect.

I open her contact, thumb hovering.

She'll want details. She'll want to plan, to know every variable. That's exactly what she needs a break from.

> Be ready at 7. Wear jeans. No questions.

The dots appear immediately. Disappear. Reappear.

I can picture her staring at her screen, analyzing every angle.

Sloane

> Where are we going? I have that North-star brief to review.

> The brief can wait. Trust me.

That's the real ask. Not the destination. Not the dress code. I'm asking her to *let go*—just for one night.

Sloane

> Fine. But if I get murdered, I'm telling my brother it was your fault.

Deal.

I'm smiling for the first time all day.

She said yes.

She's going to let me take the lead—even if she's probably already googling "mysterious date locations Minneapolis
area" and cross-referencing them with crime statistics.

"An arcade? Seriously, Sullivan?"

Sloane stares at the buzzing neon sign of The Pixel Palace
through my windshield.

The parking lot's mostly empty. Beat-up sedans, a minivan
with faded stick-figure decals.

"No questions, McKenzie. That was the deal."

She glances back through the window, eyes scanning the
blinking facade. *Classic Games! Duckpin Bowling!*

Her brow furrows. Analytical. Appraising.

She turns to me, one eyebrow lifted. "This is your big
plan?"

"When's the last time you played Skee-Ball?"

"I..." She blinks. "I don't think I ever have."

"Well, that's about to change."

Inside, it's sensory overload.

Neon lights flash in every color. 8-bit soundtracks crash
over each other in chaotic harmony. The air smells like but-
tered popcorn and nostalgia.

"This is..." Sloane trails off, watching a kid no older than ten destroy a pinball machine.

"Loud?"

"Perfect," she says, surprised.

We exchange twenty bucks for an obscene number of tokens. She pockets hers with the same careful precision she probably uses to organize media analytics.

"Okay," she says, scanning the maze of games. "Where do we start?"

"Air hockey. Hope you're ready to lose."

Her eyebrows shoot up. "Fighting words, Sullivan."

"Just setting expectations."

Three minutes later, I'm down 3–0.

Everything I thought I knew about Sloane McKenzie? Up for review.

"What the hell was that?" I point to the goal she just slotted in with a trick shot I swear defies physics.

"Hand-eye coordination," she says, twirling her paddle like a gunslinger. "Plus, you're telegraphing your shots. Your tells are terrible."

"My tells?"

"You bite your bottom lip before you shoot left. And you do this thing with your shoulder—" She mimics a subtle twitch I didn't even know I had.

I lean across the table, close enough to see the flecks of gold in her eyes. "You've been watching me that closely?"

A flush creeps up her neck. "I'm observant."

"Uh-huh."

I score while she's distracted. Even the odds a little.

"Cheap shot."

But she's laughing, and it's not the polite work-laugh or the nervous giggle. This one's pure joy.

"All's fair in love and air hockey."

The words slip out.

Her paddle stutters, the puck bouncing off the wall.

"Did you just—"

"Nope." I clear my throat. "Completely normal hockey phrase. Very common."

"Uh-huh—"

I score again. "Focus, McKenzie. I'm mounting a comeback."

She narrows her eyes, but the softness behind them makes my chest ache.

"We'll see about that. Time for a line change, Sullivan."

"Did you just use hockey terminology to trash-talk me?"

"Maybe I did." She fires a backhand shot. It lands. Clean. "What are you going to do about it?"

"Remind you that I invented trash talk."

"Prove it."

Next, we hit the Skee-Ball lanes. Sloane studies the target rings like she's developing a strategic blueprint. She tests the weight of the ball, adjusts her grip. Then destroys me.

"This is embarrassing," I mutter, watching her land another perfect 50-point shot.

"This is fun," she says, grinning wide enough to unspool me. She does a little hip-shimmy victory dance that should be illegal in public.

When she bumps her hip against mine, the contact is electric.

"When's the last time you lost at something?" she asks.

"Practice this morning. Daniels hit me into next week."

"That's work," she says. "This is..."

"Play?"

"Yeah." The word lands quiet. Soft. Like she's remembering what that feels like.

"Your turn to pick," I say.

She points to the far corner. "Duckpin bowling. I want to see if you're as bad at that as you are at Skee-Ball."

"Hey. I won two rounds."

"By cheating."

"Strategic distraction is not cheating."

"Kissing my neck while I'm trying to concentrate is definitely cheating."

I smirk. "Seemed to work."

She bumps my shoulder. "Shut up and bowl."

The duckpin lanes are tiny. The balls fit in my hand. The pins wobble like they're waiting to be knocked over by accident.

Sloane goes first, clutching the ball like it might detonate. Her wind-up is half shot put, half kitchen disaster.

She lets it fly. Three pins go down.

"That's your approach?" I ask, barely holding in a laugh.

"It worked."

"Barely."

"Your turn, hotshot."

I pick up one of the miniature balls. "The key is follow-through," I explain, lining up my shot. "You want to keep your arm straight, release at the bottom of your swing—"

My ball hits the gutter before it's halfway down the lane.

Sloane's laugh is immediate and completely unsympathetic. "Oh, that's precious. Please, continue with your expert instruction."

"That was a warm-up."

"Sure it was."

My second shot clips two pins. "Better," she says, patting my arm with mock encouragement. "You're really improving."

"You're enjoying this way too much."

"I'm enjoying this exactly the right amount."

When it's her turn again, I step behind her.

"Here, let me—"

My arms come around hers, hands settling over hers on the ball. She goes completely still.

"It's all in the follow-through," I murmur, close to her ear. The words come out rougher than intended. "Let your arm swing naturally. Like a pendulum."

She shivers. I feel it everywhere.

Slowly, I guide her through the motion, my body moving with hers. She leans into me, just slightly, just enough that I can feel her back against my chest, and the rest of the arcade dissolves.

"Like that?" she asks, her voice softer now. Breathier.

"Exactly like that."

We're not talking about bowling anymore.

"Garrett..."

"Yeah?"

"We're in public."

"I know."

"Someone could see."

"There's no one here but us and that kid who's been playing Guitar Hero for the past hour."

She glances around the mostly empty arcade, then back at me. "This is reckless."

"This is duckpin bowling."

"You know what I mean."

I do. We're forty minutes outside Minneapolis, in a no-name arcade where no one knows or cares who we are. For once, there's no spotlight, no team, no rules. Just us.

"Bowl," I say, stepping back. Every instinct wants to stay close, but I let her go.

Her form is flawless this time. The ball arcs down the lane and crashes into the pins, clearing half the deck.

"Much better," I say.

"Good teacher."

"Motivated student."

We finish the game, she wins, obviously, and head to the prize counter with our tickets. The teenage attendant stares at us, dead-eyed, as we dump them on the counter.

"How many?" he mumbles.

"Four hundred thirty-two," Sloane announces. She'd been counting, of course.

I scan the shelves, ignoring the practical prizes. Keychains, stress balls, flashlights.

"That one," I say, pointing to the largest, most absurd prize available: a giant, electric-blue sloth that's approximately the size of a small child.

"Seriously?" the kid asks.

"Seriously."

"Garrett, what am I supposed to do with that?" Sloane protests as he uses a telescoping pole to retrieve it.

"He's our son," I declare, accepting the sloth with mock solemnity.

"Our... son?"

"Our secret sloth-child. A tribute to tonight's triumph." I bow as I hand him over. "What shall we name him?"

She stares at the absurd thing, then at me. Her expression shifts. The careful guard she always wears slips, replaced by something simple and bright. Joy.

"Steve," she says, hugging the sloth's fuzzy bulk. "His name is Steve."

"Steve the Secret Sloth."

"Steve the Secret Sloth," she repeats, and when she smiles at me over his plush blue head, I could take on an entire playoff team solo.

The drive back feels like floating. Steve's buckled in behind us, and Sloane's thumb traces lazy circles on my palm where our hands rest on the console. Every red light becomes a small gift, another excuse to steal glances at her profile in the dashboard glow, to watch the way she smiles at nothing.

Neither of us mentions that we should probably let go.

When I pull up to her building, she doesn't reach for the door handle. Just sits there, still holding my hand, staring up at the familiar brick facade like she's seeing it for the first time.

I scan the street automatically. Empty sidewalks, no late-night dog walkers, no cars idling with phones pointed our way. Her building sits tucked back from the main road, shielded by trees that cast everything in shadow. Safe.

"Steve's going to need an escort," I say.

"Definitely a two-person job." But she's grinning when she says it.

Getting him out of the backseat is ridiculous. His massive blue limbs catch on everything, the seatbelt, the door frame, my jacket. Sloane dissolves into giggles when his fuzzy head gets stuck, and I have to physically wrestle our stuffed son free while she steadies his body from the other side.

"Our parenting skills need work," she gasps, still laughing. "We'll figure it out."

The words slip out easier than they should. She goes quiet, but not the bad kind. The kind that feels like settling.

We duck into the shadowed alcove by her door, hidden from the street by a brick overhang. She props Steve against the frame like he's standing guard. Her keys jingle in her hand, but she doesn't use them. Just turns to face me.

"Thank you," she says. "For tonight."

I step closer. "Thank you for saying yes."

"Even though you gave me no choice?"

"Especially because of that."

She looks up at me, and the guarded look she wears everywhere is gone. Just Sloane, relaxed and real, standing in the glow of a streetlight.

My hand finds her cheek.

"Garrett."

The way she says my name. Not rushed, not whispered like a secret. Just my name, steady and sure.

She rises on her toes and kisses me.

Her lips move against mine without urgency, without the frantic edge of stolen moments. Her hands slide up my chest, fingers curling into my jacket, and I taste cotton candy and possibility. When I pull her closer, she melts into me like she belongs there.

Like we have all the time in the world.

When we break apart, I don't step back. Her forehead rests against mine, and I count the gold flecks in her eyes while we share the same breath.

Her keys catch what little light filters into our hidden alcove.

"Garrett."

"Yeah?"

She doesn't step back either. Just looks up at me like she's making a decision.

The key slides into the lock with a soft click.

Her eyes never leave mine as the door swings open.

22

Garrett

The door closes behind us with a soft snick that might as well be a thunderclap.

We stand in her entryway, and the air between us shifts.

"Steve needs a home," she says softly, but there's something in her voice that has nothing to do with our ridiculous blue sloth and everything to do with the way I'm looking at her.

"He does," I agree, though I can barely focus on anything but the way the lamplight catches the copper in her hair.

I set Steve down carefully by the door. My eyes never leave her.

Her apartment is exactly what I expected and nothing like I imagined. Rich jewel tones and soft textures that scream sophisticated taste, but with little contradictions that make me fall harder: a ratty University of Minnesota sweatshirt draped over a dining chair, mismatched coffee mugs in the sink, romance novels with cracked spines stacked on her coffee table.

"Your place is perfect," I tell her, and I mean it. Professional Sloane and secret Sloane existing in the same space.

"It's home," she says, then pauses. "Do you want some coffee? Wine? I think I have—"

"Sloane."

She stops mid-sentence, looking at me with those green eyes that have been driving me crazy for months.

"I don't want coffee."

"What do you want?"

I take a step toward her, then another.

"You," I say. "Just you."

She rises on her toes, threading her fingers through my hair, and kisses me with a hunger that makes my knees weak. This kiss is different from the one at her door. Deeper, more intentional. Less about stolen moments and more about the luxury of time.

Her hands work at the buttons of my shirt, and I feel the exact moment she stops holding back. The tension in her shoulders dissolves, replaced by something liquid and wanting.

"Sloane," I murmur against her mouth.

"I know," she whispers, her lips trailing along my jaw.

I catch her hands, still them against my chest. Force myself to meet her eyes.

"Do you? Because this isn't about the secrecy or the adrenaline or—"

She silences me with a kiss that tastes like certainty.

"It's about you," she whispers against my lips. "About us."

My resolve crumbles. "You are," I tell her, cupping her face. "You are."

When she reaches for my shirt again, I don't stop her.

She leads me to her bedroom, all cream and sage green, with fairy lights strung around a window that overlooks the city. I feel like I'm crossing a threshold into something sacred.

"You're sure?" I ask, because I need to hear it one more time.

"I've never been more sure of anything." Her fingers trace the line of my jaw, and I turn into the touch, pressing a kiss to her palm. "Are you?"

Instead of answering with words, I show her.

We undress each other slowly, with less urgency than last time. Each piece of clothing that falls away feels like permission. Her sweater, my shirt, the careful reveal of skin that's been hidden behind professional distance.

When we come together, it's not the shock of discovery but the relief of returning. We take our time, learning each other's rhythms, discovering what makes the other gasp and sigh.

There's something profound in the way she looks at me. Not just desire, but trust. The kind of openness that comes from knowing you're safe with someone.

Afterwards, I'm sprawled on my back, Sloane curled against my side with her head on my chest. Her fingers trace lazy patterns on my skin while I play with her hair.

"That was..." she starts, then trails off with a satisfied sigh.

"Better than air hockey?" I tease, and feel her smile against my chest.

"Way better than air hockey." She lifts her head to look at me, and her expression is so open, so full of affection, that something catches in my chest. "Though I'm still not admitting defeat on that front."

"Rematch next week?"

"You're on." She settles back down, her arm tightening around my waist. "This is nice. Just being able to take our time."

"No risk of interruption," I agree, pressing a kiss to the top of her head. "No having to sneak around."

"Just us."

"Just us."

We lie in comfortable silence, and I let myself memorize this. The weight of her against me. The rhythm of her breathing.

"I should probably go soon," I say eventually, though every fiber of me rebels against the idea.

"Probably." But she doesn't loosen her grip. "Early practice tomorrow."

"And you've got that early meeting."

"Sure do."

Neither of us moves.

"Five more minutes," I say.

"Five more minutes," she agrees.

We both know it'll be longer than five minutes.

When I finally force myself to get dressed and kiss her good-bye at her door, a softer, sweeter goodbye than any we've shared, I feel like I'm walking on air.

The drive back passes in a haze of contentment. I can still hear Sloane's laugh echoing in my truck as she tried to buckle Steve into the backseat. The memory of her face when she said "This was perfect" plays on repeat, and I catch myself grinning like an idiot at red lights.

Back in my apartment, I pour two fingers of bourbon and sink into the leather chair by the window. The city glitters, but all I see is her. Lighting up the arcade. Destroying me at air hockey. Melting against me.

Perfect. She called it perfect. She was right.

Still grinning, I scroll through social media. Photos of teammates with their families. Late-night dinners. The usual.

Then I see it.

A post from Derek. My old linemate. The guy who helped wreck my last relationship. He's at a gala with his wife. She's beaming. He's holding her like she's everything.

"Couldn't be prouder of my incredible wife for chairing tonight's children's hospital fundraiser. This woman amazes me every single day. Lucky doesn't even begin to cover it. #PowerCouple #ProudHusband"

The bourbon suddenly tastes sour.

Derek looks proud. Proud in a way I feel every second with Sloane but never get to show.

My thumb freezes above the screen. And then I hear Emma's voice, sharp and painfully familiar:

"You never fought for me. When things got hard, when people talked, you just disappeared. Like you were ashamed of me."

It gutted me then. Because beneath the drama, it was true. When the press circled, when the rumors hit, I shut down. I called it discretion. Dignity. But really? I was protecting myself.

"Not once did you stand up and say you were proud to be with me."

I set the phone down.

I'm doing it again.

The realization hits like a check I didn't see coming.

Here I am, hiding the most extraordinary woman I've ever known. Making her sneak through shadows. Acting like this thing between us is some shameful secret instead of the best part of my life.

Sloane says secrecy protects her career, but what if I'm using that as armor? What if I'm using her legitimate concerns as an excuse to avoid the vulnerability of going public again? What if I'm making her pay the price for my cowardice?

Derek gets to post photos with his wife at charity galas. I can't even acknowledge that Sloane exists in my life. He gets to call her his partner. I pretend she's just another coworker.

I think of tonight. Her smile. Her trust. The way she looked at me like I was her whole world.

She deserves more than shadows.

Emma was wrong about a lot. But she was right about this: silence isn't dignity. It's cowardice.

Not this time. Not with Sloane.

I won't make the same mistake twice. When the right moment comes, when she's proving to everyone how extraordinary she is, I won't let her stand there alone.

This time, I'll fight for her.

23
Sloane

The press box smells like burnt coffee and nervous energy.

I shouldn't be here. I have a dozen emails waiting, a content calendar that needs updating, and a sponsor deck that won't finalize itself. But when Emily from social media mentioned she had an extra seat for tonight's game against Colorado, I said yes before my brain could catch up with my mouth.

Three rows down, Garrett takes the ice for warm-ups. He moves with that effortless grace that makes six-foot-three look elegant instead of hulking, stick-handling through cones like the puck is magnetically attached to his blade.

Focus, McKenzie. You're here to observe team dynamics for the Q4 campaign. This is research.

The lie tastes stale even in my own head.

The arena fills around me. Eighteen thousand fans in blue and gold, the energy building like static before a storm. The Jumbotron flashes player stats, and when Garrett's face appears, a group of women three sections over start screaming. I feel a completely irrational spike of jealousy, which is ridiculous, because they don't know what his laugh sounds like at 2 a.m., or how his voice drops when he says my name, or the way he looks at me like I'm the only person in any room.

Get it together.

The anthem. The roar. The puck drops.

Colorado comes out aggressive, testing our defense with quick transitions and heavy forechecking. I find myself leaning forward, reading the plays the way I have since I was eight years old, perched on cold bleachers watching Easton's pee-wee games. There: the way Garrett positions himself in the neutral zone, already anticipating where the puck is going before the pass is made. The subtle shift of his weight that tells me he's about to close a gap. The patience that separates elite defensemen from everyone else.

First period ends scoreless. The Zamboni makes its slow loops while I pretend to check my phone.

Second period. Colorado strikes first on a power play, their sniper finding the top corner while Easton sprawls desperately across the crease. The arena groans. I watch Garrett tap Easton's pads, a quick, wordless reassurance, before skating back to center ice.

We answer six minutes later. Daniels buries a rebound off a feed from Lucas, and the building shakes with eighteen thousand voices. I'm on my feet before I realize I've moved, clapping with everyone else, anonymous in the crowd.

This is safe. This is fine. I'm just another fan enjoying a Tuesday night game.

Then the third period happens.

Colorado's down by one with eight minutes left, and they're playing desperate. Bodies crash into boards. Sticks get tangled. The refs swallow their whistles as the game gets chippy, physical, mean.

I see it developing before it happens.

Garrett has the puck behind our net, scanning for an outlet pass. Colorado's enforcer, a hulking winger named Marchuk who's been running guys all night, builds speed through the neutral zone. He's not going for the puck. He's going for Garrett.

The hit is textbook illegal. Targeting the numbers, leaving his feet, driving Garrett headfirst into the boards with the kind of violence that ends careers.

The sound reaches me a half-second after the impact. A sickening crack that echoes through the suddenly silent arena. Garrett crumples. His stick clatters away. His helmet bounces once against the ice.

He doesn't move.

I'm standing. When did I stand? My hand is pressed against the glass partition, and I can't breathe, can't think, can't do anything except stare at the motionless figure in blue and gold lying face-down on the ice.

Get up. Get up. Please get up.

The referee's whistle screams. Players converge. Marchuk is already being escorted to the penalty box while Phil and Lucas shove at Colorado jerseys, but I can't focus on any of it. All I can see is Garrett, still down, trainers rushing across the ice with that careful urgency that means something is wrong.

Seconds pass. Five. Ten. Fifteen.

The crowd holds its breath. Eighteen thousand people suspended in collective dread.

Then Garrett moves.

It's small, just a shift of his shoulders, a turn of his head, but the relief that floods through me is so violent I have to grab the seat in front of me to stay upright. The trainers help him sit, then stand. He's wobbly, one arm wrapped around his ribs, but he's conscious. He's skating.

The arena erupts in applause as he moves slowly toward the bench, waving off assistance with that stubborn pride I've come to know so well. He disappears down the tunnel, and I finally remember how to breathe.

I sink back into my seat, pressing my palms flat against my thighs to hide the tremors. The game continues around me, we score again, the crowd roars, but I'm underwater. Watching the clock bleed down until the final horn.

Emily says something. I nod without hearing it. Smile without feeling it.

The professional mask holds. It has to.

But underneath, my hands won't stop shaking.

Steve the sloth catches the morning light streaming through my apartment windows, and I can't help but smile. He's propped in my favorite armchair like he owns the place. This ridiculous trophy from our perfect night at the arcade.

The past few days have felt like a dream. A warm, safe dream, punctuated by one moment at the arena I'm still trying not to think about. Garrett texted me after the game: *Bruised ribs, bruised ego, nothing serious. Stop worrying.* I'd laughed through the remnants of my panic, typed back something teasing about his dramatics, and told myself it was fine. Everything was fine.

I pad to the kitchen in bare feet, humming under my breath as I pour coffee into my favorite mug, the one with the little cartoon kitten. The steam rises, and I inhale deeply, savoring this moment.

This is my new normal. Secret happiness tucked into quiet mornings. The afterglow of falling for a man I never imagined I could have.

My phone erupts on the counter. Brynn's name flashes on the screen, but something's wrong. She's FaceTiming me, not texting. And it's barely seven in the morning.

I swipe to answer. "Brynn? What's—"

"Hey, sorry it's so early, but the most bizarre thing just dropped on The Sin Bin Scoop, and you're the only person who will appreciate how dumb it is." Her voice bubbles with the energy of someone who's already had too much caffeine and found something deliciously ridiculous to dissect.

My shoulders relax. This is normal Brynn, the Sports National reporter whose cult-favorite podcast is where she really lives, the place for industry gossip and dismantling the team-approved PR spin she has to tolerate all day.

"What kind of dumb?" I ask, settling against the counter. "Scale of one to 'Torres tried to trademark his own celebration dance.'"

"Oh, this is peak Torres-level stupidity. Get this: they're running a blind item about 'a certain alternate captain' on the Mammoths getting cozy with an 'ambitious, petite redhead in the marketing department.'" Her laugh crackles through the speaker. "I mean, how ridiculously specific and obviously fake is that? They're not even trying to hide that they're just making shit up to stir the pot. The word 'ambitious' alone, like, could they be more transparent about their misogyny?"

The coffee mug freezes halfway to my lips.

Alternate captain. Petite redhead. Marketing department. Ambitious.

Each detail lands with surgical precision, describing me so perfectly it's like they had a photograph.

I can't speak. Can't breathe.

"They've obviously got some grudge against the organization," Brynn continues, oblivious to my silence. "Probably trying to get back at someone. The whole thing reads like fan fiction written by someone who's never actually stepped foot in an arena. I swear, these gossip vultures get more desperate every—"

She stops. The silence stretches.

"Sloane?" Her voice changes, the amusement bleeding out of it. "That's funny, right? Just some weird coincidence they happened to describe someone who sounds vaguely like you?"

I open my mouth, but no sound comes out. The kitchen tilts around me.

"Sloane, why aren't you saying anything?"

"Wait." Her voice drops to a whisper. "Wait, wait, wait. Sloane. Tell me this isn't... tell me you're not..."

"Brynn—"

"Oh my god." The words explode out of her. "Oh my god, Sloane. It's not a coincidence, is it? It's you. It's you and Sullivan."

My throat closes completely.

"How long?" Her voice cracks, but there's something softer underneath the shock. "How long have you been carrying this alone?"

"I wasn't—I didn't—"

"Sloane." Gentler now, though I can hear her struggling to process. "I'm your best friend. I tell you everything. Every stupid date, every professional crisis, every thought in my head, and you've been—God, you must have been dying keeping this to yourself. With Sullivan?"

Tears burn behind my eyes. Not from guilt. From humiliation. This is exactly what I was trying to avoid.

"Okay, wow. I'm reeling here." Her breath catches. "But we'll figure this out. We always do. Jesus Christ, Sloane, do you have any idea what this could cost you? What it will cost you when people find out?" Her voice shifts into protective mode, the journalist in her already calculating threats. "You've worked so hard to prove you belong in that boys' club, and if this gets out wrong—"

"Now what?" The words tear out of me, raw with months of suppressed fear. "Now I'm just another woman who couldn't keep her legs closed? Is that what you think?"

"No. God, no, that's not what I meant. I'm sorry." Her voice breaks with fierce protectiveness. "That's what they'll think. That's the story they'll tell. And you know it. That's why you've been terrified, isn't it?"

The silence that follows is brutal. We both know she's right.

"Sloane," she whispers, and I can hear the tears in her voice now, but also something stronger. "What are you going to do? Because whatever it is, I'm with you."

The coffee mug slips from my fingers. It shatters against the hardwood, the sound echoing in the sudden quiet. I don't register the hot coffee splashing across my legs. I just stare.

Vivian's voice echoes in my head: *ambitious*, always laced with disdain.

This isn't just gossip. This is a strike.

Someone chose those words. Carefully. Just cryptic enough to maintain plausible deniability. But clear enough for everyone to guess.

It paints me as everything I've spent my career proving I'm not: a distraction. A manipulator. A woman using a man to climb.

Just like they did to Sarah.

"Sloane? Sloane, are you okay?" Brynn's voice cuts through my spiral, the hurt replaced by immediate concern.

"It was Vivian," I breathe. "She fed them this story."

"Wait. You think Vivian leaked this?" The protective fury in her voice sharpens. "Why would she—"

"Because she's the only one who calls me ambitious like it's a dirty word." My voice is getting stronger, my brain shifting into crisis mode. "She's been building a case against me for months. This is just the opening shot."

"Jesus, Sloane. This isn't random gossip. This is targeted."

The memory hits me. Sarah sitting in her empty office five years ago, packing her career into a cardboard box while whispers followed her down every hallway. It started just like this: a blind item on a gossip blog, making her sound like she was sleeping her way to the top instead of being the most brilliant marketing mind the league had ever seen. Three weeks later, she was gone. Blacklisted from every major sports organization in the country.

Different words. Same poison. Same ending.

"Sloane, listen to me," Brynn says. "We're going to figure this out. I'm already working my sources to find out who at Sin Bin took this tip. This isn't over."

But I'm barely listening. My mind is dissecting this like data.

This is narrative warfare. A single sentence designed to erode confidence, to shift blame, to cast shadows.

And someone tipped them off. The parking garage? The hallway outside the conference room? That moment in the film room, almost a kiss, before footsteps stopped us cold?

I press a trembling hand to my mouth.

"I have to go," I tell Brynn, my voice hollow.

"Sloane, wait. Don't shut me out. Not when you need backup the most."

"I can't think straight right now."

"Listen to me." She cuts through my panic with quiet conviction. "You're not alone in this. Whatever happens next, we face it together. That's not negotiable."

But as I'm staring at Brynn's face on the screen, a new call slides across the top.

Vivian.

I think of Garrett, probably still asleep, completely unaware that his career is now collateral damage in whatever's about to hit.

I hang up on my best friend and answer Vivian.

"Sloane McKenzie." The words come out wrong. Too high. Too tight.

"Good morning," Vivian purrs, every syllable coated in sugar and threat. "Hope I'm not catching you too early. Something's come up. I need you in my office, first thing. We need to discuss the Northstar timeline."

The campaign isn't due for two weeks. We both know it.

This isn't business. This is a summons.

"Of course," I croak. "I'll be right there."

"Wonderful. Looking forward to our chat."

The line goes dead.

Silence floods the apartment.

I glance at Steve.

Hours ago, he represented everything good Garrett and I had found together. Joy, laughter, the possibility that we could build something real.

Now he looks like evidence.

Our snow globe is cracking.

24
Sloane

The executive wing feels different at 7:30 a.m. Too quiet. Too still. Like a stage set waiting for the performance to begin.

Her assistant isn't at her desk yet, which means this meeting is off the books. No witnesses. No paper trail.

The door to Vivian's office stands slightly ajar, spilling warm light into the hallway.

"Come in, Sloane. Close the door behind you."

I step inside. Vivian sits behind her mahogany desk, perfectly put-together despite the early hour. Her blonde hair is styled in its usual severe bob, her navy blazer immaculate, her smile sharp enough to cut.

"Coffee?" She gestures to the French press on the sidebar. "I made it myself. Didn't want to wait for anyone else to arrive."

"I'm fine, thank you."

"Of course you are. Always so self-sufficient." The way she says it makes self-sufficiency sound like a character flaw. "Please, sit."

I choose the chair directly across from her desk, the one that forces me to meet her gaze head-on.

"I suppose you're wondering why I called you in so early." Vivian leans back, fingers steepled. "I heard something troubling yesterday, and I couldn't sleep until we addressed it."

My pulse kicks up, but I keep my expression neutral. "I'm listening."

"There's a podcast. Sin Bin Scoop. Apparently, they're spreading some rather salacious gossip about our organization." Her smile never wavers. "Complete nonsense, of course. The idea that anyone on our team would be inappropriate with a player is utterly ridiculous."

The word *inappropriate* drips from her lips.

"I haven't heard it," I lie.

"I'm sure you haven't. But unfortunately, perception can be just as damaging as reality in our business. Especially with the Northstar deal in such a delicate phase." She picks up a gold pen, twirling it between her fingers. "Our investors are very concerned about optics. Professional boundaries. The integrity of our brand."

Every word is carefully chosen, each one landing like a small knife.

"Which is why I wanted to check in with you personally," she continues. "As one of our most visible marketing professionals, your conduct reflects directly on the organization. I trust that's something you take very seriously."

"Of course."

"Good. Because any hint of impropriety, any suggestion that personal relationships might be compromising our professional standards, would be catastrophic. For everyone involved." The pen stops twirling. "The person in question would find themselves in an impossible position. Professionally speaking."

She knows. Maybe not specifics. But she knows enough.

"I understand," I manage.

"I knew you would. You're so intelligent, Sloane. So strategic. I'm sure you recognize that some risks simply aren't worth taking, no matter how tempting they might seem." She sets the pen down with deliberate precision. "The Northstar presentation is in two weeks. Until then, I need my entire team focused solely on the success of that deal. No distractions. No complications."

She pauses, letting the silence stretch.

"No ammunition for gossip podcasts."

I nod.

"Wonderful." Vivian's smile brightens, as if we've just discussed quarterly projections instead of my professional execution. "I knew I could count on your discretion. Your loyalty to this organization has always been exemplary."

The way she says *loyalty* makes it sound like a leash.

"Was there anything specific about the Northstar timeline you wanted to discuss?" I ask, grasping for some semblance of normal business conversation.

"Oh, we'll have plenty of time for that. I just wanted to make sure we were on the same page about priorities." She glances at her Rolex. "You should get to your office. I'm sure you have a busy day ahead."

I stand on unsteady legs.

"Sloane?" Her voice stops me at the door. "I do hope you'll keep our little chat confidential. These types of conversations can be so easily misunderstood."

"Of course."

"Have a productive day."

The door closes behind me with a soft click that sounds like a lock turning.

The cursor blinks at me from my computer screen. I've been staring at the budget spreadsheet for twenty minutes without comprehending a single number.

Any hint of impropriety would be catastrophic.

Vivian's words loop on endless repeat. The meeting wasn't a firing. It was something worse. A warning. A promise. She knows about Garrett and me, and she's given me a choice: end it, or watch her destroy us both.

I force myself to focus on the Q3 projections, but the numbers blur.

Some risks simply aren't worth taking.

A burst of laughter from the hallway makes me flinch.

No ammunition for gossip podcasts.

I need caffeine. Need something to anchor me before my 2 p.m. meeting with Garrett, a routine check-in about playoff media coverage that now feels like walking through a minefield.

The breakroom is mercifully empty when I push through the door. I'm reaching for the coffee pot when voices drift through the thin wall separating the breakroom from the marketing bullpen.

"—honestly think she's sleeping with him?"

I freeze.

"I mean, come on. Did you see the way he looked at her during that meeting last week? Like she was speaking in a secret language only he understood."

"Jennifer, you're being dramatic."

"Am I, though? She's always got those little smiles when his interviews come on. Plus, she practically glows whenever anyone mentions his name."

My blood turns to ice. The whispers are already starting.

"That doesn't mean anything," the second voice, Nikki from social media, argues. "Maybe she's just proud of her work. That campaign strategy was brilliant."

"Or maybe she's getting a little too invested in her subject. I'm just saying, if I were Vivian, I'd be asking some hard questions. Especially with everything riding on Northstar."

If I were Vivian.

This isn't organic gossip. This is Vivian's campaign in action. She's already planted seeds.

"Think it'll blow up?" Nikki asks.

"Depends how smart they are about it. But honestly? You can't have that kind of distraction during playoff season. Especially not with someone who's supposed to be managing team optics." Jennifer's tone carries the satisfied certainty of someone who's already decided the outcome. "It's exactly the kind of professional liability that gets people fired."

"Poor girl," Nikki says, but there's no real sympathy in her voice. "She's talented, I'll give her that. But talent doesn't protect you when you become the story instead of managing it."

Their conversation shifts to weekend plans. I'm no longer listening. The damage is done.

I wait until their voices fade before emerging. The coffee sits forgotten.

The conference room is a fishbowl under fluorescent lights. I've chosen the chair farthest from the door, my laptop positioned like a barrier between myself and the empty chair across from me.

When Garrett enters, he brings his usual easy confidence. His hair is still damp from the post-practice shower, and he's wearing that navy pullover that makes his eyes look more green than brown. Yesterday, the sight of him would have made my professional mask slip into something softer.

Today, it makes my chest tighten with panic.

"Hey," he says, closing the door with the quiet consideration he always shows for my corporate sensibilities. "How's the playoff media timeline looking?"

"Fine." The word comes out clipped, sharper than I intended. I don't look up from my screen. "Player availability is confirmed through next Friday. The feature interviews are scheduled with Torres, Davidson, and Williams."

He settles into the chair across from me, and I can feel his gaze. Out of the corner of my eye, I catch the small frown that creases his forehead. Confusion at my tone. At the distance I've suddenly inserted between us.

"And the community outreach coverage?" he asks, a note of uncertainty creeping in.

"Handled." I click through to another spreadsheet. "The youth clinic footage will be edited and distributed by Thursday. Social media rollout begins Friday morning."

The silence stretches between us. I can see him in my peripheral vision, leaning forward slightly, trying to catch my eye.

"Sloane." His voice is quieter now. "Is everything okay?"

"Everything's fine." I pull up another document, fingers moving across the keyboard with mechanical precision. "Did you need anything else regarding media coverage?"

I finally glance at him, and the hurt that flickers across his expression is a knife. But I force myself to maintain the facade. I can't afford to be soft right now. Can't afford to let him see how terrified I am.

He opens his mouth, probably to call out my obvious deflection, when movement in the hallway catches my attention.

Easton.

My brother's massive frame fills the corridor beyond the glass walls, moving with purpose. But as he passes our conference room, his steps slow. His head turns. And when his eyes find us through the glass, everything inside me turns to ice.

The look on Easton's face isn't casual curiosity. It's laser-focused suspicion, the kind of sharp attention he usually reserves for reading shooters in the slot. His gaze moves from Garrett to me and back again, cataloguing every detail: the distance between us, the careful positioning, the way I'm avoiding eye contact with the man across from me.

His eyes narrow slightly. I watch the pieces click into place. The blind item. My reaction at the game when Garrett got hit. The late nights I've attributed to work stress.

He knows.

The moment stretches taut. Then Easton's jaw tightens, and without a word, he continues down the hallway.

"What was that about?" Garrett's voice cuts through my paralysis. "Easton looked like he wanted to put me through the glass."

"He's protective. You know how brothers are."

The lie tastes bitter, but it's easier than the truth.

"Sloane." Garrett's voice is patient but persistent. "Talk to me. What's going on?"

"There's nothing to talk about." I close my laptop with deliberate finality, the snap echoing in the glass-walled room. "I think we've covered everything for the media schedule."

The confusion in his eyes deepens, mixed with hurt he's trying to hide.

He nods slowly, gathering his things with careful movements. "Alright. I'll see you later."

He pauses at the door, hand on the handle. I can feel him willing me to look at him. To give him some sign that this distance is temporary.

I don't look up.

It's only when the door shuts behind him that I close my eyes, letting the pain wash over me in one silent breath before I force myself back to work.

My computer chimes with an incoming email.

Subject: INVITATION: The 15th Annual Minnesota Mammoths Charity Gala

I stare at the notification. The gala. The most high-profile event of the season, where every major sponsor, every board member, every influential figure in the organization will be watching. Where Garrett and I will be forced into the same elegant ballroom, surrounded by cameras and corporate scrutiny.

I open it. The formal invitation text swims before my eyes, but all I can see is the date. Three days from now. Seventy-two hours until I'm trapped in a glittering minefield where my brother will be cataloguing my every glance, every gesture, every second of proximity between Garrett and me.

25

Sloane

The crystal chandelier above the ballroom catches the light like a thousand watching eyes. I stand near the silent auction tables, champagne flute in hand, listening to Mrs. Shaw from Northstar Bank discuss her daughter's field hockey team with practiced attention. My smile feels shellacked in place. Every inch the polished marketing executive.

But underneath the navy silk dress that felt so confident an hour ago, my skin crawls.

"—and we just think the Mammoths could really benefit from more youth outreach programs, don't you agree, dear?"

"Absolutely," I hear myself say. "Community engagement is crucial for building our fan base."

The words are automatic. My real attention is across the ballroom.

Near the bar, Vivian holds court with a cluster of board members, her hair gleaming under the lights. Every few minutes, her gaze sweeps the room. Hunting.

But it's the figure by the management table that turns my blood cold.

Easton.

My brother stands with his back to the wall, still as a goalie reading a power play. His massive frame is encased in a perfectly tailored tuxedo, but there's nothing civilized about the way he's watching me. His green eyes track my every movement. When I laugh at something Mrs. Shaw says, his jaw tightens. When I adjust my bracelet, his posture shifts.

He knows. This isn't suspicion anymore. This is certainty. And he's not here to celebrate. He's here to catch me.

"—your brother, what a season he's having—"

"Excuse me," I interrupt. "I need to use the ladies' room. It was lovely chatting with you."

I'm already moving before she can respond, weaving through clusters of Minnesota's elite. But I can feel Easton's stare on my back, following my path across the marble floor.

The conversations around me blur:

"—chemistry's been off since the Detroit series—"

"—heard there's some locker room tension—"

"—think they'll hold it together for playoffs?"

Each fragment feels aimed directly at me.

The French doors to the balcony appear like salvation. I slip through them, trading the suffocating warmth of the ballroom for November's brutal honesty.

The cold bites through silk, raising goosebumps along my arms. But it's a welcome shock. Sharp and clean and real in a way the performance inside isn't. I grip the wrought-iron railing with both hands, knuckles going white against the metal.

Minneapolis stretches below me, city lights glittering against the darkness. Up here, the corporate minefield feels distant. Manageable.

I take a breath. Then another.

"Knew I'd find you out here."

I don't turn, but every muscle in my body goes rigid.

Three days. Three days of one-word texts and avoided eye contact, of taking different elevators and timing my coffee runs to miss him entirely. Three days of treating the man I'm falling in love with like a professional liability.

"You looked like you were about to short-circuit in there." Garrett doesn't touch me, but he stands close enough that I can feel exactly where he is. The space between us hums with everything we're not allowed to say in that ballroom. "Are you okay?"

Such a simple question. But it slices through every defense I've built tonight. The practiced smile crumbles. The polished facade cracks. For the first time all evening, someone is actually seeing me.

Just me. Terrified and overwhelmed and drowning.

"No." The word slips out unguarded. "I'm not."

He shifts closer, and I feel the urge to lean into him, to let his strength anchor me. For just a moment, on this dark balcony overlooking the city, we could be real.

The French door slams open behind us.

The sound cuts through the night air, making us both freeze. I don't need to turn around to know who's standing there.

Easton.

He fills the doorway, a towering silhouette against the ballroom's glow, his face set in hard lines. His eyes flick from Garrett to me, and I watch him piece together the final puzzle. The way we're standing. The intimacy of the moment he just shattered. The look on my face that I couldn't hide fast enough.

Garrett reads the situation instantly. He gives me the smallest nod, a gesture so subtle only I would catch it. Protection, apology, and promise in a movement that lasts less than a second.

"I'll see you inside," he says, voice neutral, as he brushes past Easton without a word.

The door shuts behind him, leaving me alone with my brother.

Easton doesn't speak immediately. Just stands there, staring at me with an expression I've never seen before. Not pure rage. Something worse. The look of someone who's been bracing for bad news and just got it confirmed.

When he finally moves, it's with the deliberate precision of a man barely keeping himself in check. Three steps forward, and the balcony feels impossibly small.

"How long." Not a question. A demand.

I open my mouth, but nothing comes.

"Sloane. How long."

"Easton, it's not what you think—"

"Don't." His voice cracks on the word, and he looks away, jaw working. When he turns back, his eyes are bright. "Don't stand there and manage me. Not about this."

The crack in his voice is worse than shouting. This is my brother, who walked me to the bus stop every morning until eighth grade, looking at me like I've become someone he doesn't recognize.

"Do you understand what happens when this gets out?" He's not yelling. He sounds exhausted. "Three games from clinching home ice. Garrett's my captain. You're my sister. And when someone finds out, and they will, I'm the guy standing in the middle of that locker room who knew and didn't say anything."

"We've been careful—"

"You were on a balcony, Sloane. At the gala. With two hundred people on the other side of the glass." He drags a hand down his face. "That's not careful. That's a countdown."

Every word finds its mark. Not because he's aiming to hurt. Because he's right.

"What happens when this goes sideways and I have to choose between defending my sister and defending my captain in that room?" His voice drops, and I hear what it costs him to say this. "Because I've been thinking about it for three days, and I don't have a play for this."

"Easton—"

"I can't protect you from this." The words come out raw. Almost bewildered. Then something shifts in his face, the vulnerability closing over, and what replaces it is harder. More familiar. The Easton who blocks shots and drops gloves and solves every problem with sheer stubborn force.

"You need to end it." Flat. Decided. "Before someone else makes that choice for you."

"That's not your call—"

"You're right. It's not. But I'm making it anyway." He steps closer, and his voice drops to something low and certain that sounds nothing like a request. "Because I've watched you build this career from nothing, and I'm not going to stand here and let you torch it for a guy who—"

He stops. Swallows. I see him catch himself, pull back from whatever he was about to say about Garrett.

"Just end it, Sloane. Before it ends you."

It sounds like a threat. But I know my brother, and underneath the steel I can hear the fault line running through his voice. He's terrified. And Easton McKenzie has never once in his life known what to do with fear except turn it into action. Into control. Into making the call so no one else has to.

The problem is, this time, the call isn't his to make.

He stares at me for another heartbeat, waiting for a response I can't give. When none comes, something shutters behind his eyes. He turns and walks back through the French doors without another word.

Not because he's done talking. Because he doesn't know how to say the rest.

I don't know how long I stand there. Long enough for the cold to turn the damp tracks on my cheeks painfully numb.

Long enough for the numbness to spread from my fingers until my entire chest feels hollow.

Eventually, the cold drives me inside.

The ballroom welcomes me back with its suffocating warmth. The conversations continue, oblivious to the fact that my world just ended on a dark balcony. I smooth my dress, check my reflection in a server's polished tray, rebuild my mask with the expertise of someone who's been performing her whole life.

But as I move through the crowd, my eyes find a familiar figure across the room.

Vivian stands near the media corner, a champagne flute in her manicured hand. She's not talking to anyone. Not networking or schmoozing.

She's watching.

Her gaze moves from me to the French doors I just emerged from, to Garrett near the management table, to Easton rejoining his teammates at the bar. I watch her catalog every detail.

When her gaze returns to me, I see something that makes my stomach drop.

It's not professional disapproval. It's not corporate calculation.

It's recognition. Personal. Vicious. The look of a woman who's seen this exact scenario before and knows how it ends.

But there's something else underneath.

Satisfaction.

Like she's been waiting for this. Like she's been building toward it. Like everything that just happened on that balcony was exactly what she needed.

I stand frozen in the middle of the glittering ballroom, watching Vivian smile at me with the precision of a woman who's just won a game I didn't know we were playing.

And I finally understand.

The threat was never about policy or team chemistry or corporate image.

This is personal.

And I've just given her everything she needs.

26

Sloane

The sound of my heels on hardwood echoes through my apartment. Back and forth across the living room, still in this damn navy dress that felt flawless three hours ago and now clings like evidence.

Click-clack. Click-clack.

Each step drives Easton's words deeper into my skull. *End it, Sloane. Before it ends you.*

I rip the pins from my hair, sending strands cascading over my shoulders. The polished image from tonight unravels one bobby pin at a time, scattering across the floor in sharp, metallic clinks.

I whirl toward the kitchen where Garrett stands, still and silent. His bow tie hangs loose around his neck, jacket draped over a chair, but his eyes never leave me as I carve another trench into the rug.

He doesn't speak. Doesn't offer comfort or platitudes. Just steps into the kitchen with quiet determination, fills a glass with water, and sets it on a coaster in the middle of my path. A subtle act that says *I'm here*, without needing to say anything at all.

I ignore it. Spin to face him.

"He'll go to Kowalski. He'll ruin everything, my career, yours. Just because—" The words catch in my throat. *Because I fell for you. Because for once, I wanted something that wasn't part of the plan.*

Garrett crosses his arms, leaning against the doorframe. He's not detached. He's reading the moment, giving me space to spiral, anchoring me without interfering. The patience of someone who's been in overtime and knows you can't force the win.

"Three passes," he says quietly, after my next lap around the coffee table.

"What?"

"You've walked past that water three times. Your feet have to be killing you."

They are. These heels made me feel untouchable earlier. Now they're just punishment. But stopping feels like surrender.

Garrett moves. No hesitation. He kneels in front of me, smooth and sure. His hands wrap around my ankle, fingers working the strap.

"Garrett, you don't have to—"

"Shh."

The buckle gives way. He slips the heel off with a gentleness that almost undoes me. His thumb brushes my arch.

"Other foot."

I rest a hand on his shoulder, off balance in more ways than one. He removes the second heel, and the relief is immediate.

Not just physical. Someone seeing my pain and easing it without needing to be asked.

When he stands, I'm barefoot and somehow more grounded than I've felt all night.

"Whatever you decide," he says, calm and quiet, "I'll understand. This is your career. Your family. If you need me to leave, I will."

That breaks me.

The adrenaline collapses, and everything I've been holding back comes flooding out. A sob tears from my throat, raw and jagged. My knees buckle, and I have to grab the back of the couch to keep from falling.

"But I don't want you to go."

The words come out in a whisper. It's the first time I've said what I want instead of what I fear.

"I don't want you to go. And that terrifies me more than losing my job, more than Easton, more than anything." My voice cracks. "Because I know how this story ends."

The trembling starts in my hands and spreads through my entire body. I can't stop it. Can't control it.

"I was eight years old," I whisper, and suddenly I'm not in my apartment anymore.

I'm standing in our old kitchen, clutching my Barbie lunchbox, home from another day of pretending everything was normal.

The house is too quiet.

That's the first thing I notice when I push through the front door, my backpack heavy with homework I'm excited to show

Mom. Usually, there's music playing. She always has the radio on while she does the dishes or folds laundry. But today, there's nothing. Just this thick, cottony silence that makes my ears feel funny.

"Mom?" I call out, dropping my backpack by the door the way she's always telling me not to. "I'm home!"

No answer.

The afternoon sunlight slants through the kitchen windows at the wrong angle, casting everything in this golden, underwater glow that makes the familiar feel strange. The coffee pot is still on from this morning, the bottom of the glass carafe burned black. I reach up on my tiptoes to turn it off, the way she taught me, because leaving things on is dangerous.

That's when I see her.

Mom is sitting on the kitchen floor in her nightgown. The pink one with tiny flowers that she only wears to bed. It's three in the afternoon. I know because the big hand is on the six and the little hand is almost on the three, and that means it's time for my after-school snack.

She's not crying. She's not doing anything. Just sitting there with her back against the cabinets, staring at the wall like there's something really interesting written there that only she can see.

"Mom?" I drop my lunchbox, and it clatters against the linoleum. The sound echoes in the weird quiet, but she doesn't even blink. "Are you okay?"

I kneel down beside her, the cold from the floor seeping through my school dress. Up close, I can see that her eyes are open, but they look empty. Unfocused and utterly blank.

"Did you hurt yourself?" I ask, because maybe she fell down and can't get up. Sometimes grown-ups fall down. "Do you need a Band-Aid?"

Nothing. She doesn't even look at me.

A scary feeling starts growing in my stomach, like when you're on a swing and you go too high and suddenly you're not sure if the chains will hold. I wave my hand in front of her face, the way kids at school do when they're trying to be annoying, but she doesn't react.

"I'm hungry," I tell her, because maybe that will make her remember she's supposed to take care of me. "Can I have a snack?"

Still nothing.

So I get up and make myself a peanut butter sandwich, standing on the step stool to reach the counter. I put it on my special plate, the one with the rainbow, and I sit at the kitchen table to eat it. The chair feels too big, and my feet don't touch the floor, so they swing back and forth while I chew.

Mom doesn't move.

I do my math homework at the table, writing the numbers carefully the way Mrs. Peterson taught us. Seven plus five equals twelve. Nine plus three equals twelve. When I get stuck on a hard one, I look over at Mom to see if she'll help, but she's still just sitting there.

The shadows in the kitchen get longer and darker. My stomach starts growling again, but Mom hasn't moved to start dinner. She always starts dinner by now. Always.

That's when I notice the papers scattered on the counter. White envelopes with red writing that says things like FINAL NOTICE and PAST DUE. I can't read all the words, but I know red writing means something bad. It means you're in trouble.

I climb down from my chair and walk over to Mom again, these papers clutched in my small hands.

"Mom, there's scary mail," I say, my voice smaller now, because the feeling in my stomach is getting bigger and scarier. "The red kind that makes you upset."

But she doesn't answer. Doesn't even look at the papers. Just keeps staring at that empty wall with those empty eyes.

And that's when I understand, with the terrible clarity that sometimes comes to children: Daddy isn't coming home. Not tonight, not tomorrow, not ever. And Mom is broken. Like a toy that stops working, or a TV that only shows static.

I'm going to have to take care of everything now. The bills with the red writing. The dinner that needs to be made. The bedtime stories and the good-morning hugs and all the things that make a house feel like home instead of just a place where broken people sit on kitchen floors.

I'm eight years old, and I'm the grown-up now.

The memory releases me, and I'm back in my apartment, gasping. Garrett's face swims into focus.

"She sat there for three days," I whisper. "Three days on that kitchen floor, and I had to do everything. Make my own meals, get myself ready for school, forge her signature on permission slips. I learned to pay bills before I learned long division."

Garrett doesn't speak. Doesn't try to fix it or explain it away. He just moves closer, slowly, giving me time to object. When his arms come around me, they're cautious. Not trying to trap me. Just offering shelter.

"I'm sorry," he says into my hair. "I'm so sorry that happened to you."

I break apart then, sobbing against his chest while he holds me through the storm.

"She gave up everything," I gasp between sobs. "Her job, her friends, her whole identity. All for a man who decided she wasn't worth staying for. And when he left, she had nothing. Was nothing. I watched her disappear, and I swore I'd never need anyone that much."

"But you're not her," Garrett says quietly, his hands moving in slow circles on my back. "You're not disappearing, Sloane. You're fighting."

I pull back just enough to look at him. This man who's seen me at my most broken and hasn't run. Who's offering to walk away to keep me safe.

"Easton thinks he's protecting me," I whisper, the pieces starting to shift. "But it feels like being eight years old again. Being told I can't trust my own judgment. That I'll make the same mistakes she did."

Garrett nods. "What if he's wrong?"

"What if—" I take a shaky breath, and somewhere deep in my chest, a familiar gear clicks back into place. "What if this isn't about protecting me at all? What if it's about controlling me? Keeping me small and manageable and grateful?"

"What do you think?" he asks. Not pushing. Not directing. Just opening space.

I think about the way Easton looked at me tonight. The disappointment. The assumption that I couldn't handle the consequences of my own choices.

"I think I've been playing defense my whole life. Trying to prove I'm not her. Trying to show I can handle everything alone. But maybe that's not strength. Maybe that's just another kind of cage."

Garrett's thumb brushes away a tear I didn't realize was still falling. "So what's the play?"

The question unlocks something. Not a transformation. A gradual straightening of my spine. A slow return to myself. The woman who built impossible campaigns from nothing. Who turned crisis into opportunity.

"The play is that I stop being afraid of becoming my mother," I say, and my voice finds its footing. "Because I'm not eight years old anymore. I'm not sitting on a kitchen floor waiting for someone else to fix everything. I'm Sloane fucking McKenzie, and I build solutions."

I step back from his arms. Not because I don't want them. Because I need to stand on my own two feet. The tears have stopped, and something sharp has taken their place.

"Easton thinks he's protecting the team by managing me. But what if he's wrong about the threat?" I start to pace, my mind kicking into gear. "What if it was never about us at all?"

Garrett watches me move, a slow smile spreading across his face. "What are you thinking?"

"I'm thinking about Vivian's face tonight. The way she watched us. That wasn't professional disapproval. That was personal. Like she was seeing something that triggered her."

The strategy crystallizes. Clean. Sharp.

"The Northstar presentation," I say, and my voice is steel now. "That's not just about getting a sponsorship deal. That's about proving I'm not a liability to be managed. I'm an asset they can't afford to lose."

Garrett nods. "What do you need?"

I look at him, really look, and see not the man who tried to save me tonight, but the man who's willing to stand beside me while I save myself. The difference is everything.

"I need you to trust me," I say. "And I need you to let me win this my way."

"Done," he says. "What else?"

"If I don't just win that room, but dominate. If I make myself undeniable. Vivian can't touch me. Once the deal is inked, she'll be too exposed to come after my personal life without looking like she's sabotaging her own department's biggest win."

My voice is steadier with every word.

"This is what I do. I win impossible rooms. I change the narrative. I don't disappear. I become the reason they can't afford to lose me."

Outside, Minneapolis gleams. No longer a threat. A battlefield.

"Let's get to work," I say.

27

Sloane

The office is quiet this early. I should be working on quarterly projections, but instead I'm hunting for the truth about Vivian Lamore.

I sink onto the couch and pull my laptop closer, opening the folder labeled "V.L." Everything I've collected since that moment at the coffee machine when Anna Reyes went white and fled.

The Columbus staff photo stares back at me. Anna's open smile. Vivian's guarded expression. Both of them younger, before whatever happened.

"I don't know what you mean."

Anna's lie was terrible. Unconvincing. But effective, because what could I do? I had timing and a photograph. I had Vivian's paranoia and Anna's terror. Coincidence, not proof.

I need proof.

My mind drifts to that photo on Vivian's screen. Her and Jake Morrison, arms around each other, both grinning at a team event. The photo she was staring at until she noticed me. The photo that meant something.

I've been circling around the timing of Vivian's departure, but I never actually investigated Morrison himself. What happened to Columbus's golden boy captain who retired at twenty-nine?

Twenty minutes of digging later, I've pieced together what the team tried to bury: Morrison's retirement coincided with whispers of infidelity and "internal restructuring." His ex-wife's family had major sponsor connections. A local news article about "inappropriate conduct" has been scrubbed from the internet, but the Google cache remains.

Morrison had a scandal. Vivian left in the aftermath. Anna ran from my questions like her life depended on it.

This is the thread.

I grab my phone and check the time. 7:47 a.m. I need to catch Anna before she disappears into meetings, before she has time to see me coming.

I find her at her desk, headphones in, already deep in spreadsheets. She doesn't notice me approach until I'm standing right beside her.

"Anna."

She jumps, yanking out her earbuds. The look that crosses her face tells me everything I need to know.

"Sloane. Hi. I didn't—"

"I need to talk to you." My voice is steady, but my hands shake. "And this time, you can't say 'nothing comes to min d.'"

Her face goes pale. "I have a meeting—"

"No, you don't. Not for another hour." I lower my voice. "Anna, I know about Jake Morrison. I know he retired the same summer Vivian left. I know there was a scandal, something bad enough that the team scrubbed articles from the internet. And I know it's happening to me now."

She stares at me, frozen.

"Someone is setting me up," I continue. "They're going to try to make me look incompetent or worse. And I think Vivian is using the same playbook on me that someone used on her in Columbus." I meet her eyes. "You have to tell me what happened. Please."

Anna's fingers clench around her pen so hard I think it might snap.

"There's a conference room," she whispers finally. "Second floor. Empty until nine."

I follow her there.

She closes the door behind us with shaking hands, then leans against it like she needs the support.

"If I tell you this," she says, "and it gets out... if she finds out I told you..."

"Then we go down together," I say. "But at least we go down fighting."

Anna nods once. When she speaks again, her voice is stronger but still trembling.

"I was unemployed for eight months after Columbus. No interviews. Nothing. It was like I'd been blacklisted." She presses her hands flat against the table. "I don't know everything. But people said Morrison was involved with someone.

Not Vivian. Someone else. A woman whose family had big connections to our top sponsors."

"An affair."

She nods slowly. "That's what people whispered. And when his wife found out, she didn't just threaten to expose the affair. She threatened to blow the whole thing open. Financial irregularities, shady contracts, sponsor money getting funneled through back channels."

"Morrison needed a scapegoat."

"Vivian was young. Talented. She'd been working on his personal branding. It was easy to spin that into something inappropriate."

"But nothing happened between them."

"Nothing." Anna's voice hardens. "Vivian was married. Happy. She was building something real. But once the rumors started, who was going to believe her? He was the face of the franchise. She was a marketing girl."

This wasn't a relationship gone bad. This was a calculated sacrifice.

"Her marriage fell apart?"

Anna nods, voice breaking. "The whispers. The looks. The way people treated her husband at events. He couldn't handle it. Filed for divorce six months after she got fired. She lost everything, Sloane. And she didn't do a damn thing wrong."

I sit back. The ugly picture becomes sickeningly clear. Vivian's expression at the gala wasn't jealousy. It was recognition.

She wasn't seeing two colleagues in the early stages of an office romance. She was seeing herself. Watching history repeat.

"Anna?"

She takes a breath, then looks at me. Really looks at me. Her voice drops to a whisper.

"Last night, I saw the way Vivian was watching you. Watching Garrett. And I recognized it."

Her eyes go glassy.

"It's the same way she used to look at herself in the mirror. After it all fell apart." A pause. "Like she was seeing a ghost."

28

Garrett

The morning light cuts through my loft windows, and I'm watching Sloane the way I used to study game film. Completely locked in.

She's turned my dining table into a command center: laptop open, printouts fanned out in perfect rows, her phone charging beside a stack of color-coded folders.

I've seen that look before. On captains in the tunnel before Game 7. Someone who knows what's at stake and has no intention of losing.

She tucks that one stubborn strand of auburn hair behind her ear without glancing away from the screen, her entire world reduced to whatever data she's dissecting. Her coffee mug sits empty at her elbow, and I catch the subtle bounce of her left knee under the table. A tell only I'd notice. She's channeling her nerves into precision.

I push off the counter and roll my shoulders, trying to work out the pre-game tension that's settled there overnight. Old habits. My body still thinks today's a playoff game. Maybe it's not wrong.

I grab the protein shake I made earlier, take a long pull, and move to the coffee pot.

"Thanks," she murmurs as I set the refilled mug beside her hand, still not looking up. She reaches for it automatically. Her fingers flex slightly. Another tell. She's been at this for hours.

The apartment smells like dark roast and clean paper. Outside, commuters are scraping frost off their windshields. But in here, it's warm and focused. Ours.

"Ready for a scrimmage?" I ask, sliding into the chair across from her.

That gets her attention. She looks up, and there it is. That small, fierce smile that hits me square in the chest. "Hit me."

The shift is instant. I straighten, let my voice lose its warmth, take on the edge of an exec who wouldn't hesitate to make her sweat.

"Alright, Ms. McKenzie. I've got a dozen proposals on my desk. Why are the Mammoths anything more than a tax write-off?"

Her posture snaps straight. Shoulders back, chin up, green eyes locked on mine. The knee bounce stops dead.

"Because you're not just buying a hockey team. You're buying a community. Our fan engagement metrics show—"

"Your Q3 projections are optimistic, considering the broadcast-rights negotiations are stalled," I cut in, leaning forward. "Prove this isn't wishful thinking."

She doesn't blink. "Page fourteen of the appendix shows we built those projections around the uncertainty. The streaming partnership we're proposing creates revenue streams independent of traditional networks. In fact, the current stall gives us leverage because—"

She's ripping through clauses and market models like she's calling plays. Every word precise. I throw a curveball about competitor analysis, referencing the Rangers' recent streaming pivot. She twists it back into a strength so seamlessly I almost forget I'm supposed to be playing defense.

This is her zone. Every tell vanishes. She references data like line pairings, stacks logic like power plays, and anticipates my next move before I make it.

"The Sacramento deal you mentioned actually reinforces our approach," she says, spinning her laptop toward me and tapping a chart. "Their numbers seem strong until you factor in market saturation and service overlap. Our proposal targets an untouched segment that—"

I push again on long-term sustainability, and she lights up as she dismantles the concern piece by piece. She's not just good. She's surgical. The kind of strategist who sees plays no one else notices.

And somewhere between her explanation about revenue diversification and scalable models, it hits me. A clean blindside.

This is it.

I can't imagine my life without her. I want all of it. Forever.

"—and that's why the Northstar partnership isn't just profitable. It's essential for both organizations moving forward." She leans back, flushed. "Next question?"

The mock meeting dissolves. I'm just Garrett again, staring at her like she invented the moon. "Damn, Sloane."

She grins, the fierce executive falling away to reveal the woman who steals my hoodies. "Too much?"

"Not even close." I stand, glance at my watch. "We should get moving."

She nods and closes her laptop with the kind of care that says every detail is locked and loaded. We move around each other in the narrow space between kitchen and table like we've done it for years instead of weeks. That silent rhythm of two people who just fit.

I'm fixing my tie when she appears in front of me, reaching up to adjust the knot I've apparently screwed up. Lucky break that the GM invited the captain and alternate captains to the Northstar meeting. Miller's office said the request came down from Henderson's people to show player buy-in, not just a corporate pitch. Probably just for show, but I'm grateful. I get to see her do this live.

Her fingers graze the column of my throat, and the air shifts. Business to personal.

I cover her hand with mine. Then I reach up and tuck that stubborn piece of hair behind her ear. It'll fall out again in twenty minutes, and I love that I know that.

"You're going to kill it today," I tell her. "You're the most brilliant person I know."

She looks up, and something in her softens. The tension she's been carrying for days finally releases.

"We're a good team."

The words land with weight. Not just about the meeting. Not just about today. Everything.

29

Sloane

The boardroom smells like expensive leather and day-old coffee.

My final slide glows on the wall-mounted screen, our legendary coach's quote about legacy positioned beside the Northstar Bank logo.

"This isn't just about market share," I say, voice steady despite the pounding in my chest. "It's about legacy. Our legacy. And now, Northstar's."

Mr. Blackwood, Northstar's CEO, leans forward. His steel-gray eyes haven't left me once.

"Your Q4 projections are ambitious, Ms. McKenzie. What's your defense against market saturation?"

I don't flinch. My fingers find the clicker, flipping back two slides to the data chart I built specifically for this question. The motion is smooth. Practiced. Reflex from a dozen dry runs with Garrett grilling me from the couch.

"It's not saturation, sir. It's diversification. We're not chasing the same audience. We're creating a new one. The youth hockey initiatives outlined on page twelve don't just drive ticket sales. They cultivate multigenerational brand loyalty."

Frank Miller, the GM, smiles from his corner seat. The skepticism that clung to him at the start is gone. Even the other Northstar execs shift forward in their chairs.

Just land the plane, McKenzie. Don't look at Garrett. Don't let yourself be distracted by his stupid, proud face.

But I feel him watching me. Steady. Across the table, Vivian's fingers tap against her leather portfolio, her smile razor-thin.

She checks her phone when she thinks no one's watching. A knot forms in my stomach. I push it aside.

"Walk me through your revenue acceleration timeline," Blackwood says.

I flip to the rollout schedule. "Phase one launches with opening night. Community partnerships initiate bi-weekly through December. By February, we'll have early engagement data tied to season ticket retention."

"The digital media allocation looks conservative," one of the other suits chimes in.

"Because traditional advertising doesn't work on Gen Z," I shoot back. Crisp. No hesitation. "Authenticity does. Player-generated content outperforms professional campaigns three to one and costs a fraction. We're not buying attention. We're earning it."

The questions keep coming, but now they're soft. Pro forma. I can see it in Blackwood's posture. His arms have relaxed. His tone has warmed. The subtle nod when I explain our community impact metrics.

It's happening.

"Impressive work," he says. "The cultural integration component is especially compelling."

This is it. The respect. The promotion. The career I've bled for. One breath away.

Blackwood inhales. I can already see the shape of the words forming.

And then I hear it. A soft scrape. Chair leg against polished floor.

Heads turn.

Garrett is standing.

No. No, no, no.

My eyes snap to him across the table, and I give the smallest shake of my head. A silent *please*. A warning.

He doesn't see it. He's looking at me like I just scored the overtime winner in Game 7. So full of pride and love that he's blind to what he's about to do.

His posture is steady. Certain. The stance of a captain taking the mic in the post-game presser.

"Mr. Blackwood," he says, voice strong and low in the pin-drop silence. "If I may."

30

Garrett

God, she's incredible.

Watching Sloane command this room is like watching a master strategist execute the perfect play. Every word calculated, every gesture precise. She's dismantling their skepticism piece by piece, turning doubt into investment, resistance into enthusiasm.

Blackwood is sold. I see it in his posture, in the way his jaw has unclenched, the approving nod when she walked them through the community engagement metrics. Miller is already looking at her like she reinvented the sport.

She did it.

But as I watch her field their final questions, Emma's voice cuts through my euphoria:

"You never fought for me. When things got difficult, you just shut down."

The accusation still burns three years later. Not because Emma was right about everything. She wasn't. But because she was right about that. When the media circus started, when the rumors flew, I retreated into silence. Called it dignity. Called it taking the high road.

Really, I was just protecting myself.

And now I'm watching the most brilliant woman I've ever known prove her worth to a room full of executives, and I'm sitting here like a spectator. Again. Letting her stand alone.

Not this time.

I'll give the player's perspective. Show them she's not just a suit. She's the one who gets us. They need to see why her vision works. This will help. This will seal it.

I stand before I can second-guess myself. The motion is instinctive. Like stepping up for the game-winning shot.

Every head in the room turns, but all I see is her. The slight widening of her eyes, the way her fingers tighten around the clicker. She's surprised, but she'll understand. She has to understand that this is me finally doing it right.

"Mr. Blackwood, if I may," I begin, keeping my voice level. "I'd like to offer a player's perspective on what you just heard."

The room settles. This is plausible. An athlete providing ground-level insight to complement the executive strategy. Blackwood nods.

"What Ms. McKenzie has presented isn't just a marketing campaign," I continue. "It's a cultural shift. And as someone who lives in that culture every day, I can tell you: this vision works because she understands us."

I catch Sloane's expression. Still shocked, but there's something else. Pride, maybe. Relief that I'm supporting her vision instead of undermining it.

Good. She should be proud.

"The community engagement metrics she showed you? Those aren't just numbers on a spreadsheet. They represent every kid who'll see hockey as accessible instead of elite. Every family who'll feel welcomed instead of excluded." My voice gains strength. "She's not just expanding our fan base. She's expanding our identity."

The executives are listening. Blackwood leans forward. This is working.

But as I continue, the careful professional framing begins to dissolve.

"I've watched her develop this vision," I say, my tone shifting. "Seen her work late into the night, not because she had to, but because she believed in it. Believed in us."

Her face changes. The pride flickers, replaced by something that looks almost like panic. But she's always been modest about her achievements. She needs to hear this.

"She sees connections others miss. Patterns others ignore. When she talks about hockey, she's not talking about a sport. She's talking about a movement."

The words pour out faster now, my restraint cracking under the weight of months of admiration I've kept contained.

"This isn't theoretical for her. It's personal. Every strategy session, every late-night revision, every moment she's poured into this vision. It comes from someone who doesn't just work for this organization. Someone who believes in its potential to be extraordinary."

I'm leaning forward now, my entire focus narrowed to her. The woman whose brilliance I've watched in secret for too

long. The woman who deserves to have someone recognize
her genius publicly.

"She doesn't just see hockey players. She sees leaders. She
doesn't just see fans. She sees community. She doesn't just
see a business. She sees a legacy."

The room has gone silent.

"That's the kind of strategic thinking that doesn't just
build profitable partnerships," I say, my voice dropping. "It
builds the future. And there's no one I trust more to architect that future."

I meet her eyes across the room. She's gone very still, her
composure slipping to reveal something raw underneath.

This is it. The moment I stop hiding. Stop protecting
myself.

"This isn't just about endorsing a proposal," I say. "It's
about endorsing the person."

I look directly at her, letting everyone in the room see
the conviction in my eyes. And then, because words aren't
enough, my hand moves across the polished table, and for
one brief, catastrophic moment, I cover her hand with mine.

"I trust Sloane McKenzie with the future of this team.
And with mine."

The touch is fleeting. But the contact is a detonation.

The words hang in the air, heavy and irreversible.

And in the silence that follows, I watch her face transform
from emotion to absolute, devastating horror.

For the first time since I stood up, I see what she sees. Not a colleague offering professional support. Not a teammate backing her play.

A man who just publicly claimed her. In front of executives. In front of investors. In front of the entire corporate structure she's spent years navigating.

I fought. I finally fought.

But I think I just lost everything anyway.

31

Sloane

The atmosphere curdles instantly. I watch Blackwood's expression shift. His brows draw together. His jaw tightens. Across the table, Frank Miller lets his smile drop completely.

Every word of Garrett's speech lands like a blow. He might as well have stood up and announced we're sleeping together.

Then Vivian leans forward, and I see it. The calculated gleam. The move she's been waiting to make.

"Well," she says, voice sweet as honey laced with arsenic. "As you can see, Garrett's passion for Sloane's work is... considerable."

She lets the implication hang.

"It's hard to ignore, isn't it? Especially now that podcasts are hinting about a certain alternate captain and a 'petite redhead in marketing.'"

The words detonate.

"But I hesitated to act," Vivian says, shaking her head with performative regret. "It felt like malicious gossip. And I refused to jeopardize careers based on rumors. I hoped it was a misunderstanding."

She turns her gaze on Garrett. Her expression softens into what almost looks like sorrow.

"But now, after this public declaration, after witnessing this personal bias firsthand, it confirms my worst fears. His speech wasn't a professional endorsement. It was a confession. This relationship has compromised their judgment. We're watching the consequences unfold right here in this boardroom."

She's not accusing. She's regretting. Not striking, but sacrificing. It's genius. She's framed it perfectly: the concerned executive forced into action by someone else's recklessness.

Blackwood sets his pen down with slow, quiet finality.

"Frank," he says, cool and clipped. "Our partnership discussions were built on the promise of a professional, no-tolerance environment. We're a bank, not a tabloid. Our brand can't afford this kind of public drama. This—" he gestures to the space between Garrett and me, "—is precisely the kind of liability we require our partners to avoid."

Liability. The word hangs there, final.

Frank turns to me. The rage I feared isn't there. Something worse has taken its place. Cold, quiet disappointment.

He addresses Blackwood first. "Mr. Blackwood, please accept my apologies. This organization upholds its standards, and we act decisively when they're violated."

Then his gaze shifts, and the full weight of his authority lands on me.

"Ms. McKenzie, you've put this organization in an untenable position. This is a blatant breach of conduct, made worse by the timing, the venue, and the company present."

Each word strips something from me.

"Effective immediately, you are suspended pending a full HR investigation," Miller says, flat and final. "You may leave. Now."

My world reduces to two points of focus: the gleaming conference table and Garrett's face as it finally hits him.

He didn't protect me. He destroyed me.

I watch his expression crumble. The exact second his pride morphs into horror.

The promotion. The respect. The career I bled for. Gone.

My hands move mechanically, closing my laptop with a quiet click that sounds unnaturally loud. I gather my portfolio, the same one I thought would secure my future.

I don't cry. Don't argue. There's nothing left to say.

I rise, each step toward the door loud in the silence. Behind me, I hear Garrett's sharp intake of breath, the scrape of his chair as he starts to move.

"Sloane—"

I don't turn around.

The heavy boardroom door clicks shut behind me.

The hallway stretches before me. Polished marble reflecting fluorescent lights.

One step. Then another.

The elevator is ahead.

My fingers clutch the portfolio. The leather is slick with sweat.

Behind me, the boardroom door explodes open.

I freeze. There's an alcove ahead, a recessed nook where they keep the emergency equipment, and I press myself against the wall. The marble is cold against my back.

"Sullivan."

Frank Miller's voice cuts through the corridor. Not yelling. That would be unprofessional. Instead, it's low and tight with a fury that's infinitely more terrifying than shouting. One word, delivered with the absolute authority of a man who holds careers in his hands.

Heavy footsteps echo toward me. I hold my breath.

They stop.

"Let me be crystal clear." Frank is right outside the alcove. "Your little performance just jeopardized a nine-figure partnership. You've made this organization a joke."

Nine-figure partnership. Jeopardized.

"Pursuant to Section 8 of the Standard Player Contract and the CBA," Frank says, "you are being fined the maximum allowable amount for conduct detrimental to the team. That's fifty thousand dollars."

The number lodges in my brain. Fifty grand. For one reckless act of love.

"Furthermore, you are suspended. Indefinitely. You will not attend practice. You will not enter the facility. You will not speak to media. Understood?"

Indefinitely. During playoff season.

Garrett says nothing. For a moment, I wonder if he's still breathing.

Then: "Understood."

His voice is level. Steady. Too steady. And that breaks me more than anything.

Fight it, I want to scream. *Say it was worth it. Say I was worth it.*

But he doesn't. He just accepts the sentence. Shoulders the blame. Like he always does.

Then he speaks again, and it cuts through every defense I have left.

"Which way did she go? Was she okay?"

Not *Is she suspended?* Not *Will she be investigated?* Just me. Was I okay.

Even in the wreckage, he's looking for me.

Frank doesn't flinch. "Worry about yourself, Sullivan. You've got bigger problems than her hurt feelings."

Footsteps retreat. Silence.

I press the elevator button. It glows blue beneath my finger. The reflection in the polished metal stares back at me. Pale. Hollow-eyed.

The doors open, and one truth follows me in:

I didn't just lose my career today. I destroyed his too.

32

Sloane

My apartment door swings open to reveal my sanctuary from this morning. Coffee mug still on the counter with my lipstick stain. Morning paper folded beside it. Everything exactly as I left it when I thought I was walking into triumph.

My eyes land on Steve.

The ridiculous blue sloth grins at me from my armchair, that dopey, permanent smile stretched across his fuzzy face.

My phone buzzes. Then again.

Steve keeps grinning, and suddenly I can't breathe past the rage tightening in my chest.

"You think this is funny?" My voice cracks. "You think any of this is fucking funny?"

I grab Steve by his ridiculous blue throat and hurl him across the room. He hits the wall with a satisfying thud, landing face-down on the hardwood.

It's not enough.

He took my moment.

The thought explodes through my brain. MY moment. The presentation I'd spent months perfecting, the deal I'd crafted from nothing, the victory that was supposed to prove

I belonged in that boardroom, and he took it and made it about himself. About us. About his guilt and his need to play the hero.

I storm to the kitchen where Garrett's coffee mug sits beside mine, the one with the little chip I never had the heart to return. The ceramic feels solid in my grip. Real. Something I can actually break.

"You ruined everything!" I scream at the empty apartment. "It was MINE! It was supposed to be MINE!"

I hurl the mug at the wall. It explodes in a shower of ceramic shards, coffee staining the white paint.

Still not enough.

I whirl toward my workstation where neat stacks of papers sit organized like the life I used to have. Quarterly projections. Marketing strategies. All evidence of the career that just died because the man I loved couldn't keep his mouth shut for five minutes.

My hands shake as I sweep the first stack off the counter. Papers flutter through the air. I grab another stack, my presentation notes, the backup materials, and send them flying too.

"Ten years!" I'm sobbing now, but I can't stop. "Ten years I worked for this! Ten years proving I was more than what they wanted to see!"

Books tumble from shelves. Picture frames shatter.

And through it all, my phone won't stop buzzing.

I stumble to the counter, grabbing the device with trembling fingers. The screen floods with notifications.

Nineteen missed calls from Garrett.

Text after text: *"Sloane, please answer." "I'm sorry. God, I'm so sorry." "Let me fix this. I can fix this."*

Fix this. There is no fixing this.

A sharp knock on my door cuts through the destruction.

"Sloane!" Garrett's voice, muffled but unmistakable. "Please, I know you're in there. Your car's in the lot."

I freeze among the wreckage.

"Sloane, please. Just let me explain—"

"GO AWAY!" The words tear from my throat. "I don't want to hear it!"

"I know you're angry—"

"ANGRY?" I'm at the door now, pressing my palms against the wood. "I'm not angry, Garrett. I'm destroyed. Do you understand that? You destroyed me."

"Let me in. Please. Let me apologize—"

"No." My voice drops to something cold and final. "You don't get to do this. You don't get to show up here and make this about your guilt."

But he's still talking through the door. "I know I fucked up, but I was trying to show them how proud I was of you. I was fighting for you—"

"FIGHTING FOR ME?" The words explode out of me. "I DIDN'T NEED DEFENDING! I needed a partner!"

"I was your partner! I am your partner!"

Something in his tone unlocks my door. Not because I want to let him in. Because I need him to see what he's done. Need him to witness the wreckage.

I tear the door open, and he stumbles back. His eyes go wide as they take me in. Tear-streaked, shaking, standing in the doorway of my destroyed apartment.

"Jesus, Sloane—"

"Look at it." My voice is steady now. Cold. "Look at what your grand gesture cost me."

He steps inside, his gaze sweeping over the scattered papers, the broken ceramic, the chaos that used to be my ordered life. When his eyes meet mine again, they're bright with unshed tears.

"I can fix this," he says. "I'll talk to Miller. I'll release a statement explaining that I acted alone, that you had nothing to do with—"

"Stop." The word is a blade. "Just stop talking."

But he can't stop. "I'll make them understand that you're brilliant, that your presentation was flawless—"

"You still don't get it." I'm backing away from him. "You still think this is about the presentation failing. About me getting fired."

His brow furrows. "Isn't it?"

"No, you fucking moron. It's about what you said. How you said it." I can barely speak past the rage. "You stood up in that room and made my professional competence about your personal feelings. You turned me into someone who needed defending instead of someone who earned respect."

"That's not—I didn't—"

"You did." Each word is deliberate. "You took my moment, the biggest moment of my career, and you made it about you. About your pride. Your need to be the hero."

He takes a step toward me, hands raised. "Sloane, that's not how I meant it—"

"It doesn't matter how you meant it!" My voice cracks. "What matters is what you did! In front of a room full of executives, you reduced me to someone's girlfriend instead of someone's colleague. You confirmed every sexist assumption they've ever made about me."

The words hang between us, and I watch understanding finally dawn in his eyes. Too late.

"I was trying to support you," he whispers, and there's something broken in his voice that makes my chest ache even through the fury.

"No, you were trying to save me. There's a difference." I wipe my eyes with the back of my hand. "I didn't need saving, Garrett. I needed you to trust that I could handle myself."

"I do trust you—"

"Do you? Because from where I'm standing, it looks like you couldn't stand watching me succeed on my own. Like you needed to insert yourself into my victory so you could matter."

He flinches. "That's not—"

"Isn't it? Tell me the truth, Garrett. When you stood up in that room, was it really about showing them how great I am? Or was it about proving to yourself that you matter in my success?"

The silence stretches. I watch him open his mouth to deny it, then close it again.

"Maybe..." His voice is barely audible. "Maybe I needed them to know. Maybe I needed to matter."

There it is. The confession.

"Thank you," I say quietly, and he looks up with something like hope. "Thank you for finally being honest."

The hope dies when he sees my face.

"I can't be with someone who sees me as a project to be rescued," I continue. "I can't love someone who needs to diminish me to feel important."

"Sloane, no—"

"Yes." The word is final. "I've spent my entire life proving I'm not my mother. Proving I won't disappear into someone else's definition of who I should be. And you..." I laugh, but there's no humor in it. "You turned me into exactly what I swore I'd never become."

"We can work through this—"

"No, we can't." I move to the door, holding it open with trembling hands. "Because you don't see the problem. Even now, after everything, you're trying to fix me instead of understanding that you broke something that can't be repaired."

He doesn't move. Just stands there in my destroyed living room, looking utterly gutted.

"Love isn't enough," I whisper. "Not if it comes with the price of making me smaller."

"Sloane, please—"

"Get out."

"I love you."

"Then leave."

He stares at me for a long moment, and I see the exact second he realizes this isn't something he can talk his way out of. Can't charm or explain or hero his way through.

He walks past me to the door, pausing on the threshold. "For what it's worth," he says without turning around, "you were magnificent in that room. Before I ruined it. You were everything I said you were and more."

The door clicks shut behind him, and I slide the deadbolt home with shaking fingers.

I lean against the wood, listening to his footsteps fade down the hallway.

The adrenaline drains away, leaving me hollow. I slide down the door until I'm sitting on the floor, surrounded by debris. Papers scattered everywhere. Broken ceramic glinting in the afternoon light. Steve the sloth lying face-down among the ruins.

I pull my knees to my chest and close my eyes.

The sobs come, and when they finally stop, something cold and hard has taken their place. The grief was a fire, and it burned away everything but the anger.

And anger is useful.

33
Sloane

I stand in the wreckage of my apartment, counting casualties.

But I'm not mourning anymore. The fury from our fight has cooled into something useful.

Garrett's footsteps faded down the hallway long ago, but his absence doesn't bring relief. It brings clarity about what needs to happen next.

I step over a scattered stack of quarterly reports and grab my phone from the counter. My fingers are steady as I scroll through my contacts.

"Brynn." My voice cuts through her phone's first ring. "Get over here. Now. We have work to do."

"Sloane? Jesus, I've been worried sick. I heard about the meeting and—"

"I don't need sympathy. I need your investigative skills and whatever evidence you can gather on Vivian." I pause. "Bring everything."

There's a beat of silence, then I hear her shift into professional mode. "I'll be there in twenty minutes."

The second call is harder, but necessary.

"Easton." His name tastes bitter, but I force it out anyway.

"Sloane, thank God. I've been trying to reach you for hours. After what happened in the boardroom, I—"

"Save it." I don't let him finish. "Apologies don't rebuild careers. Evidence does. Are you going to help me fight this, or are you going to keep trying to protect me from my own decisions?"

Silence on the line. When he speaks again, his voice has changed.

"What do you need?"

"Your moral support and your complete silence about anything I'm planning until I tell you otherwise." I move through my living room, already picturing the transformation from wreckage to workspace. "Get here. Fast."

By the time Brynn's key turns in my lock, I've cleared the coffee table and organized what's left. Papers stacked by priority. Evidence, timelines, financial records. The broken ceramic swept into a neat pile. Everything useful separated from everything that isn't.

"Holy shit," Brynn breathes, taking in the apartment. But it's not the destruction that stops her. It's me. Still wearing the navy dress from this morning, but standing straighter now.

"You look ready," she says.

"Good." I gesture to the cleared table. "Sit. Show me what you have."

Easton arrives five minutes later, moving through the doorway carefully. He takes in the cleaned-up apartment, me standing over the coffee table with Brynn, and his shoulders drop an inch. Relief.

"Sloane—"

"We're not doing emotional processing right now," I cut him off, pointing to the table where Brynn is already spreading documents. "We're doing strategic planning."

Brynn slides a thick manila folder across the coffee table. "I've been building this case for weeks. Ever since that blind item dropped about you, I felt like something was off."

"It's not just a pattern; it's a receipt. The Sin Bin Scoop blind item was sent from a public WiFi hotspot. But look at this..." She points to a line item on a printout. "Vivian's corporate card. A coffee charge from that exact hotspot, nine minutes before the tip was sent. She wasn't just enjoying the fire, Sloane. She lit the match."

"Do I want to know how you got all of this?" I don't wait for Brynn to answer.

I flip open the folder and start reading. Email threads with highlighted timestamps. Financial records showing suspicious budget reallocations. A timeline correlating the anonymous tip with Vivian's calendar entries.

"This isn't just about me," I murmur. "She's done this before."

"Three times that I can prove," Brynn confirms. "Always successful women. Always manufactured scandals. Always plausible deniability."

Easton leans over my shoulder. "Jesus. It's a playbook."

I spread the documents across the table. The pattern is right there once you see it. Not just sabotage, but systematic elimination. Brynn's research confirms Anna's story. Confirms that she's done this before.

"She didn't get lucky with Garrett's outburst," I say. "She orchestrated it. Manipulated him into giving her exactly what she needed to destroy me."

"The question is," Brynn says, pulling out her laptop, "what do we do with this information?"

I study the evidence.

"We go through proper channels first," I decide. "We present this to Frank Miller in a formal meeting. Give the organization a chance to do the right thing. I'm suspended right now pending the HR investigation, but this should give them everything they need to wrap it up and reinstate me."

Brynn frowns. "Sloane, are you sure? This could leak. We could lose control of the narrative—"

"No. Frank's a company man. He cares about liability, about protecting the organization from lawsuits. When he sees this evidence, when he understands what Vivian's been doing, he'll have no choice but to act."

I start pacing. "We schedule a formal meeting. We present the evidence systematically. Financial irregularities, pattern of behavior, documentation of gender-based discrimination. We make it clear that this isn't just about reinstating me. This is about protecting the organization from a massive lawsuit."

"And if he refuses to meet with you?" Easton asks.

"Then we go nuclear," I say. "But we give him the chance to be the hero first."

Brynn nods slowly. "It's elegant. Shows good faith on our part."

"Exactly." I stop pacing. "We're not disgruntled employees making wild accusations. We're concerned parties presenting irrefutable evidence of corporate misconduct."

The three of us spend the next hour refining the approach, building talking points, anticipating counterarguments. The apartment starts to feel less like wreckage and more like a campaign headquarters.

"When?" Brynn asks as we finalize the strategy.

"Tomorrow morning. First thing. Before Vivian has time to spin whatever story she's planning."

Easton checks his phone. "I can get us a meeting. Frank respects me, trusts my judgment. If I tell him it's urgent, he'll make time."

"Do it."

As Easton steps into the hallway to make the call, Brynn studies me.

"You're different," she says. "Harder."

"Good. Soft got me destroyed. Hard gets me justice."

She nods. "Just... be careful not to lose yourself in the process."

But I'm not worried about losing myself. For the first time in hours, I know exactly who I am: the woman who turns crisis into opportunity. Who fights back with intelligence, evidence, and precision.

Easton returns. "Nine a.m. tomorrow. Frank's office."

"Perfect." I close the folder of evidence. "Vivian Lamore thinks she broke me. She thinks she can destroy careers and move on to her next target."

I look at my brother, who chose loyalty over team politics, and my best friend, who spent weeks building this case.

"She has no idea what's coming."

My heels echo through the executive wing, sharp on the marble. Fifteen floors above the rink where my brother guards the net, we move toward Frank Miller's office with the focused energy of people who've rehearsed.

My briefcase is heavy with months of evidence. Documented patterns of sabotage, financial irregularities, a timeline that tells one story and only one story. This isn't speculation. This is data. The language Frank Miller speaks.

"Remember," I murmur to Brynn and Easton, "we lead with the timeline, follow with the financial trail, close with legal exposure. Clean. Professional."

Brynn adjusts her folder against her chest. "The systematic pattern alone should be enough."

Easton's legal pad is covered in bullet points we've rehearsed. "Just stick to facts. No emotion. Let the evidence speak."

The elevator opens onto the executive floor. Championship banners line the walls. Miller's assistant doesn't look up as we approach.

"Mr. Miller is ready for you. First door on the left."

We move down the corridor. Through the glass office walls, I can see other executives conducting business. Budget meetings, contract negotiations, the ordinary machinery of professional sports.

Miller's office is large and designed to remind you of that fact. Championship trophies line the shelves. Floor-to-ceiling windows frame the Minneapolis skyline. Team photos document decades of success.

Miller himself sits behind a mahogany desk with the posture of a man who doesn't stand for visitors. Mid-fifties, silver hair, a suit that fits too well to be off the rack.

"Ms. McKenzie." His voice is warm in the way that press statements are warm. "Please, have a seat. I can give you fifteen minutes."

Fifteen minutes for a case that took months to build. Fine. Fifteen minutes is enough.

I settle into the chair and place my briefcase on the desk.

"Mr. Miller, thank you for making time. I'm here to present documented evidence of systematic workplace sabotage by a senior member of your executive team."

His eyebrows rise slightly. Good. He's paying attention.

"That's a serious accusation, Ms. McKenzie."

"It's a documented pattern." I slide the first folder across his desk. "This contains timeline analysis showing eight distinct instances where Vivian Lamore deliberately undermined my work, altered reports, and fed false information to external parties."

Miller glances at the folder but doesn't open it. He leans back and presses his fingertips together.

"Ms. McKenzie, before we dive into workplace dynamics, perhaps we should address the obvious issue." His tone shifts, turning paternal. "Your relationship with Mr. Sullivan, in direct violation of company policy, created this entire situation."

I expected the pivot. I recover, reaching for the second folder.

"My personal life is irrelevant to the evidence of corporate sabotage. Brynn, would you walk Mr. Miller through the investigative timeline?"

Brynn straightens. "The anonymous tip that started this gossip campaign was sent from a public Wi-Fi network. My sources provided the IP address and timestamp."

She lays photographs across his desk with steady hands. Coffee shop receipts. Time-stamped security footage. Corporate expense reports showing Vivian Lamore's company card used at the exact location nine minutes before the tip was sent.

"That's not workplace dynamics, Mr. Miller. That's documented libel with clear intent to damage my professional reputation."

Miller studies the photographs the way you'd study a menu you've already decided against. His pen taps a rhythm on the desk.

"Ms. Callahan, I appreciate your investigative enthusiasm." His politeness doesn't bother trying to hide what it really is. "But what I'm seeing is a series of coincidences and assumptions. Nothing that would withstand legal scrutiny."

The dismissal stings. I lean forward with the financial analysis.

"Mr. Miller, these aren't assumptions. These are budget reallocations, strategic resource withdrawals, and documented interference with client relationships. The pattern—"

"Which brings us to legal exposure," Easton cuts in. He flips through his legal pad. "By failing to investigate documented harassment and selectively enforcing policies that disproportionately punish female employees, this organization faces significant liability."

Miller's posture changes. The warmth drops out of his face completely.

"Mr. McKenzie, I appreciate your concern for your sister's career." He leans forward. "But let's be crystal clear about what we're actually discussing here."

This isn't the reasonable businessman I expected. This is the man who runs the machine.

"This organization has a zero-tolerance policy regarding relationships between players and staff," he continues, each word measured. "Ms. McKenzie signed a contract explicitly acknowledging that policy. She violated it. End of discussion."

He's not engaging with the evidence. Not even pretending to consider it. Just closing the door.

"Mr. Miller," I begin, keeping my voice level, "you're ignoring months of documented evidence to focus on a relationship that had zero impact on my professional performance—"

"Zero impact?" He laughs, and the sound is empty. "Your relationship became the subject of a gossip podcast. It was discussed in my boardroom. It became a distraction that cost us a nine-figure partnership deal."

He stands and moves to the window, looking out over the practice rink below.

"You want to talk about patterns, Ms. McKenzie? Every organization that blurs personal and professional lines ends up exactly here. Accusations. Counter-accusations. Drama that belongs in a soap opera, not a championship-caliber franchise."

My chest tightens. "This isn't drama. This is systematic harassment designed to—"

"This," he says, turning back, "is precisely why we have these policies. To prevent employees from making judgment calls that compromise the organization's interests."

He returns to his chair and sits down. His expression is closed.

"Ms. McKenzie, I've given this matter serious consideration. While I appreciate your passion for your work, it's clear that your continued presence here is untenable." He pauses. "And you've just confirmed the relationship violation yourself, in front of witnesses."

My stomach drops. "Excuse me?"

"The relationship. The violation of policy. The disruption to our organization." He speaks slowly. "For the stability of this franchise, we're moving forward without these complications."

He opens a drawer and slides a manila folder across the desk. The motion is practiced.

"Your employment with the Minnesota Mammoths is terminated, effective immediately. The severance package includes six months' salary and benefits, contingent upon your signature of the non-disclosure agreement included in the packet. Your final paperwork will be processed within the hour."

Terminated. Effective immediately. Non-disclosure agreement.

This isn't a meeting.

This is an execution.

"You can't be serious," Brynn says.

"I'm resolving a personnel issue that threatens organizational stability," Miller replies. "The results of our HR investigation are conclusive. Ms. McKenzie violated clearly established company policy, and the consequences, as outlined in her employment contract, are unambiguous."

"What about Vivian?" Easton's voice is barely controlled. "What about all of this evidence?"

Miller gestures at the folders on his desk the way you'd wave off a fly. "Ms. Lamore is a valued executive with an exemplary service record. I see no compelling reason to pursue what amounts to office gossip and speculation."

I stare at the termination folder lying between us. Silence in exchange for erasure. Six months' pay to make this disappear.

"The decision is final, Ms. McKenzie." Miller reaches for his phone. "Security will escort you to clear your office once we've concluded here. I trust this transition can be handled with appropriate discretion."

I stand. My hands close the briefcase with mechanical precision.

Brynn and Easton flank me as we move toward the door. No one speaks. The case we spent hours building, dismantled in minutes by a man who was never going to listen.

The hallway stretches long and glassed-in. Through the office walls, other executives continue their meetings. They don't look up as we pass.

In the elevator, I catch my reflection in the steel doors. The blazer that felt like armor this morning is just a blazer. The briefcase that was supposed to save me holds nothing that matters anymore.

"Sloane," Easton says, gentle.

I shake my head. Not yet. The numbness is the only thing keeping me upright. When it breaks, I need to be somewhere without an audience.

The elevator opens onto the lobby. The same marble, the same glass. But I'm not an employee fighting for justice anymore. I'm a terminated liability being processed out.

The city moves past the windows. Traffic, people hurrying to jobs they still have. The world continuing.

I step into the afternoon sunlight, unemployed and si-
lenced.

And standing on the sidewalk, watching my former workplace behind the tinted glass, I understand what Frank Miller
just taught me:

Sometimes the system doesn't fail you.

Sometimes it works exactly as it was designed to.

34

Sloane

The knock comes again. Sharp. Insistent.

I remain frozen beneath my blankets, wrapped in fleece and denial. Through the fabric, I can hear movement in the hallway—shuffling feet, whispered consultation. They know I'm in here. My car is in the parking garage. The lights have been on day and night because I lack the energy to turn them off.

"Sloane?" Brynn's voice, muffled but unmistakable. "Come on, we know you're in there. I know you said you wanted to be left alone, but—"

I close my eyes tighter, willing them to disappear. Willing everything to disappear.

"We're worried about you," Easton's deeper voice joins the chorus. "It's been three days. You haven't answered your phone, your emails—"

Three days. Has it really been that long? Time has become elastic, meaningless. Hours blur together into numbness, punctuated only by brief, brutal moments where I remember exactly how I've destroyed everything.

"Sloane, please." Brynn again, and there's something in her voice—a crack of desperation that makes my chest tighten. "We just need to know you're okay. You don't have to talk to us. Just... knock on the wall or something. Give us a sign."

The silence stretches. I can picture them standing there in the hallway, probably holding coffee they brought for me, probably with new evidence or strategies or well-meaning advice about moving forward. They still think this is fixable. They still believe in justice, in truth winning out, in good people being rewarded for their integrity.

Frank Miller cured me of that delusion on Monday morning.

He hadn't even looked at our evidence. The financial irregularities. The pattern of sabotage. The documented proof of Vivian's systematic campaign to destroy careers. None of it mattered. The narrative had already been written: I was the distraction who cost them a major sponsorship. I was the liability who needed to be excised.

"Furthermore, any attempt to publicize these allegations would be considered a violation of your non-disclosure agreement and would result in immediate legal action."

The trap had been sprung. They'd built the trap perfectly—allow me to present my case so they could appear fair and reasonable, then dismiss it while threatening me into silence. Even my righteous anger had been anticipated, planned for, neutralized.

The footsteps in the hallway move closer to my door. I hear Easton's voice, lower now, probably meant to be private but carrying anyway.

"Maybe we should call my mom. Get her down here."

The suggestion is a shock of ice water. Mom, who spent two years catatonic on a kitchen floor after Dad left. Mom, who lost herself so completely in someone else's love that when it vanished, there was nothing left but an empty shell. Mom, who would take one look at me and see her worst fears confirmed—that I've inherited her weakness, her inability to survive without external validation.

No. I can't face that recognition in her eyes. Can't handle the gentle disappointment, the careful suggestions about "getting help," the underlying assumption that this breakdown was inevitable because I am, at my core, just like her.

I pull the blanket tighter around my head and wait.

After what feels like an hour but is probably only minutes, I hear Easton sigh. "She's not going to answer."

"This isn't like her," Brynn says, and there's frustration mixed with the worry now. "Even when she's hurt, she fights. She doesn't just... disappear."

But that's exactly what I've done. Disappeared. Not just from their concern, but from everything. I've deleted my LinkedIn profile, blocked news alerts, muted every group chat that might remind me of the professional world I used to inhabit. I am lost in the ruins of my own ambition.

"Tomorrow," Easton says finally. "If she doesn't answer tomorrow, we're getting the building manager to let us in."

The threat should motivate me to respond, to give them some sign of life before they stage an intervention. Instead, it just adds another layer to my exhaustion. Tomorrow, I'll have to force a mask of normalcy. Pretend I'm healing when really I'm just hollow.

Their footsteps retreat down the hallway, leaving me alone again with the silence and the weight of my failure.

I drift.

The afternoon light fades to evening gray, then to the artificial orange glow of streetlights filtering through windows I haven't bothered to cover. Somewhere in the building, a door slams. A car alarm wails briefly before cutting off. The normal sounds of people living normal lives, pursuing normal dreams that won't detonate in boardrooms full of men who mistake cruelty for strength.

My phone sits facedown on the coffee table where I abandoned it yesterday, its silence now less merciful than ominous. No doubt there are messages accumulating—job recruiters with opportunities that pay half what I was making, former colleagues offering hollow condolences, maybe even media requests from outlets that want to turn my destruction into content.

I should check it. Should start the grim process of rebuilding from the ashes. Should prove to Easton and Brynn that I'm not completely broken.

Instead, I close my eyes and give in to the darkness again.

When awareness returns, it's to the sharp buzz of my phone vibrating against the wooden table. The sound cuts through my numb state like a fire alarm, jarring and impossible to ignore. I check the time through bleary eyes—4:47 a.m. Nothing good happens at 4:47 a.m. Medical emergencies. Family crises. The kind of catastrophes that make losing a job seem like a minor inconvenience.

With sluggish effort, I reach for the phone and flip it over. The screen blazes with an intensity that makes my adjusted eyes water. One new text message, from a number I don't recognize.

For a moment, I consider deleting it without reading. Whatever new problem this represents—another reporter digging, another job recruiter, another reminder of how far I've fallen—I don't have the strength to process it.

But something about the timestamp stops me. What kind of crisis makes someone text a stranger at 4:47 in the morning?

I open the message.

The photo loads first, and my heart stops.

Maya. Ten years old, gap-toothed grin bright enough to power the city. She's holding up a report card—straight A's marching across the page in perfect formation. But it's what she's wearing that resonates deep in my chest: a Minnesota Mammoths jersey, number 19, hanging loose on her small frame. Garrett's number.

555-237-9862

Hi Sloane, this is Emily, Maya's mom. Just wanted to reach out before I head into work—Maya was so excited this morning she made me promise to text

> you right away. She got all A's on
> her report card! She keeps saying it's
> because hockey taught her discipline
> and focus, and she wanted to make
> sure you knew. Thank you for believing
> in her. It's made all the difference.

I stare at the screen until my eyes blur with tears I didn't know I still had. Maya. Sweet, brilliant Maya whose mother works double shifts to afford equipment, whose dreams of working in hockey seemed impossible until I helped design programs specifically for kids like her. Maya, who still believes I matter. Who still sees me as someone worth thanking.

While I've been buried in despair, convinced my career is over, Maya has been out there living the vision I created. Proving that what I built had value beyond corporate politics and poisonous colleagues.

The analytical part of my brain—dormant for days—begins to stir. I sit up slowly, pushing the blanket away from my face, and read the message again. Then again. Each word lands with increasing weight as the heavy despair finally begins to recede.

Thank you for believing in her.

But Maya doesn't know that I've been fired. Doesn't know that the programs she's benefiting from are being dismantled by executives who see community outreach as an expense rather than an investment. In her world, I'm still the woman who believed kids like her deserved opportunities. I'm still the architect of her success.

And suddenly, with sharp clarity, I understand my fundamental mistake.

I've been fighting the wrong battle.

For three days, I've been consumed with the injustice of my termination, the corruption of the system, the unfairness of Vivian's sabotage campaign. I appealed to Frank Miller's sense of ethics, presented evidence of wrongdoing, demanded accountability from an organization that had never once prioritized integrity over image.

But business doesn't care about wrong. Business cares about indispensable.

I've been trying to prove what had been done to me was unjust, when I should have been proving what they lost when they let me go was irreplaceable.

My laptop sits buried under three days of takeout containers and self-pity. I clear the debris with sudden, sharp movements, my body finally responding to commands from a brain that's fully awake for the first time since the boardroom disaster.

The screen flickers to life, and I navigate to the locked folder I haven't opened in months: "MCCP - Master." The Mammoth Community Champions Program. My passion project. The comprehensive vision that stretched well beyond any single sponsorship deal.

I'd pitched pieces of it to Vivian over the past year, but she'd always dismissed it as "too ambitious" or "not commercially viable." So I'd developed it in secret, refining the framework in stolen moments between official duties, building something that could transform not just the team's brand, but their entire relationship with the community.

As I scroll through pages of research, projections, and strategic frameworks, Maya's photo burns bright in my peripheral vision. This isn't just about youth hockey programs. This is about urban development, educational initiatives, creating a sustainable model for sports franchises that want to matter beyond their win-loss record.

The Northstar deal had been thinking too small. A single corporate partnership, impressive but ultimately limited in scope. What if instead of chasing one major sponsor, we created a comprehensive community engagement platform that attracted dozens of corporate partners? What if we turned the Mammoths into the sports franchise that other teams tried to emulate?

My fingers fly across the keyboard, pulling together market research, demographic data, revenue projections. I integrate case studies from successful community programs in other markets, add my own innovations, weave it all together into a vision that's audacious enough to make even corporate executives pay attention.

The numbers are staggering. Conservative estimates put the potential annual revenue at thirty-seven million dollars. And that's just year one.

This isn't about proving I was wrongfully terminated. This is about proving they can't afford to let me stay terminated.

The apartment around me has gone silent except for the rapid clicking of keys. Outside, Minneapolis sleeps, unaware that in this small corner of the city, something is being born from the ashes of destruction. Not revenge—though that will be a sweet side effect. Revolution.

I save the file and reach for my phone, Maya's message still glowing on the screen. Sweet, brilliant Maya who believes in me even when I've stopped believing in myself. Who sees possibility where I saw only ending.

Time for me to return the favor.

I open a new message and type.

> Brynn. I know I've been MIA and I owe you a massive explanation. I promise I'll give you one. But first—I need a huge favor. Can you get me Robert Blackwood's personal number? Please.

I hit send before I can second-guess myself, then lean back in my chair and smile for the first time in three days. It's sharp enough to cut glass, cold enough to freeze flames.

Frank Miller thinks he buried me. Vivian thinks she destroyed me. The entire organization thinks I'm a cautionary tale about the dangers of mixing business with pleasure.

They have no idea what's coming.

But they're about to find out.

35
Garrett

The silence in my loft has weight. Four days of suspension, and the stillness is making me stupid. No morning skate. No practice. Nothing to do with my hands.

I pace from the kitchen to the windows overlooking the Mississippi, the same loop I've been walking for two days. Outside, the world keeps going. I'm stuck in this glass box with my own thoughts and the sound of Sloane's voice on repeat:

"You took my moment and made it about you."

I stop at the window and press my forehead against the glass. Cool. Solid. It doesn't help. I keep replaying our fight the way I watch game film, frame by frame, looking for the play I should have made. The thing I should have said differently.

But the more I replay it, the more lost I get. I was trying to support her. Trying to show them how brilliant she was. How is that wrong? How does fighting for someone you love become the thing that destroys everything?

My phone sits dark on the coffee table. I've drafted a dozen texts to her in four days. Deleted every one. What's left to say when everything out of your mouth apparently makes things worse?

"You don't see the problem," she'd screamed at me. "Even now, after everything, you're trying to fix me instead of understanding that you broke something that can't be repaired."

The accusation sits under my ribs. I wasn't trying to fix her. I was trying to protect her. There's a difference.

Isn't there?

My phone buzzes. Marcus's name on the screen. I grab it before the second ring.

"Tank, buddy—how're you holding up?"

Marcus Rodriguez. My agent for six years. He's using the voice. The one that says everything's under control when nothing is.

"Not great, Marcus. Not great at all."

"Hey, I get it. This whole thing's a nightmare. But I've got good news—I've been making calls all morning, and I think we can shut this down quickly."

Shut this down quickly. Like it's a PR fire to stamp out. A speed bump.

"The suspension?" Marcus continues. "I've already reached out to the league office. They're open to negotiation. We're probably looking at five games, ten at the most. And the fine?" He makes a dismissive sound. "Steep, sure, but hey—it's a business expense. Part of the job."

Business expense. My stomach turns.

"We'll schedule a soft interview," he goes on, building speed. "Something local, friendly. You'll express regret, talk about lessons learned, emphasize your commitment to the team. Classic crisis management. You'll be back on the ice in a week, two max."

I close my eyes. Standard playbook. Manageable problem. Career barely scratched.

"Marcus." My voice comes out quieter than I mean it to. "What about Sloane?"

Three seconds of silence. Three seconds that tell me everything.

"Tank, I know you care about her, but that's not really our concern right now. My job is protecting your career. Her situation is... unfortunate, but it's separate."

Separate.

The word lands like a blindside hit.

Separate. Like we weren't in the same room. Like we weren't destroyed by the same moment, the same words, the same spectacular failure of judgment.

"She got fired, Marcus." I can barely say it. "Forced to sign an NDA. Career destroyed. And you're telling me I'll be back next week with a slap on the wrist."

"That's..." He sounds genuinely surprised. "That's harsh. I'm sorry to hear that. But Tank, you can't take responsibility for decisions above your pay grade. You've got to focus on what you can control."

What I can control.

I hang up without saying goodbye.

The quiet after is different. Heavier.

Separate.

I stand from the couch and walk to the window. The city spreads out below, going about its business.

Sloane lost everything. Her job. Her reputation. Her career. Fifteen years of work, gone in one afternoon because of what I said. How I said it.

And me?

A fine I can cover without noticing. A suspension already being negotiated down to nothing. Marcus scheduling soft interviews and planning my image rehab while she's—what? Updating her résumé? Explaining to potential employers why security walked her out?

I play the boardroom scene again. But this time I'm not watching it through my own confusion. I'm watching it through Sloane's eyes.

I see myself standing up. Commandeering her presentation—the one she'd worked on for months, the deal that was supposed to cement her future—and making myself the center of it.

"I trust Sloane McKenzie with the future of this team... and with mine."

Jesus Christ.

I didn't support her. I claimed her. In front of a roomful of executives, I turned her professional triumph into a declaration about us. I took the most important moment of her career and made it a love story.

I painted her as my girlfriend instead of their colleague.

I confirmed every bias in that room. Every assumption they'd ever made about women in sports marketing. Every whispered suspicion that she got here on her back instead of her brain.

I sit down hard. Head in my hands. The full picture coming into focus.

She didn't need defending. She was winning. She had them convinced, ready to sign, ready to see her exactly as she is. And I stood up and turned her into someone who needed a man to speak for her.

"You still think this is about the presentation failing," she'd said. "It's about what you said. How you said it. You stood up in that room and made my professional competence about your personal feelings."

She was right.

"You turned me into someone who needed defending instead of someone who earned respect."

I think about Emma. About what she said in those last fights.

"You never fight for me. When things get difficult, you just shut down. Made me feel like I was bothering you by existing."

So when it mattered—when Sloane needed me to trust her—I overcorrected. I fought. But wrong. Loud. Public. Possessive. I turned her achievement into a display of my feelings instead of evidence of her talent.

I let Emma walk away because I was afraid to fight for her.

And I destroyed Sloane because I needed to be seen fighting for her.

Same cowardice. Different costume.

I didn't lose Sloane because I failed to protect her. I lost her because I failed to see her. The competent, brilliant woman who didn't need protection. She needed partnership. And I gave her a performance.

I stand and walk to my office. On the wall hangs my contract, framed behind glass. Eight years, sixty-four million dollars. My leverage. My value to this organization.

I take it down. It's heavy. The weight feels different now. Not like a trophy. Like a tool.

I remove the document, fold it carefully, and put it in my briefcase next to my laptop. Not a grand gesture. Not the kind of move I would have made a week ago—charging in, making noise, making sure everyone saw me doing the right thing.

Something quieter. Something that requires me to swallow every instinct that's led me wrong.

I pull out my phone and text the last person who wants to hear from me.

> *Need to talk. About Sloane. Name the place.*

Nothing for ten minutes. Then:

Easton

> *Why.*

I stare at the screen. Type. Delete. Type again.

> *Because I need to fix this and I can't do it without you.*

Another long pause.

Moose Tavern. 9pm.

Not one of our usual spots. A dive on the south side where nobody gives a shit who you are. Message received.

I get there early. Order a whiskey. Take a corner booth.

Easton shows up at 9:15. The fifteen minutes is deliberate—I've known him long enough to recognize a power move. He slides into the booth, doesn't order anything, and just looks at me.

I wait for him to say something. He doesn't.

"Thanks for—"

"Don't." He cuts me off. "Don't thank me. I'm here because you mentioned my sister. That's it."

"Okay."

Silence. He's going to make me do the work. Fair enough.

"I fucked up," I say.

"Yeah."

"In the boardroom. What I said—"

"I know what you said. I was there." His voice is flat. "Watched you stand up and tell a room full of executives that you trust Sloane McKenzie with your future. Real romantic. Great timing."

"I was trying to—"

"I don't care what you were trying to do." He leans forward. "I care about what happened. She got fired. Escorted out by security. Had to sign an NDA so she can't even defend herself. And you got, what, a suspension? A fine?"

I don't have an answer for that.

"You know what she's doing right now?" Easton continues. "She's in her apartment, alone, trying to figure out how to rebuild a career that took her fifteen years to build. Fifteen years, Garrett. And you blew it up in thirty seconds because you couldn't keep your mouth shut."

"I know."

"Do you? Because from where I'm sitting, it looks like you thought you were being some kind of hero. Big man standing up for his woman." The contempt in his voice is worse than if he'd hit me. "She didn't need you to stand up. She was winning. She had them."

"I know," I say again. "I didn't see that. I should have, but I didn't."

"Why not?"

The question sits there. I turn my whiskey glass in my hands, not drinking.

"Because I was so focused on proving I'd fight for her that I didn't notice she was already fighting for herself." I make myself look at him. "I made it about me. What I needed to prove. And I turned her into someone who needed a man to vouch for her."

Easton's expression doesn't change. "Keep going."

"She was right. Everything she said when she kicked me out. I didn't see her—I saw someone to protect. And that's just as bad as not caring at all. Maybe worse."

He's quiet for a long moment.

"You know what my problem is with you right now?" he finally says. "It's not that you screwed up. People screw up. It's that you screwed up in exactly the way I told Sloane you would."

"What do you mean?"

"I told her this would end with her getting hurt. I told her guys like us—athletes, guys with big egos and bigger platforms—we don't know how to love someone without making it a performance." He shakes his head. "She said you were different. Said you understood her. And then you stood up in that boardroom and proved me right."

I absorb that. Don't deflect.

"She trusted you," Easton says. "She doesn't trust anyone. Not like that. And you—"

He stops. Looks away. Works his jaw.

"I want to make it right," I say.

"How." Not a question. A challenge.

I pull the folded contract from my jacket. Set it on the table.

"What's that?"

"My contract. Eight years, sixty-four million."

Easton looks at it but doesn't touch it. "And?"

"I want to give it to her. To use however she wants. Negotiate her job back, force Henderson's hand, blow the whole thing up—whatever she decides. It's hers."

He stares at me. "You're serious."

"Yeah."

"You'd throw away your career."

"If that's what it takes for her to have options." I push the contract toward him. "But I'm not trying to be her hero. That's not what this is. I just want her to have leverage. Whatever she needs to fight this her way."

Easton doesn't respond. The bartender glances over, probably wondering if we're about to throw down.

"She won't take it," Easton finally says.

"Maybe not. But I want her to know it's there."

"And what do you want in return?"

"Nothing."

He laughs—short, humorless. "Bullshit. You want her to forgive you. Take you back."

"I want her to know I understand what I did. That's it. If she never wants to see me again, I'll live with it."

"Will you?"

I think about Sloane. Her laugh, her stubbornness, the way she looked at me like I was the only solid thing in her world.

"No," I admit. "But I'll do it anyway. Because that's her call to make. Not mine."

Easton picks up the contract. Turns it over. Sets it back down.

"You know what pisses me off the most?" he says, and his voice is different now. Still hard, but something underneath has loosened. "I gave her an ultimatum. At the gala. Told her she had to choose—you or her career. You or this family."

I wait.

"Told her I'd go to Kowalski myself if she didn't end it."
He's not looking at me anymore. "I thought I was protecting
her. Thought I knew better."

"And now?"

"Now she lost her career anyway, and all I did was make
her feel like she couldn't come to me when it happened." He
shakes his head. "I was so worried about her repeating old
patterns that I didn't notice I was repeating mine. Ultima-
tums. Deciding what's best for everyone."

I don't push.

"Sloane doesn't need you to save her," he says. "Doesn't
need me to save her either. She's been handling her own life
since before either of us knew what responsibility meant."
He meets my eyes. "What she needs is people who show up
and ask what she wants instead of deciding for her."

"I can do that."

"Can you? Because so far your track record isn't great."

"I know." I hold his gaze. "I'm asking for the chance to
prove I've learned something."

Easton is quiet for a long time. Long enough that I think
he's going to stand up and leave.

Then: "I'll tell her you want to talk. That's all I'm offering.
She decides if she wants to see you."

"That's enough."

"And Garrett?" He stands, looks down at me. "If she gives
you another chance, and you pull anything like this again—I
don't care how long we've been friends. I don't care about
the team. I will make your life very difficult."

"Understood."

He nods once. Doesn't say goodbye. Turns to leave.

He's almost to the door when he stops. Doesn't turn around.

"Poker's at Webb's on Thursday. You missed last week."

I look at the back of his head. "Didn't think I'd be welcome."

"You're not." A pause. "But you still owe me sixty bucks, and I intend to collect."

He pushes through the door and into the parking lot.

It's not forgiveness. It's not even close.

But it's poker on Thursday. It's sixty bucks. It's fifteen years of friendship saying we'll figure this out even when everything else is broken.

I sit there a while longer, turning the glass I still haven't touched.

For the first time since that boardroom, I'm not trying to force my way through a door.

I'm waiting to be invited.

36

Sloane

The numbers on my laptop screen blur, but I keep typing. Revenue projections. Market penetration analysis. The framework that will either resurrect my career or confirm its burial. The coffee beside me went cold hours ago.

The Mammoth Community Champions Program. Not the watered-down version I'd pitched to Vivian in fragments over the past year, but the full vision. Thirty-seven million in projected first-year revenue. A sustainable model that transforms sports franchises from entertainment into community institutions.

Maya's gap-toothed grin watches me from where I've propped her photo against my monitor. Thank you for believing in her. The words that pulled me off the couch and back to work.

The knock on my door comes sharp and sudden.

I freeze, hands above the keyboard. No one should be here. Easton and Brynn know better than to interrupt when I'm working. The building manager would call first.

Unless—

"No," I whisper. He wouldn't. Not after what I said.

The knock comes again. Three raps, too fast.

I close my laptop. Cross the apartment in bare feet. My hand hovers over the deadbolt for a second, then I turn it.

Garrett Sullivan stands in my hallway, and he looks terrible.

His hair is a mess, his gray Henley is wrinkled, and there are shadows under his eyes that suggest he hasn't slept. But his eyes are clear. He's here on purpose.

"Sloane." My name comes out rough.

The memory of our fight flashes through me—ceramic shattering against my wall, the look on his face when I told him to leave. I push it down.

"What do you want, Garrett?" Cold. Professional.

He doesn't try to push past me. He takes a small step back, giving me space I didn't ask for.

"Could I talk to you for a moment? Please?"

I step aside just enough to let him in. I don't move far.

He enters and stops. He doesn't pace or fill the room the way he usually does. He stands still, hands at his sides.

"I need to apologize to you," he says. "And I need to do it right this time."

"I'm listening." I cross my arms.

He takes a breath, then looks me in the eye.

"I didn't see you in that boardroom. I saw someone I needed to save. Someone whose victory belonged to me because I cared about it. Because I loved you."

This isn't the defensive justification I expected.

"My help wasn't about supporting you," he continues. "It was about me. My need to matter in your success. I erased your competence because I needed to be the hero of your story."

"I didn't respect you as an equal in that moment," he says, quieter now. "I respected you as someone I loved. Someone I was proud of. Someone who reflected well on me. And that was my failure, Sloane. Not the outcome—the perspective."

I didn't expect this. Not from him. Not from anyone. The real betrayal named, out loud, without hedging.

"You didn't need defending," he says. "You were winning. You had them convinced, ready to sign, ready to see you as the strategist you are. And I stood up and turned you into someone who needed a man to speak for her."

"You turned me into exactly what I've spent my life proving I'm not," I say, and my voice comes out rougher than I want.

"Yes." No hesitation. "And I'm sorry doesn't begin to cover what I took from you. Your moment. Your victory. Your professional identity."

He takes a step closer, then catches himself. Stops.

"But I'm not here to ask for forgiveness. I'm here to offer you something."

"What?"

He reaches into his jacket and pulls out a folded document—his contract. Sixty-four million dollars over eight years. The thing that makes him untouchable in this organization.

"My contract. My name. My position as their franchise player." He holds it out between us. "It's leverage, Sloane.

And I'm not here to use it for you. I'm here to hand it over. You decide how it gets used. Tell me what to do. I'll follow your lead."

I stare at the contract in his hand. This isn't him riding to the rescue. This is him making himself a tool I can pick up or put down.

With his leverage, my plan transforms. The offer I'm building for Blackwood becomes exponentially stronger when paired with the threat of franchise instability.

"You're serious," I say.

"Dead serious." He doesn't look away. "I can't undo what I did. I can't give you back what I stole. But I can give you what I have left and let you decide how to use it."

"You understand what you're offering? You're talking about potentially destroying your own career to fix mine."

"I'm talking about finally putting my money where my mouth should have been four days ago. You're the most brilliant person I know. If anyone can make this work, it's you."

I study his face. Looking for the hero complex in disguise. Looking for the version of this where he gets to feel good about himself.

All I see is a man who finally understands what he broke and is handing me the only tool he has to help fix it.

My laptop sits closed on the dining table. The plan inside it just became something much bigger.

"Alright, Sullivan." I step back, and the distance between us feels like the start of a negotiation. "If you're serious, here's the play."

"I'm listening."

"I don't just want my job back. I want to remake this entire organization. Turn it into something that matters beyond wins and losses."

I open my laptop. The screen fills with projections and frameworks. "I've been building a comprehensive community engagement platform. Thirty-seven million in first-year revenue. It's ambitious. It's risky. And it requires the kind of leverage only a franchise player has."

He moves closer, studying the screen the way he studies game film. "What do you need from me?"

"Your contract gives us leverage with ownership. Your reputation gives us credibility with sponsors." I pull up partnership projections. "But I need more than your name. I need your complete, public support for something that goes far beyond hockey."

"You have it."

Immediate. No conditions.

"You don't even know what you're agreeing to."

"I know you." Quiet. Certain. "Whatever you're building, it's going to be extraordinary."

The words land differently than his boardroom declaration. No audience. No performance. Just recognition.

"This isn't forgiveness," I say. "This is strategy. You're not my boyfriend in this scenario. You're my partner. My equal. Nothing more."

"Understood. What's the timeline?"

"Fast. Before they regroup or spin the narrative. I've already reached out to Blackwood directly. He's agreed to a meeting."

"When?"

"Tomorrow afternoon." I close the laptop. "We walk in with an offer he can't refuse and consequences he can't ignore. You're the stick to my carrot."

"What do you need me to do?"

"Help me prepare." I nod toward the couch. "We have twenty-four hours to build something they've never seen before."

He moves toward the couch but stops at the edge of my workspace. "Sloane?"

"Yeah?"

"Thank you. For letting me try to do this right."

I don't answer right away. Instead, I focus on the work ahead. On the fight we're about to pick together.

But as I settle beside him—keeping distance—I let myself notice that for the first time in four days, the apartment doesn't feel like a bunker.

It feels like a war room.

37
Sloane

The silence in the apartment didn't break; it just sharpened.

Four hours. That's how long it took for the leverage to settle. I'd spent that time watching the light shift across the floor, listening to the muffled rhythm of Garrett's pacing and the frantic, staccato clicking of Brynn's keyboard. We weren't a team in a movie; we were four people holding our breath in a room that had started to feel too small for the size of the fire we'd just lit.

"Social media is a mess," Brynn said, not looking up. The blue light of her screen washed out her face, making her look as tired as the rest of us. "The trade demand leaked. Henderson's office is ghosting the press, which is basically an admission of guilt in this town."

Easton stopped by the bookshelf, his phone vibrating against the wood. He didn't answer it. He just looked at the screen, his jaw tight. "The locker room is leaking like a sieve. Everyone's looking for Garrett. Miller hasn't left his office since the trade demand hit the wire."

I didn't feel like a general. I felt like a strategist who had just pushed her last stack of chips into the center of the table.

When my phone finally buzzed, the sound felt like a physical strike. I didn't look at the name; I knew the area code. I hit speaker.

"This is Sloane," I said. My voice was thinner than I wanted, but it was steady.

"Henderson's office. Five minutes," Frank Miller's voice was flat, stripped of its usual condescending gravel. He sounded like a man who had already been told he was being replaced.

The line clicked shut.

"Well," Brynn said, her voice barely a whisper. "The king is calling."

I stood up, and for a second, my knees felt like they belonged to someone else. I didn't give myself a manifesto in my head. I just reached for my laptop bag. My fingers were cold, but they didn't shake. I checked the strap, adjusted my blazer, and looked at Garrett.

He didn't give me a speech. He just stood up and held the door open.

The walk through the Mammoth Center wasn't a victory march—it was a gauntlet.

The atmosphere in the executive suite had curdled. It was 4:45 PM, but no one was packing up to leave. Usually, this hallway smelled like expensive espresso and ambition; today, it smelled like ozone and sweat.

Phones were ringing at desks that were usually silent. We passed the junior marketing coordinator's cubicle. She didn't look at me with "reverence"—she looked at me with the wide-eyed, terrified curiosity of someone watching a car wreck. She looked at Garrett, then at me, then quickly back at her monitor, her hands hovering uselessly over her keys.

Conversations died as we passed glass-walled offices. I saw a VP of Sales pull his blinds shut as we approached. It wasn't respect I felt coming off them; it was the frantic, selfish fear of people wondering if their names were on the same list as Miller's.

We reached Conference Room A. Through the glass, I could see them. Henderson was standing by the window, his back to the door. Vivian was staring at a legal pad like it held the secrets to the universe. Miller was there, too, looking smaller than I'd ever seen him.

I didn't wait for an invite. I didn't knock. I just turned the handle and let the heavy door swing open.

The air in the room was stale, heavy with the scent of Miller's cologne and the sharp, metallic tang of a crisis in progress. Henderson turned slowly. His face was a mask of practiced corporate neutrality, but his eyes were bloodshot.

He didn't look at Garrett. He didn't look at Easton. He looked at me.

"Sloane," he said. Just my name.

I didn't sit down. I walked to the head of the table, set my laptop down, and felt the cool grain of the wood under my palms.

"We have a lot to get through, Paul," I said. "And I have a 6:00 PM call with Robert Blackwood. Let's not waste time."

38
Sloane

The executive conference room was a vacuum of glass and cold marble, designed to make anyone who wasn't Robert Henderson feel like an intruder. Four hours ago, I'd been a woman in a bunker; now, I was a strategist stepping onto the ice for the final period.

Henderson sat at the head of the table, his presence as heavy and unmovable as the championship banners hanging in the rafters. Beside him, Frank Miller was a study in casual arrogance, his tie loosened just enough to suggest he was bored by the life-or-death stakes of my career.

Then there was Vivian. She looked like the mentor I had once admired, but her fingers were drumming a frantic, silent code against the mahogany. It was the only crack in her armor, and I stared at it until she stopped.

I took my seat, the click of my laptop opening sounding like a hammer cocking in the silence. Garrett moved beside me—not as a savior, but as a shadow. His hand brushed mine as he pulled out my chair, a brief, jolting reminder of everything we had risked. For a split second, the professional mask slipped, and I was just a woman whose heart was hammering against her ribs. I forced it down. This wasn't about the man; it was about the work.

"Gentlemen. Ms. Lamore," I said. My voice was cool, stripped of the desperation that had lived in it for the last four days. "I'm not here to litigate my suspension. I'm here to show you the thirty-seven million dollars in first-year revenue you're currently ignoring."

I spent the next ten minutes burying them in data. I watched Henderson's eyes. He didn't care about the glossy photos of kids in jerseys; he cared about the ROI and the Gen-Z market penetration. I gave him exactly what he wanted—a plan so sound it made Miller's traditional marketing strategy look like a relic from the nineties.

"It's a nice PR story, Sloane," Miller interrupted, leaning back with a scoff that made my skin crawl. "But this is the Mammoths, not a non-profit. I think we've entertained this little 'redemption' tour long enough."

"It's only a PR story if you're incapable of reading a projection, Frank," I countered. I didn't look at him. I kept my eyes on Henderson. "If you want the Northstar renewal, you don't give them a logo. You give them a legacy."

Henderson shifted, the leather of his chair creaking. "Vivian. You've been overseeing Sloane's department. Why am I seeing this for the first time today?"

The room went lethal. The air didn't just feel cold; it felt thin.

Vivian leaned back, her face a mask of weary disappointment. "Because, Robert, this is what I warned you about.

Sloane has a talent for narrative, but she lacks the professional boundaries to execute it. She and Garrett have been... 'collaborating' on this for months." She let the word hang there, a sharp, ugly insinuation. "I have to wonder if this entire proposal is just a play to rehabilitate her reputation after a very public lapse in judgment."

She looked at me then, her gaze a glittering brittleness. "Ambition doesn't justify fabricating a business strategy to hide a scandal, Sloane. Did you and Sullivan cook this up during your pillow talk?"

The shame hit me like a physical blow—a hot, stinging flush that started at my collarbone and worked its way up. It was the ultimate weapon, designed to reduce my ten years of expertise to the status of a "distraction."

In my peripheral vision, I felt Garrett go perfectly still. I waited for him to speak—for the "Hero Complex" to kick in and for him to roar in my defense. But the silence stretched. He didn't move. He didn't breathe. He gave me the one thing Vivian didn't think I had: the floor.

"I'm glad you mentioned fabrication, Vivian," I said, my voice steadying as the anger took over. I clicked the remote.

The screen shifted to a raw, unformatted spreadsheet. It was the "rubble" I had been building from.

"These are the original projections I submitted three months ago. And these," I clicked again, the numbers turning red, "are the versions that reached Miller's desk. The revenue was slashed. The community metrics were deleted. The metadata shows these modifications were made from your terminal, Vivian. On a Sunday night while I was at a scouting event."

Vivian's face didn't change, but her knuckles went white. "Metadata can be spoofed. This is a desperate woman reaching for a conspiracy to save her job."

"It wasn't just my reports," I continued, pushing through the ringing in my ears. "Three of our legacy sponsors received 'anonymous' briefings warning them about organizational instability. I spoke with my contact at Northstar an hour ago. They were told my department was being dissolved for misconduct. Your misconduct, Vivian. Not mine."

I looked at Henderson, whose face was now a mask of cold gray stone. "I think Vivian saw a pattern she recognized from Columbus, and she decided to burn the work before the work could burn her."

The name *Columbus* was a grenade. The room didn't just go quiet; it went dead.

"I hired you because I thought you were a survivor, Vivian," Henderson said. His voice was a low, terrifying rumble. "I knew the story in Columbus was a mess. I hired you because I thought you'd be the one person in this building who *wouldn't* scapegoat a talented woman to protect a brand."

"Robert, I was trying to protect the organization from another scandal—"

"You were trying to protect your own ghost," Henderson cut her off. He looked at the red numbers on the screen. "The reports were altered. The work was real, and you buried it. The 'why' doesn't change the 'what.'"

He didn't look at her as he delivered the verdict. "I'm asking for your resignation. Effective immediately. I won't make the metadata public, but I won't sign a reference either. We're done."

Vivian stood. She didn't cry. She didn't beg. She gathered her portfolio with the precision of someone who had packed up her life before. She walked to the door, her back straight, looking like a woman who was already a ghost. As she passed me, the scent of her perfume—the same one I'd once thought smelled like "success"—felt cloying. She didn't look at me. She just left.

The door clicked shut, the sound echoing like a gavel.

Henderson turned to Miller. "Frank. Your VP was cooking the books under your nose for a year. We'll discuss your future later. Right now, I need the room."

Miller left, looking smaller than I'd ever seen him, his "casual dominance" replaced by the frantic calculations of a man trying to save his pension.

Then, it was just me. And Garrett, standing like a silent sentry. And Henderson.

"Your proposal is approved," Henderson said. He closed his legal pad with a definitive snap. "I'm creating a new position: Vice President of Strategic Partnerships. You'll report directly to me. I want a full implementation timeline on my desk by Friday."

The words hit me, and for a second, I couldn't draw air. VP. Reporting to the owner. Ten years of "proving myself" finally crashed into the reality of actually being seen. My vision blurred, and I had to press my hands flat against the mahogany to keep from trembling.

Henderson stood, adjusted his jacket, and paused at the door. "I should have looked at the numbers sooner, Sloane. Don't make me regret the promotion."

Then he was gone.

The room was suddenly too quiet. The presentation was still glowing on the wall—my name, my vision, my victory. I stared at the screen until the letters started to swim. I didn't feel triumph. I felt a strange, hollow weight. I had finally reached the top of the mountain, and the air was freezing.

Behind me, I heard the scrape of a chair.

I turned around. Garrett was still there. He hadn't rushed over to kiss me or take credit for the play. He was just waiting. For the first time, he was waiting for my lead.

The Sloane who had walked into this building a year ago was gone. The woman standing here now didn't need a hero. But as I looked at Garrett, I realized I finally had something better.

"Well, Sullivan," I said, my voice finally breaking into a shaky, sharp smile. "I think we have a meeting on Friday."

39

Garrett

The silence in the conference room feels profound, like the quiet awe after a perfectly executed play. But this isn't about hockey. This is about watching the most extraordinary woman I've ever known completely remake her world through sheer force of brilliance.

I can't stop staring at her.

Sloane stands at the head of that massive mahogany table like she was born to command it, her hands flat against the polished surface, shoulders squared beneath her navy blazer. The presentation still glows on the wall behind her—her vision, her strategy, her revolution—now backed by Henderson himself.

She did it. She didn't just win her job back—she transformed defeat into dominance, turned her termination into promotion, weaponized their dismissal into absolute victory. And I got to watch it happen. Got to be here when she proved to everyone in this room that underestimating Sloane McKenzie is the kind of mistake that costs you everything.

The pride coursing through my veins is so intense it's almost painful. Not the possessive pride of a man claiming credit for his woman's success, but something cleaner, purer—the deep satisfaction of watching someone you love become exactly who they were always meant to be. She didn't need me to save her. She saved herself. All I did was give her the tools and get out of her way.

Finally. Finally, I got it right.

Across the room, Easton and Brynn are gathering their things with the quiet efficiency of people who know the real show is just beginning. Brynn's laptop disappears into her bag with a soft snap, and she moves toward Sloane with predatory satisfaction gleaming in her eyes.

"Jesus Christ, Sloane," she breathes, pulling her into a fierce hug. "You didn't just win—you conquered."

Easton reaches them in two long strides, his massive frame radiating the protective satisfaction of a goalie who just shut out the opposing team's power play. When he wraps his arms around both women, his voice carries the rough edge of someone processing relief and pride in equal measure.

"I'm sorry," he says into Sloane's hair. "For the ultimatum. For not trusting you to handle this. For thinking I needed to protect you from your own choices."

"You were protecting the team," Sloane replies, and there's no edge to it now, no lingering resentment. Just understanding. "I get it. But next time, trust that I know what I'm doing."

"There won't be a next time," Easton says firmly. "You just proved you're untouchable."

They hold each other for another moment, siblings who've weathered the storm and emerged stronger. Then

Brynn steps back, her mind already shifting toward the story she'll craft from today's victory.

"I need to get back to work," she says, but her gaze flicks meaningfully between Sloane and me. "This story writes itself, but I want to get it published before anyone tries to spin the narrative."

She pauses at the door, turning back with a grin that could power the city. "Enjoy your moment. You both earned it."

The words hang in the air like a benediction, and then Easton smiles too before he follows her out, leaving us alone in this cathedral of corporate power with nothing but the truth between us.

I watch Sloane's shoulders drop as the warrior persona she's worn for days finally begins to fade. The brilliant strategist is still there—will always be there—but underneath it, I can see glimpses of the woman who used to steal my hoodies. Who laughed at my terrible jokes. Who trusted me with her secrets and her dreams before I broke that trust with my need to be her hero.

She turns toward me, and when our eyes meet, the impact is like a clean hit to the chest. Everything I've been holding back—relief, love, hope, the desperate need to touch her—crashes through me with enough force to make my knees wobble.

"Garrett," she says, and my name in her voice sounds different now. Softer. Less guarded.

"Sloane." I take a careful step toward her, then stop. This is her moment, her victory, her choice. I've learned to wait for her cue.

She's studying my face with that analytical intensity I know so well, but there's something new there too. Something that looks almost like wonder.

"You didn't speak for me in there," she says quietly.

The observation hits me like a revelation. She's right. When Vivian tried to reframe her evidence as fabrication, every instinct I had screamed at me to defend her. To stand up and deliver some passionate declaration of her competence. To be her champion.

Instead, I stepped back. Gave her the floor. Trusted her to fight her own battle while knowing I'd be there when the smoke cleared.

"No," I agree, my voice rough with emotion. "I didn't."

"You stood with me."

Four words. Four simple words that rewrite everything between us.

The relief that crashes through me is so overwhelming I have to grip the back of a chair to stay upright. She sees it. She understands what I've learned, what I've become. I'm not her hero anymore—I'm her partner. Her equal. The man who trusts her competence completely and loves her fiercely enough to let her shine without dimming her light with my own need to matter.

"Always," I manage. "I'll always stand with you."

Something in her expression shifts, the last wall between us crumbling. She's crossing the space between us before I can process the movement, her hands coming up to frame my face with a gentleness that makes my chest ache.

"I'm sorry," she whispers, and the words hit me like absolution. "For shutting you out. For not seeing that you were trying to learn. For not giving you the chance to show me you'd changed."

"You had every right—"

"No." Her thumbs trace my cheekbones, and I lean into the touch, starved for the contact. "I was scared. Scared of wanting you so much that I'd lose myself the way my mother did. Scared of trusting someone with that kind of power over me. But you..." She shakes her head, wonder bright in her green eyes. "You gave the power back. You made yourself my weapon instead of my savior."

The truth of it settles between us, a connection finally solidified. She's right. That's exactly what I did. What we did together.

"I love you," I say, the words coming out rough and unguarded. "I love your brilliant mind and your fierce heart and the way you turn impossible situations into victories. I love that you don't need me to rescue you—you rescue yourself. And I love that you're strong enough to let me stand beside you while you do it."

Her smile transforms her entire face. "I love you too. God, I love you so much it terrifies me. But not the bad kind of terrified anymore. The good kind. The kind that means something matters enough to be worth the risk."

When she rises on her toes to kiss me, I meet her halfway, my arms coming around her waist to pull her against me. There's no desperation here, no frantic hunger—not yet. Just the quiet confidence of a promise being kept, the gentle press of lips that says we found our way back to each other.

This is forgiveness and promise and profound love, tasting like forever.

Her lips are soft and sure beneath mine, and when I deepen the kiss, she sighs into my mouth with a deep contentment. But as our tongues dance together, as her hands slide up to tangle in my hair, something shifts. The gentle reunion kiss transforms into something deeper, warmer. More intent.

"So," she says, and I can hear the smile in her voice. "What now?"

Before I can answer, her briefcase catches my eye where she set it beside the conference table. I move to collect it, lifting the weight that represents everything she's accomplished. Not because she can't carry it herself, but because I want to. Because supporting her load is different from carrying her burden.

"Now," I say, offering her my arm, "we go downstairs. Together. Then you're coming home with me. I'm cooking you a proper celebration dinner. No arguments."

Her smile turns wicked, her eyes dancing with a light I thought had been extinguished forever. "Oh, so the master chef is finally going to perform? I was beginning to think all those cookbooks on your shelf were just for show."

I grin back, pulling her close as we walk. "They've been waiting for an occasion special enough. Get ready, McKenzie."

She laughs, the sound bright and unguarded, and takes my arm with the kind of easy trust that makes my chest tight with gratitude. "Dinner sounds perfect. Though I should warn you—I'm starving. Destroying corporate empires works up an appetite."

The elevator arrives with a soft chime, its polished interior reflecting our joined image like a preview of our future. When the doors slide shut, the sudden privacy wraps around us like a cocoon, intimate and charged with possibility.

"Garrett," Sloane says, turning to face me fully. The warrior is gone. In her place is the woman I fell in love with—brilliant and fierce and beautifully, perfectly human.

"Yeah?"

"Thank you." Her voice carries the weight of everything we've been through, everything we've overcome. "For trusting me to fight my own battles. For being my partner."

The elevator descends through the floors, carrying us from the corporate stratosphere back toward earth, back toward the real world where we'll have to figure out how to be together without secrets, without hiding, without shame.

"Thank you," I reply, "for giving me the chance to get it right. For seeing who I was trying to become instead of just who I'd been."

Her hand finds mine in the space between us, fingers threading together with the perfect fit of puzzle pieces finally finding their proper place. "I want to try again," she says quietly. "Not hiding. Not pretending we're just colleagues. I want to try being us. Really us."

The elevator slows as we approach the main floor, and through the small window, I can see the expansive lobby of the Mammoth Center opening before us. In thirty seconds, those doors will part, and we'll step out into the public space where our relationship will be visible to anyone who cares to look.

"Are you ready for that?" I ask, studying her face for any trace of hesitation. "For everyone to know? For all the speculation and gossip and judgment that comes with being public?"

Her smile is radiant, fearless. "I'm ready to stop being afraid of what other people think about my choices. I'm ready to be with the man I love without apology or explanation." She squeezes my hand. "I'm ready to be proud of us."

The elevator chimes softly as we reach the ground floor. Through the gap in the doors, I can see the soaring space of the lobby beyond—marble floors that reflect the afternoon light streaming through floor-to-ceiling windows, the distant sounds of the arena coming to life for tonight's game, the normal flow of staff and visitors moving through the space that houses our dreams.

As the doors begin to part, something settles in my chest—a deep, abiding certainty that feels like coming home after a long journey through hostile territory. This woman beside me isn't just my girlfriend or my lover. She's my partner in every sense of the word. My equal. My match. The person who makes me better not by completing me, but by challenging me to become the man worthy of standing beside her.

The lobby opens before us like a stage, and without hesitation, without fear, without the slightest trace of shame, our hands remain laced together.

The simple gesture feels like a declaration of war against everyone who ever tried to make us smaller. Let them see. Let them talk. Let them judge. We're done hiding, done apologizing for taking up space in each other's lives.

"Ready?" I ask.

"Ready," she says.

We step out of the elevator together, hand in hand, into the bright expanse of our future. The afternoon sun streams through the massive windows, casting everything in golden light that makes the ordinary lobby feel like a cathedral celebrating new beginnings.

I can feel eyes on us as we cross the marble floor—staff members doing double takes, visitors recognizing the familiar face of the team's alternate captain, the whispered speculation that follows in our wake. But none of it matters. For the first time since this all began, the judgment of strangers feels irrelevant compared to the weight of her hand in mine.

We push through the main doors together, and Minneapolis opens before us like a promise. The city air carries the scent of possibility and change, and I realize this isn't really an ending at all.

It's a beginning.

The drive to my loft passes in comfortable conversation about everything and nothing—her plans for restructuring the partnerships division, my thoughts on the upcoming road trip, whether Steve will adjust well to a new environment. Normal couple things. The kind of easy back-and-forth that makes the ordinary feel precious.

The door swings open and she steps inside. I close it behind her, the soft click echoing in the sudden, charged silence, sealing us off from the world.

She drops her briefcase by the door, the sound loud in the quiet room. The work is done.

A soft, familiar smile touches her lips as she looks around. She wanders toward the mantel, her fingers gently tracing the glass of the ridiculous little Zamboni snow globe. "I missed this place," she says, her voice quiet.

Having her here again, not as a storm refugee but as my partner, changes the very air in the room. The loft finally feels complete.

She turns to face me, and the warrior from the boardroom is gone. In her place is just Sloane, her green eyes shining with unshed tears of relief and victory. I don't know what to say, what words could possibly capture the immensity of what she just accomplished, of what I feel for her.

"You were..." is all I manage to get out, my voice thick with emotion.

That's all it takes. She meets me halfway, her hands coming up to frame my face as my own find her waist, pulling her flush against me.

The kiss is everything. The relief, the triumph, the certainty. It's all the pent-up fear and hope and love from the past few weeks crashing together in a moment of pure, unadulterated release. It tastes like victory and promise and coming home.

Her hands are confident now, working at my shirt buttons while I map the familiar territory of her mouth. When she pushes the shirt off my shoulders, I break away just long enough to capture her gaze.

"Are you sure?" I ask, because I need to hear it, need to know this is what she wants and not just adrenaline from the day's victories.

Her answer is to reach for the zipper of her skirt, the sound of it sliding down loud in the quiet of my apartment. The navy fabric pools at her feet, leaving her in the silk blouse that has been driving me crazy all day.

"I've never been more sure of anything," she says, her voice full of a deep and settled certainty.

What follows is a slow unraveling of everything we've held back. We undress each other with reverent hands, each piece of clothing that falls away representing another barrier overcome, another wall torn down between us.

When we come together, it's with the relief of two people finding their way back to each other. The connection is overwhelming—physical, emotional, complete. We move together, bodies and hearts finally aligned.

"I love you," she whispers against my skin, and the words are everything.

"I love you too," I reply, capturing her mouth with mine as we hold nothing back.

Afterwards, we lie tangled together on my couch, her head on my chest, both of us still catching our breath. The late afternoon light streams through the windows, painting everything in gold, and I can't remember ever feeling this complete.

"So," she says after a while, her voice lazy with satisfaction. "About that celebration dinner..."

I laugh, the sound rumbling through my chest. "Give me a few more minutes to remember how my legs work, and I'll make you the best carbonara you've ever had."

"Promise?"

"Promise."

She lifts her head to look at me, her green eyes bright with love and contentment and the kind of deep satisfaction that comes from finally being exactly where you belong.

"I'm proud of us," she says softly.

"Me too," I reply, pulling her up for another kiss. "Me too."

This, right here, is what comes next. And it's everything.

40

Epilogue - Garrett

The smell of sourdough batter hits the griddle with a perfect sizzle, and I can't help but grin. Three months of Sunday mornings like this, and I still get that same kick of satisfaction watching the pancakes bubble and rise. It's the little things—the routine, the normalcy, the way Sloane hums while she works at the kitchen table behind me—that make this feel real.

Real in a way that our secret stolen moments never could.

I flip the first pancake with perfect timing, then glance over my shoulder. Sloane sits cross-legged in one of my old hockey t-shirts, laptop balanced on her knees, completely absorbed in whatever she's reading. Her hair falls in soft waves around her face, and there's this little crease between her eyebrows that appears when she's deep in concentration.

God, I love that crease.

"How's the program looking?" I ask, sliding the golden pancake onto the growing stack.

She looks up, and that brilliant smile that's mine now—completely mine, no hiding, no apologies—lights up her face. "Maya's group had twelve girls show up yesterday for the financial literacy workshop. Twelve, Garrett. We started with three."

The pride in her voice does something to my chest, makes it tight and warm and full. "That's incredible."

"The community center director called this morning. They want to expand the program to include career mentorship. Apparently, half the girls are asking about marketing and business development after hearing me talk about strategic planning." She laughs, shaking her head. "Who knew that explaining market analysis could be inspiring to teenagers?"

I pour more batter onto the griddle, letting the comfortable domestic rhythm settle around us. This is what I never knew I was missing—not just Sloane, but this version of us. The easy Sunday morning conversations about her work, the way she gets excited about connecting with those kids, how natural it feels to support her while she changes the world one strategic partnership at a time.

"I knew," I say quietly.

"Knew what?"

I turn to face her fully, spatula still in hand. "That you'd be incredible at this. That you'd take something everyone else saw as a consolation prize and turn it into exactly what you wanted to build."

The way she looks at me in that moment—soft and grateful and completely unguarded—reminds me why I was willing to walk away from everything rather than let anyone dim that fire. She fought for this. Fought Easton, fought Vivian, fought for the right to have both her career and me. And now she's sitting in our kitchen in my t-shirt, revolutionizing youth programming like it's the most natural thing in the world.

She's not my redemption story. She's not the prize I won for finally growing up.

She's my partner. My equal. The woman who sees my protective instincts for what they really are—love, not ownership—and lets me take care of her because she knows the difference.

"Come here," she says softly, setting the laptop aside.

I abandon the pancakes without hesitation, crossing to her in three quick strides. She reaches up as I lean down, her hands framing my face as I kiss her slow and deep. It tastes like coffee and contentment and the promise of a thousand more Sunday mornings exactly like this one.

When we break apart, she keeps her forehead pressed to mine. "I love you," she whispers. "I love this. I love that we don't have to hide anymore."

"Best decision I ever made," I murmur against her lips. "Going public."

She laughs. "Best decision *we* ever made."

We. Us. Together.

The words still give me that same rush they did three months ago when she stood in front of Kowalski and half the team brass and announced that she was keeping both her job and her relationship, and anyone who had a problem with that could take it up with her directly.

My phone buzzes on the counter, and I'm about to ignore it when Sloane's starts ringing too. She frowns, reaching for it.

"It's Brynn," she says, glancing at me before answering and putting it on speaker. "Hey, what's—"

"Sloane, you're not going to believe the nightmare assignment I just got." Brynn's voice is sharp with fury, but there's something raw underneath it. "Two weeks shadowing Zac fucking Torres for an in-depth profile. Two weeks with the man who seems to enjoy destroying people."

I watch Sloane's face change, recognition and concern flickering across her features.

"Oh no," Sloane breathes. "Brynn—"

"I can't do this. Not with him. Not after—" Brynn's voice cracks, then hardens again. "God, I have to go. I need to figure out how to get through this without committing murder."

The line goes dead, leaving us in sudden silence.

Sloane sets the phone down slowly, her expression troubled. I move behind her, wrapping my arms around her waist.

"That sounded complicated," I murmur against her hair.

"Very," she says quietly, then turns in my arms to face me. "But that's their mess to sort out. Right now, I'm more interested in our pancakes."

The smile she gives me is soft and real, pushing away the shadow of our friends' drama. I kiss her forehead, then her nose, then her lips, tasting coffee and contentment.

"Our pancakes are probably burned," I tell her.

"Then make new ones," she says, pulling me down for another kiss. "We have all morning."

And we do. Here in our kitchen, with Sunday sunshine streaming through the windows and nothing to hide, we have all the time in the world.

"I love our life," I tell her, and mean it completely.

"Me too," she says, kissing me again. "Me too."

THE END

A Note from Sena

Thank you for spending your time with Sloane and Garrett. Writing their story was a joy, and I hope you loved reading it.

Want more Mammoths?

Brynn's book is next. Newsletter subscribers get first look at covers, bonus content, and a **free prequel novella** — the story of Brynn's on-air rampage after a spectacularly bad date.

JOIN THE LIST →

Or go to: **subscribepage.io/senavoss**

Ready for Brynn and Zac's story?

Mics and Misconduct is available for preorder now.

PREORDER ON AMAZON →

Or search "Mics and Misconduct Sena Voss" on Amazon.

Flip the page for an exclusive sneak peek at Chapter One.

If you loved this book, a review on Amazon or Goodreads helps other readers find it. Even a sentence or two makes a difference.

Keep reading for an exclusive sneak peek at *Mics and Misconduct* — a second-chance hockey romance about the journalist who ran and the enforcer who never stopped looking.

Mics AND Misconduct

41

Mics and Misconduct - Brynn

C hapter 1 - Brynn

"Chicago's locker room chemistry was so toxic it needed a hazmat suit, and somehow Zac Torres got blamed for the smell."

I lean into the mic, letting my voice drop into that conspiratorial register my listeners love. The "On Air" light glows red above my bedroom-turned-studio door, and Riley's laugh crackles through my headphones from her apartment across the city — I picture her in her usual uniform of oversized glasses and a hoodie she probably slept in.

"Okay, you beautiful degenerates," I continue, "buckle up, because we need to unpack the trade that broke hockey Twitter and my personal will to live. The Minnesota Mammoths just acquired six-foot-three of stone-faced controversy, and I have thoughts."

"You always have thoughts," Riley says. "That's literally the premise of this podcast."

"Rude. Accurate, but rude." I glance at my whiteboard, where I've scrawled TORRES = ENIGMA OR ASS-

HOLE?? in aggressive red marker. The question marks mock me. "So here's where we're at: Zac Torres, twenty-nine years old, five seasons with Chicago, career plus-minus that makes strong men weep with joy, and yet somehow—somehow—this man has been labeled a 'locker room problem.'"

I make air quotes even though no one can see me. The lavender candle on my desk is fighting a losing battle against the ghost of last night's kung pao chicken.

"The advanced stats tell a different story," Riley says. "Torres's on-ice impact was actually—"

"Riley." I hold up a hand she can't see. "I love you, but if you say 'expected goals above replacement' one more time, I'm going to need you to translate that into a language that includes feelings and drama."

A pause. Then, dry as toast: "Fine. He made his teammates better. They just didn't like him for it."

"See? Was that so hard?" I grab my stats printout and fan myself with it, even though the apartment's February chill has me in two sweaters. "He's the vegetables your mom hid in the mac and cheese. Nutritious but unappreciated. And now he's our problem."

"Minnesota's problem."

"Our city, our team, our problem. I'm nothing if not a homer." I pull up my notes, scanning bullet points I've practically memorized. "Right, so—the official line from Chicago's front office is 'pursuing a different direction.' Which is corporate-speak for 'we needed a scapegoat and he doesn't fight back.'"

"You think he was scapegoated?"

"I think—" I stop. Take a breath. "I think it's interesting that a guy whose teammates scored more when he was on the ice is somehow blamed for bad vibes. The advanced metrics don't lie, even if I need you to translate them for me."

"The eye test says he's difficult. Media-averse. Doesn't do the whole 'personality' thing."

"Right, because personality is definitely the same as performance." I hear the edge in my voice and dial it back. "Look, the man once answered twelve questions with variations of 'we played hard.' He makes a brick wall look chatty. Granite has more charisma. But that doesn't make him a cancer—it makes him boring in post-game scrums."

Riley makes a thoughtful sound. "We've got a listener question on this, actually. Lee from Duluth asks: 'Is Torres actually a locker room problem, or is he just media-averse and we're conflating the two?'"

Lee from Duluth, asking the questions I don't want to answer.

"Right. Okay." I lean back in my chair, the springs creaking. "So here's the thing about media-averse guys. Some of them are just... they're not built for the performance part. Doesn't mean there's nothing there. It means—"

I catch myself. The words forming are too specific, too knowing. Too much.

"—it means I'm projecting my romance novel brain onto a guy who probably just really hates microphones. Moving on." I shuffle papers I don't need to shuffle. "What we do know is that the Mammoths got him for pennies on the dollar because Chicago was desperate to move on. Their loss, potentially our gain, assuming the vibes check out."

"You think they will?"

"I think—" I stop again. Pull the professional mask tighter. "I think we'll find out. That's literally why we have a podcast. Speaking of which—" I glance at my rundown, "—we should probably talk about the upcoming road trip and whether Kowalski's going to keep juggling the second line like a circus performer, but that's a topic for next week."

"Teasing content. Very professional of you."

"I learned from the best. That's all for today, degenerates. Keep your sticks on the ice and your DMs unhinged. Riley?"

"May your fantasy teams prosper and your exes' teams tank."

I punch the stop button. The red light flickers off.

Silence rushes in—not normal silence, but the dead, flat quiet of soundproofing foam and closed windows. I pull off my headphones and the pressure against my temples releases. My reflection stares back at me from the dark computer monitor: blonde ponytail gone messy, two sweaters, lipstick I put on three hours ago and mostly chewed off.

I exhale. Rub my face with both hands.

"Jesus Christ," I mutter to no one.

My phone buzzes. Riley.

RILEY: How much of that Torres take were you actually believing and how much was podcast voice?

I stare at the text. She always knows. Three years of co-hosting and she can hear the difference between me riffing and me... whatever that was.

BRYNN: All podcast voice. You know me. Drama for the content.

Three dots appear. Disappear. Appear again.

RILEY: K. You good? You sound weird today.

I almost laugh. I sound weird because I just spent forty-five minutes talking about a man whose hoodie is currently shoved in my closet, behind dry-cleaning I will never pick up, and I've never told anyone why I still have it. Not Riley. Not even Sloane.

I told them both a version. That I met someone in Vegas. That it was intense. That I left before it got complicated.

I didn't tell them that I gave him a fake name. That I woke up at 4 AM with his arm heavy across my waist, looked at his face in the gray light, and felt so terrified of being seen that I slipped out before he could open his eyes.

I didn't tell them that for one night, I wasn't performing. Wasn't "on." Wasn't the clever one, the funny one, the one who fills silence because silence is where feelings live.

I was just... there. With him. And it scared me so much I ran.

BRYNN: I'm good. Long week. Talk tomorrow?

RILEY: You know where to find me. Same bat time, same bat channel.

BRYNN: Love you, weirdo.

RILEY: Love you too, disaster.

I set the phone down. The apartment is quiet again, but different now. Heavier.

The apartment feels too small suddenly, too close. I stand, joints cracking from two hours in my podcast chair, and move without thinking toward my bedroom. Past the white-board. Past the graveyard of half-drunk coffee cups with lipstick kisses on the rims.

My closet door doesn't latch properly. It never has. I tug it open, push past the dry-cleaning bag I've been meaning to pick up for six months, and there it is.

Gray. Soft. A gas station logo across the chest that's faded from too many washes—not by me. By him, before.

I pull the hoodie out and hold it. The cotton is pilled under my fingers, worn thin at the cuffs. It smells like dust and something fainter underneath. Something I can't quite name anymore but would recognize anywhere.

Two years. This thing has lived in my closet for two years.

I should throw it out. I've told myself that approximately nine hundred times. It's just fabric. Just threads and stitching and a gas station logo from a town I'll never visit again.

Except it's not.

It's proof.

Proof that for one night, someone looked at me—really looked, not at the performance or the punchlines—and didn't look away. Proof that I can be that person, the one who stays, the one who's honest, the one who doesn't fill every silence with a joke because jokes are armor and armor is safe.

I was her for eight hours. Then I woke up with his arm across my waist and I looked at his face in the gray pre-dawn light, and I thought—

He's going to figure out I'm not this.

That the woman he talked to all night, the one who laughed without performing and listened without planning her next line—she was a fluke. A one-time anomaly. And when he woke up and looked at me in actual daylight, he'd see the real version. The one who's too much and not enough all at once. The one people leave.

So I left first.

I always leave first.

I told Riley about it a month later. Sat on her couch with a bottle of wine and said, "I met someone in Vegas and I think I ruined it."

She didn't ask for details. Just said, "Oh, B," in that way she has, and handed me more wine, and we watched four episodes of a dating show where everyone made worse decisions than me.

She didn't push. She never does. That's why I can tell her the almost-truth—because she holds the almost and doesn't demand the rest.

The rest is this: I kept his hoodie because it's the only evidence I have that I can be soft. That I can stay. That somewhere, under all the armor, there's a person worth knowing.

I just don't believe it most days.

My phone buzzes on the desk in the other room. I don't move.

It buzzes again.

I carry the hoodie with me when I go to check it, which is a choice I don't let myself think too hard about. The screen glows:

MIRA CHEN (Sports National): Call me. Torres profile just came up. You're my first choice.

I stare at the text. Then at the hoodie in my hands. Then back at the text. What the fuck is happening.

My thumb hovers over Mira's contact.

I don't call back.

Instead, I fold the hoodie—carefully, corners matched, the way I always do—and carry it back to the closet. Slide it behind the dry-cleaning. Close the door as best I can, which isn't all the way.

It never closes all the way.

Just like the rest of it.

Three hours later, I'm pacing my living room with my phone in my hands.

This is my second call to Sloane tonight. The first one was pure emotion—fury, outrage, words spilling out before I could filter them. "Zac fucking Torres, Sloane. Of all the players in this goddamn league—" I'd hung up before she could ask questions. Before I had to manufacture answers.

I've pulled myself together. A scalding hot shower always does the trick. This call is different. I'm actually trying to decide.

My phone sits on the coffee table, Sloane's contact pulled up but not yet dialed. Outside, a siren wails past and fades

into the distance. February in Minneapolis means dark by
five and cold that seeps through walls, and I've already
turned the heat up twice.

I sink onto the couch and stare at the ceiling. Two years
I've managed to avoid this. Two years of carefully not cov-
ering Chicago games, not Googling his name, not letting
myself think about what might have happened if I'd stayed
for breakfast.

And now he's here. In my city. On my team. And my
editor wants me to spend two weeks following him around
like the universe has a sick sense of humor.

I tap Sloane's name before I can talk myself out of it.

She answers on the second ring. "Okay, I was giving you
space, but it's been three hours and you hung up on me
mid-sentence, so—"

"I've calmed down." I don't sound calm. I try again. "Okay,
I've mostly calmed down. I need your PR brain."

"My PR brain is concerned about your life brain."

"Career advice. That's all I'm asking." I stand up, sit back
down, press my palm flat against my thigh to stop fidgeting.
"A profile on Zac Torres for Sports National. Good visibility
or career suicide?"

Sloane pauses. In the background, I hear what might be a
hockey game—Garrett's probably watching tape. "It's good
visibility," she says carefully. "If you can deliver."

"I can always deliver."

"Brynn."

"What?"

Another pause. Gentler this time. "You don't have to take this. He's worse with the press than Garrett was when I met him. Wasn't it Zac a few years ago that—"

"Nothing happened." The words come out too fast, too sharp. I force my voice lighter. "I told you, we crossed paths once. He was difficult. End of story."

"You said 'not after' and hung up on me earlier. That's not 'nothing happened.'"

My chest tightens. I stand up, move to the window, press my forehead against the cold glass.

"It was a long day," I say. "I was being dramatic. You know me—I make everything a bit."

"That's exactly what worries me."

Silence stretches between us. The city bleeds through my thin walls—traffic, distant bass from a neighbor's apartment, someone laughing too loud in the hallway.

"There's something I should probably—"

The words form in my mouth. *He wasn't difficult. He was—*

I shut it down. Pivot.

"—consider," I finish. "Like whether his whole thing with journalists is going to make this piece impossible. He once answered twelve questions with variations of 'we played ha rd.'"

The silence that follows tells me Sloane knows. Not the specifics—she can't know those—but she knows I pivoted. She knows she's being handled.

"Sure," she says. "That's definitely what you were about to say."

"It was."

"Okay."

"Sloane—"

"You know," she says, and her voice shifts—softer, less pointed, "Garrett was media-averse when we met. Still is, mostly. Walls aren't always personality. Sometimes they're protection."

I latch onto the deflection like a lifeline. "Speaking of Garrett, how's the—"

"Subtle."

"I'm never subtle. How's the cohabitation? Has he reorganized your closet by color yet?"

Sloane laughs, and the tension in my chest loosens by exactly one degree. We talk about her for a while—the apartment, Garrett's season, the upcoming road trip. Normal friend things. Things that don't require me to lie or tell the truth.

When we hang up, I take a breath. Let it out.

He probably won't remember "Rebecca" anyway. I'm making this a bigger issue than it needs to be.

But I pull up Mira's text anyway.

BRYNN: I'm in. When do I start?

Send.

The phone goes dark. I stare at it for a long moment, waiting for something—buyer's remorse, panic, the universe intervening to save me from myself.

Nothing happens.

I glance toward the bedroom. The closet door is still ajar, the way I left it. I can't see the hoodie from here, but I know exactly where it is—shoved in the back corner, behind dry-cleaning I'll never pick up.

I don't go back for it.

I turn off the lights and don't look back.

Acknowledgements

Writing a book is a solitary job, but it's never a solo effort.

To my husband: thank you for being the one who actually kept our world spinning while I was busy building this one. For every meal you handled, every time you checked in on me, and for never doubting that I'd finish this—thank you. I couldn't have done this without you in my corner.

To my two kids: thank you for your hugs, your patience, and for the constant reminders of what really matters. You guys are my favorite story, and I'm so lucky I get to be your mom.

To my editors and beta readers and everyone who looked at these early drafts: thank you for your honesty and for helping me see what this book could be. Your encouragement was the fuel I needed to reach the end.

And finally, to you, the reader. Thank you for spending time with these characters and letting them into your head for a while. If you aren't ready to leave this world just yet, I've included the first chapter of Book Two on the following pages. I can't wait to show you what happens next.

About the author

Sena Voss writes steamy, heartfelt contemporary romance where the banter is just as important as the happily ever after. She believes in the power of a good cup of coffee, the thrill of a last-minute power play, and the timeless magic of a well-written love story. When she isn't forcing her characters to fall in love, she's probably rewatching a classic 90s rom-com for the hundredth time.

Connect with Sena and be the first to hear what's next!

For news about upcoming books, exclusive deleted scenes, and special offers, sign up for the newsletter at:

www.senavoss.com

Find her on Instagram: **@senavossauthor**

And on TikTok: **@senavoss**